*The
Corridors
of
Time*

The Corridors of Time

POUL ANDERSON

Doubleday & Company, Inc. Garden City, New York

*All of the characters in this book are fictitious,
and any resemblance to actual persons,
living or dead, is purely coincidental.*

TO ANTHONY BOUCHER

for much more than introducing me

to Storm Darroway

1

The guard said, "You got a visitor," and turned the key.

"What? Who?" Malcolm Lockridge rose from his bunk. He had been lying there for hours, trying to read a textbook—keep up with his course work—but mostly with his gaze held to a crack in the ceiling and his mind awash in bitterness. If nothing else, the noises and stinks from the other cells distracted him too much.

"I dunno." The guard clicked his tongue. "She's a dish, though." His tone was more awed than otherwise.

Puzzled, Lockridge crossed the floor. The guard stepped back a little. One could read his mind: Careful, there, this guy's a killer. Not that Lockridge appeared vicious. He was of medium height, with crew-cut sandy hair, blue eyes, blunt snub-nosed features that reflected no more than his twenty-six years. But he was wider in chest and shoulders, thicker in arms and legs, than most men, and he moved like a cat.

"Don't be scared, son," he fleered.

The guard reddened. "Watch yourself, buster."

Oh, hell, Lockridge thought. Why take my feelings out on him? He's been decent enough. —Well, who else is there to hit back at?

Anger died away as he walked down the corridor. In the grindstone sameness of the past two weeks, any break was treasured. Even a talk with his lawyer was an event, though one to be paid for afterward with a sleepless night, raging at the man's bland unwillingness to fight his case. So he gnawed the question of who this might be today. A woman—his mother had flown back to Kentucky. A dish—one girl friend had come to see him, and she was kind of pretty, but that had been a morbid "How *could* you?" scene and he didn't expect her to return. Some female reporter? No, by now the local papers had all interviewed him.

He came out into the visiting room. A window opened on the city, traffic noises, a park across the street, new-leafed trees and heartbreakingly blue sky full of swift little clouds, a breath of Midwestern springtime that made him doubly aware of the stench he had left. A couple of guards kept watch on those who sat at the long tables and whispered to each other.

"Over there," said Lockridge's escort.

He turned and saw her. She stood by the assigned chair. The heart jumped in him. My God!

She was as tall as himself. A dress, simple, subtle, and expensive, showed a figure that might have belonged to a swimming champion, or to Diana the Huntress. Her head was carried high, black hair falling to the shoulders and shimmering with a stray sunbeam. The face—he couldn't quite tell what part of the world had shaped it: arched brows over long and tilted green eyes, broad cheekbones, straight nose with slightly flaring nostrils, imperious mouth and chin, tawny complexion. For a moment, though the physical resemblance was slight, he recalled certain images from ancient Crete, Our Lady of the Labrys, and then he had time only to think of what was before him. Half frightened, he approached her.

"Mr. Lockridge," she said, not as a question. He couldn't place her accent either; perhaps just a too perfect enunciation. The voice was low-pitched and resonant.

"Y-yes," he faltered. "Uh—"

"I am Storm Darroway. Shall we sit down?" She did so herself, as if accepting a throne, and opened her purse. "Would you like a cigarette?"

"Thanks," he said automatically. She flared a Tiffany lighter for him but did not smoke herself. Having something to do with his hands steadied his nerves a little. He took his chair and met her gaze across the blank surface that divided them. In some corner of turmoil he wondered what anyone of her appearance was doing with an Anglo-Saxon name. Well, maybe her folks had been unpronounceable immigrants and changed. Yet she had none of the . . . the humbleness, the desire to please, which that suggested.

"I'm afraid I haven't had the, uh, pleasure of meetin' you before," he mumbled. Glancing at her left hand: "—Uh, Miss Darroway."

"No, of course not." She fell silent, watching him, her countenance gone expressionless. He began to fidget. Stop that! he told himself, sat straight, looked back and waited.

She smiled with closed lips. "Very good," she murmured. Crisply: "I saw an item about you in a Chicago paper which interested me. So I came to learn more for myself. You seem to be the victim of circumstances."

Lockridge shrugged. "I don't want to give you a sob story," he said, "but yes, that's right. Are you a reporter?"

"No. I am only concerned with seeing justice done. Does that surprise you?" she asked on a sardonic note.

He considered. "I reckon so. There're people like Erle Stanley Gardner, but your kind of lady—"

"Has better ways to spend her time than crusading." She grinned. "True. I need some help myself. Perhaps you are the one who can give it."

Lockridge's world was tilting around him. "Can't you hire somebody, Ma'm—Miss?"

"Some qualities cannot be bought, they must be given, and I have not the means to search deeply." Warmth entered her tone. "Tell me about your situation."

"Why, you saw the papers."

"In your own words. Please."

"Well—gosh—there isn't much. I was headin' back to my apartment from the library, one night a couple weeks ago. That's in a kind of run-down district. A bunch of teen-agers jumped me. I reckon they figured to beat me up for kicks and for what little money I had. I fought back. One of 'em hit the sidewalk and cracked his head. The rest made off quick, I called the police, and the next thing I knew, I was charged with second degree murder."

"Can you not claim self-defense?"

"Sure. I do. It doesn't do me a lot of good. No witnesses. I can't identify any of those punks; the street was dark. And there's been a lot of trouble lately between their sort and the college. I was caught up in one small riot before, when some of the high school crowd tried to bust into a picnic. Now they say this fellow and me must've had a grudge fight. Me, with combat trainin', pickin' on a chee-ild." Rage welled up in him, tasting of vomit. "Child, hell! He was bigger and hairier than I am. And there were a good dozen of 'em. But we got an ambitious D.A."

She studied him. He was reminded of his father, long ago on the farm in Kentucky's hills, watching the ways of a young bull he had acquired. After a pause, she asked, "Are you remorseful?"

"No," he said. "That's countin' against me too. I'm no good at actin'. Oh, I sure didn't set out to kill anybody. I pulled my punches right along. Pure accident that the punk fell the way he did. I'm sorry it happened. But my conscience feels clear. There I was, mindin' my own business, and—suppose I hadn't known how to handle myself. I'd've ended in the hospital, or dead. Everybody would've said, 'How awful! We must build still another youth recreation center.'"

Lockridge's shoulders slumped. He crushed out his cigarette and stared at his hands. "I was foolish enough to say that to the press," he continued dully. "Along with a few other remarks. They don't seem to like Southerners much around here, these days. My lawyer says the local liberals are also makin' me out a racist. Shucks, I hardly ever saw a colored man where I came from; and you can't get to be an anthropologist and keep superstitions about race; and those hoodlums were white anyhow. But none of that seems to make any difference to people's feelin's."

His anger turned on himself. "I'm sorry, Miss," he said. "I didn't mean to whine."

She reached toward him, but checked herself. He looked up and saw that the strange, beautiful face had taken on a pride that came near to arrogance. Yet she spoke low, almost tenderly: "You have a free heart. I was hoping for that."

At once she became all impersonal business. "What are your prospects at trial?"

"Not so good. The court appointed me a lawyer who says I ought to plead guilty to manslaughter and get off with a lesser sentence. I can't see that. It's not right."

"I gather you have no money for a protracted contest."

Huh? he thought. A woman like her, talkin' like a stage professor? "No," he said. "I been livin' on a graduate fellowship. My mother swears she'll mortgage her place to raise a stake, she bein' widowed and none of my brothers rich. I hate for her to do that. Course, I'll pay the debt off if I win. But if I don't—"

"I think you may," she said. "Am I correct in believing that William Ellsworth in Chicago is one of the nation's best criminal lawyers?"

"What? Why—why— He's hardly ever lost a case, they say." Stupefied, Lockridge gaped. He began to tremble.

Storm Darroway stroked her chin. "A good staff of private investigators could track down the members of this boy-gang," she said thoughtfully. "Their whereabouts that night could be established in court, and skilled cross-examination break their lies. We could also find character witnesses for you. Your life has been blameless, has it not?"

"Well—" Lockridge clamped teeth together. He achieved a sort of smile. "Reasonably so. But look, this'd cost a fortune!"

"I have a fortune." She brushed the question aside. Leaning forward, the luminous eyes searching out every detail about him: "Tell me of yourself. I shall need information. Where did you get this combat training you mentioned?"

"Marines. And I was stationed on Okinawa, got interested in karate and attended a dojo." In his hammering daze he

scarcely noticed how she drew his life from him: the boyhood
of work, forests, hunting and fishing; restlessness that ended
in his enlistment at seventeen; the enlightening shock of other
lands, other peoples, a world more wide than he had imagined;
the birth of a wish to learn. "I read quite a lot in the service.
Afterward, back in the States, I went to college on my savin's,
decided to go in for anthropology. They have a good depart-
ment in the university here, so I am—I was buckin' for my
master's. Ph.D. later on. Could be a good life. I like primitive
people. They're nothin' to get romantic about, they've got
troubles as bad as ours or worse, but there's somethin' there
that we've lost."

"You have traveled, then?"

"Some field trips, to places like Yucatán. We were goin' back
this summer. I reckon that's washed up for me, though. Even
if I got off the hook in time, I'm probably not very welcome
around here any more. Well, I'll find another place."

"Indeed you might."

Storm Darroway glanced around, lynx careful. The guards,
less bored than usual, were watching her, but they were out
of earshot if she talked softly.

"Listen, Malcolm Lockridge," she said. "Look at me."

With pleasure, he thought. His spine tingled.

"I am going to engage Ellsworth to defend you," she said.
"He will be instructed not to consider expense. If you are convicted, he will appeal. But I do not think that will be necessary."

Lockridge could only whisper, "Why?"

She tossed her head. The long locks flew back and he saw
a tiny, transparent button in her left ear. Hearing aid? Somehow the thought that she was also troubled and imperfect
warmed him. The walls between him and the world came
down and he sat in spring sunlight.

"Let us say it is wrong to cage a lion," she answered. There
was no coquetry about her; the words rang.

Her mask clamped down. She sat utterly relaxed and went
on, cool of tone: "Besides, I require assistance. The task is

dangerous. You seem much better fitted than some *slogg* I might hire off the street. The payment will not be niggard's."

"Miss," he stammered, "I don't want any pay for—for anything at all."

"You will need travel funds, at least," she told him. "Immediately after the trial, Ellsworth will give you an envelope with a check and instructions. Meanwhile, you are not to speak a word about me. If asked who is financing your defense, say a wealthy distant relative. Is that clear?"

Only later, trying to make sense of the whole fantastic matter, did he wonder if she was some kind of criminal, and refuse to believe that she could be. In this moment, he knew a command when he heard one, and nodded dumbly.

She rose. He stumbled to his feet. "I will not return here," she said. Her hand clasped his, a swift firm gesture. "We will meet again when you are free, in Denmark. Now good-bye and good heart to you."

He stared after her until she was gone, and then down to the hand she had taken.

2

September 14, her letter had said, at nine in the morning. Lockridge woke early, couldn't get back to sleep, and finally went for a long walk. He wanted to say farewell to Copenhagen anyhow. Whatever the job Storm Darroway had for him, it would scarcely be here—not when he was directed to buy backpacking equipment for two, a rifle, and a pistol—and he had fallen in love with the city.

Bicycles swarmed the streets, weaving in and out of auto traffic, the last workward rush. Their riders didn't have the beaten look of American commuters: placid portly men, young fellows in business suits or student caps, girls with fresh faces and blowing blonde hair, all openly enjoyed life. The gay glitter of Tivoli was like champagne in the blood, but you needn't go there to taste the Old Vienna spirit. Sufficient was to walk down Langelinje, sea winds in your nostrils, ships bound by for the outposts of the world; stop to pay your respects to the Little Mermaid and Gefjon of the Oxen; go past royal Amalienborg, left along the canal through Nyhavn where centuries-old seamen's taverns sleepily recalled last night's fun, across Kongens Nytorv with a pause for a quick beer at an outdoor café; and on among Renaissance churches, palaces, counting houses, whose slender copper-sheathed spires pierced the sky with loveliness.

I got so damn much to be grateful to that woman for, Lockridge reflected, and not least that she had me arrive here three weeks ahead of time.

He had wondered why. Her instructions were to get ordnance maps and familiarize himself with the Danish topography, spend many hours in the Old Nordic section of the National Museum, and read several books that thoroughly explained the exhibits. He obeyed conscientiously, puzzled but not questioning his luck. There were ample chances for recreation, and no lack of companionship. The Danes were friendly, delightfully so in the case of two young ladies he had met. Maybe that was Storm Darroway's idea: for him to recover from the ordeal behind him, and work off enough biological steam that he wouldn't be making passes at her—wherever they were bound.

The reminder was jolting. Today! He quickened his steps. The hotel she had ordered him to use hove into view. Trying to ease the tension that gathered in him, he took the stairs to his room rather than an elevator.

He had not long to pace and chain smoke. The phone rang. He yanked it off the hook. The clerk said, in excellent English, "Mr. Lockridge? You are asked to meet Miss Darroway outside in fifteen minutes, with your baggage."

"Oh. Okay." For a moment he bristled. She was treating him like a servant. No, he decided. I've been so long in the northern states I've forgotten what a real lady expects. No reason to get a bellhop. He slipped a pack onto his shoulders, took the other one and his suitcase in his hands, and went down to check out.

A gleaming-new Dauphine stopped by the curb. She was at the wheel. He had not forgotten her looks, that was impossible, but when her dark head leaned out the window, he drew a breath and the Danish girls fell from his awareness.

"How do you do," he said lamely.

She smiled. "Welcome back to freedom, Malcolm Lockridge," the husky voice greeted him. "Shall we start?"

He put the gear in the trunk and joined her. She was wearing slacks and sneakers, but looked no less imperial than before.

She slipped the car into traffic with more skill than he could have shown. "Whew!" he said. "You don't waste time, do you?"

"There is little to spare," she answered. "I want to be across this country before nightfall."

Lockridge pulled his eyes from her profile. "I, uh, I'm ready for whatever you've got in mind."

She nodded. "Yes, I read you aright."

"But if you'll tell me—"

"In a moment. I gather you were acquitted."

"Completely. I don't know how I can ever thank you."

"By helping me, of course," she said with a touch of impatience. "But let us discuss your own situation first. I need to know what commitments you have."

"Why—none, really. I'd no idea how long this job would take, so I haven't applied for another. I can stay with my mother till I do get one."

"Does she expect you back soon?"

"No. I stopped off in Kentucky to see my folks. Your letter said not to let on, so I only told them my defense had been handled by somebody rich who thought I was gettin' a raw deal and now wanted me in Europe as a consultant on a research project that might or might not take quite a while. Okay?"

"Excellent." She dazzled him with a look. "I did not misjudge your ingenuity either."

"But where are we headed, anyway? What for?"

"I cannot tell you much. But, briefly, we are to recover and transport a treasure."

Lockridge shaped a whistle and fumbled for a cigarette.

"You find that unbelievable? Melodramatic? Something from a bad novel?" Storm Darroway chuckled. "Why do people in this age think their own impoverished lives must be the norm of the universe? Consider. The atoms that built you are clouds of sheer energy. The sun that shines on you could consume this planet, and there are other suns that could swallow *it*. Your ancestors hunted the mammoth, crossed oceans in rowboats, died on a thousand red fields. Your civilization stands at the edge of oblivion. Within your own body, at this instant, a war is fought without quarter against invaders that would devour you, against entropy and time itself. There is a norm for you!"

She gestured at the street, where folk were about their daily business. "A thousand years ago they were wiser," she said. "They knew the world and the gods would go under and nothing could be done but meet that day bravely."

"Well—" Lockridge hesitated. "Okay. Maybe I'm just not the Ragnarok type."

She laughed. The car hummed onward. They were out of the old city, into a district of high apartment buildings, before she continued:

"I will be brief. Do you remember that the Ukraine rebelled against the Soviet government, a number of years ago? The revolt was savagely put down, but the fight lasted long. And the headquarters of the freedom movement was here, in Copenhagen."

Lockridge scowled. "Yes, I've studied foreign politics."

"There was a—a war chest," she said, "that was hidden away when the cause began to look hopeless. Now, lately, we have found someone who knows the place."

His muscles tautened. "We?"

"The liberation movement. Not for the Ukraine alone any more, but for everyone enslaved. We need those funds."

"Wait a minute! What the dickens?"

"Oh, we do not hope to set free a third of the planet overnight. But propaganda, subversion, escape routes to the West —such things cost money. And nothing may be looked for from governments that blither of a *détente*."

He needed time to collect his wits. So he said, "That's right. I used to claim, in bull sessions and so forth, there seems to be a will to suicide in America these days. The way we sit up and beg for any kind word from anybody, whether or not he's sworn to wreck us. The way we turn over whole continents to idiots, demagogues, and cannibals. The way, even at home, we twist the plain words of the Constitution to buy off any bunch of—

never mind. My arguments didn't make me any too well liked."

An odd exultation flitted across her face, but she said flatly:

"The gold is at the end of a tunnel in western Jutland, dug by the Germans during their occupation of Denmark for an ultra-secret research project. The anti-Nazi underground raided that base near the end of the war. Apparently everyone there who knew of the tunnel was killed, because its existence was never revealed in public. The Ukrainians learned of it from a man on his deathbed, and took it over as a hiding place. After their revolt was crushed and they disbanded, their treasury was left. You see, those few who had been told about it would not betray their trust by appropriating the gold for their private use, yet they had no more cause. Most of them are dead now, of age or accident or murder by Soviet agents. The last survivors finally decided to let our organization have the fund. I have been assigned to fetch it. You are my helper."

"But—but—why me? You've got men of your own."

"Have you never heard of using an outside courier? An East European might too likely be watched, or searched. But American tourists go everywhere. Their luggage is seldom opened at the frontiers, especially if they are traveling cheaply.

"Beaten into leaf, the gold can be sewn into our garments, the linings of our sleeping bags, and so on. We will go by motorcycle to Geneva and there turn it over to the proper person." Her eyes challenged him. "Are you game?"

Lockridge bit his lip. The thing was too weird to swallow in a piece. "You don't think they'll wave us on with this arsenal I bought, do you?"

"The guns are mere precaution while we prepare the gold to go. We will leave them behind." Storm Darroway fell silent a while. "I will not insult your intelligence," she said gently. "This involves certain violations of law. They might become very great violations, if there is a fight. I need a man who will take the risks and is capable of meeting trouble, and tough if he must be, yet not a criminal tempted by the chance of personal gain. You seemed right. If I have been mistaken, I beg you to tell me now."

"Well—that is—" Lockridge recovered some humor. "If you wanted James Bond, you sure were mistaken."

She gave him a blank glance. "Who?"

"Never mind," he said, largely to cover his own astonishment. "Uh— All right, I'll speak plain. How do I know you are what you say? This could be an ordinary smugglin' ring, or a con game, or . . . or anything. Even a Russian stunt. How do I know?"

The city was falling behind, the road so clear that she could give him a long regard. "I cannot tell you more than I have done," she said. "Another part of your task is to trust me."

He looked into those eyes and surrendered with joy. "Okay!" he exclaimed. "You got yourself a smuggler."

Her right hand fell on his left and squeezed. "Thank you," she said, and that was ample.

They drove on in silence, through green countryside and little red-roofed villages. He ached to talk with her, but you wait for the queen to open conversation. They were entering Roskilde when he finally ventured: "You'd better give me some details. The layout and so on."

"Later," she said. "This day is too fair."

He could not read her expression, but a softness lay on the mouth. Yes, he thought, in your kind of life you must grab after everything beautiful you can, while you can. They passed near the great three-spired cathedral and he wished he could find better words than, "Quite a church yonder."

"A hundred kings lie buried there," she said. "But under the market square are the still more ancient ruins of St. Lawrence's; and before that rose, there was a heathen temple with the gable ends carved into dragon heads. For this was the royal seat of Viking Denmark." Somehow it ran a shiver down his nerves. But her mood passed like a blown cloud and she smiled. "Did you know that the modern Danes call the Perseid meteors the tears of St. Lawrence? They are a people of charming fancies."

"You seem right interested in them," he remarked. "Is that why you wanted me to study up on their past?"

Her tone stiffened. "We need a cover story in case we are observed. Archeological curiosity is a good excuse for poking about, in a land this old. But I said I do not wish to think about these matters now."

"I'm sorry."

Again she bewildered him with change. "Poor Malcolm," she teased. "Is it that hard for you to be idle? Come, we are to be a pair of tourists, camping out at night, eating and drinking at poor men's inns, winding down back roads and through forgotten hamlets, from here to Switzerland. Let us begin to practice the part."

"Oh, I'm good at bein' a bum," he said, eager to please.

"Have you traveled much, besides your field trips?"

"Sort of. Hitchhiked around some, and used to go into the hinterlands on Okinawa when I had a pass, and took a leave in Japan—"

He was sophisticated enough to admire the skill with which she encouraged him to talk about himself. But that didn't make the process less enjoyable. Not that he was given to bragging; however, when a gorgeous woman listened with so much interest, he naturally obliged her.

The Dauphine purred down the island, Ringsted, Sorø, Slagelse, and so to Korsør on the Belt. There they must take the ferry. Storm—she had awarded him permission to be on first-name terms; it felt like an accolade—led him to the restaurant aboard. "This is a good time to have lunch," she said, "especially since drinks are tax free in international waters."

"You mean this channel is?"

"Yes, around 1900 or so, Britain, France, and Germany held a conference and grew touchingly unanimous in their opinion that the straits through the middle of Denmark are part of the high seas."

They sat down to akvavit and tall beer chasers. "You know an awful lot about this country," he said. "Are you Danish yourself?"

"No. I have an American passport."

"By ancestry, then? You don't look it."

"Well, what do I look like?" she invited.

"I'm blessed if I know. A sort of mixture of everything, that came out better'n any of the separate parts."

"What? A Southerner with a good word for miscegenation?"

"Now come off it, Storm. I don't go for that crap about would you want your sister to marry one. Mine has the sense to pick the right man for herself regardless of race."

Her neck lifted. "Still, race does exist," she said. "Not in the distorted twentieth-century version, no. But in genetic lines. There is good stock and there are scrubs."

"M-m-m—theoretically. Only how do you tell 'em apart, except by performance?"

"One can. A beginning is being made in your current work on the genetic code. Someday it will be possible to know what a man is fit for before he is born."

Lockridge shook his head. "I don't like that notion. I'll stick with everybody bein' born free."

"What does that mean?" she scoffed. "Free to do what? Ninety per cent of this species are domestic animals by nature. The only meaningful liberation is of the remaining ten in a hundred. And yet, today, you want to domesticate them too." She looked out the window, to sunbright waters and skimming gulls. "There is the civilization suicide you spoke of. A herd of mares can only be guarded by a stallion—not a gelding."

"Could be. But a hereditary aristocracy has been tried, and look at its record."

"Do you think your *soi-disant* democracy has a better one?"

"Don't get me wrong," he said. "I'd like to be a decadent aristocrat. I just can't afford to."

Her haughtiness dissolved in laughter. "Thank you. We were in danger of becoming serious, were we not? And here come the oysters."

She chattered so brightly through the meal, and afterward up on the throbbing deck, that he hardly noticed how adroitly she had turned the talk away from herself.

They drove off at Nyborg, on across Fyen, through Hans Christian Andersen's home town of Odense—"But the name means Odin's Lake," Storm told Lockridge, "and once men were hanged here, in sacrifice to him." And at last they crossed the bridge to the Jutish peninsula. He offered to take the car, but she refused.

The land grew bigger when they swung northward, less thickly populated, there were vistas of long hills covered with forest or with blooming heather, under a dizzyingly high sky. Sometimes Lockridge glimpsed *kæmpehøje,* dolmens sur-mounted by rough capstones, stark in the lengthening light. He made some remark about them.

"They go back to the Stone Age, as I hope you remember," Storm said. "Four thousand years and more ago. Their like may be found all down the Atlantic coast and on through the Mediterranean. That was a strong faith." Her hands tightened on the wheel; she stared straight before her, down the flying ribbon of road. "They adored the Triune Goddess, they who brought those burial rites here, Her of Whom the Norns were only a pallid memory, Maiden, Mother, and Hellqueen. It was an evil bargain that traded Her for the Father of Thunders."

Tires hissed on concrete, the split air roared by open win-dows. Shadows lay deep in the folded uplands. A flight of crows winged from a pinewood. "She will come again," Storm said.

Lockridge had begun to expect such passages of darkness through her. He made no reply. When they turned toward Hol-stebro, he checked the map and realized with a clutch at his throat that they didn't have far to go—not unless she meant to skate across the North Sea.

"Maybe you'd better brief me now," he suggested.

Her face and voice were alike uninterpretable. "There is little to tell you. I have already reconnoitered. We need expect no trouble at the tunnel entrance. Further along, perhaps—" Intensity flashed forth. She gripped his arm so hard that her fingernails pained him. "Be prepared for surprises. I have not told you every detail, because the attempt to understand would engage too much of your mind. If we meet an emer-gency, you must not stop to wonder, you must simply react. Do you see?"

"I-I reckon so." It was good karate psychology, he knew. But— No, damnation, I'm committed. Crazy, stupid, quixotic, whatever you want to call me, I'm on her side—with no more advance warnin' than this—whatever happens!

The blood raced in him. His hands felt cold.

Not far beyond Holstebro, Storm turned off the pavement. A dirt road snaked west among fields that presently gave way on the right side to a timber plantation. She pulled over to the shoulder and stopped the engine. Silence flowed across the world.

3

Lockridge stirred. "Shall we—"

"Hush!" Storm's hand chopped at his words. From the glove compartment she took a small thick disc. Colors played oddly over one face. She shifted it about, her head bent between sable wings of hair to study the hues. He saw her relax. "Very well," she muttered. "We can proceed."

"What is that thing?" Lockridge reached for it.

She didn't hand it over. "An indicator," she said curtly. "Move! The area is safe *now*."

He reminded himself of his resolution to go along with anything she wanted. That seemed to include not asking silly questions. He got out and opened the trunk. Storm unlocked a suitcase of her own. "I assume you have full camp gear in those packsacks," she said. He nodded. "Take yours, then. I will carry my own. Load both guns."

Lockridge obeyed with a sharp, not unpleasant prickling in his skin. When the frame was on him, the Webley holstered at his side and the Mauser in his hand, he turned about and saw Storm closing her suitcase again. She had donned a sort of cartridge belt like none he had ever seen before, a thing of darkly shimmering flexible metal whose pouches appeared to seal themselves shut. Hanging on the right, as if by magnetism, was a slim, intricate-barreled thing. Lockridge did a double take. "Hey, what kind of pistol is that?"

"No matter." She hefted the disc of colors. "Expect odder sights than this. Lock the car and let us be gone."

They entered the plantation and began walking back, parallel to the road, hidden from it by the ordered ranks of pines. Afternoon light slanted through a sweet pungency and cast sunspeckles on the ground, which was soft with needles underfoot. "I get you," Lockridge said. "We don't want the car to draw attention to where we're headed, if somebody happens by."

"Silence," Storm ordered.

A mile or so beyond, she led the way to the road and across. There a harvested grain field lay yellow and stubbly, lifting toward a ridge that cut off view of any farmhouse. In the middle stood a hillock topped by a dolmen. Storm slipped agilely through the wire fence before Lockridge could help and broke into a trot. Though her pack was not much lighter than his, she was still breathing easily when they reached the knoll, and he was a little winded.

She stopped and opened her belt. A tube came out, vaguely resembling a large flashlight with a faceted lens. She took her bearings from the sun and started around the hillock. It was overgrown with grass and brambles; a marker showed that this relic was protected by the government. Feeling naked under the wide empty sky, his pulse thuttering, Lockridge looked at the dolmen as if for some assurance of eternity. Gray and lichen-spotted, the upright stones brooded beneath their heavy roof as they had done since a vanished people raised them to be a tomb for their dead. But the chamber within, he recalled, had once been buried under heaped earth, of which only this mound was left. . . .

Storm halted. "Yes, here." She began to climb the slope.

"Huh? Wait," Lockridge protested. "We've come three-quarters around. Why didn't you go in the other direction?"

For the first time, he saw confusion on her face. "I go widdershins." She uttered a hard laugh. "Habit. Now, stand back."

They were halfway up when she stopped. "This place was excavated in 1927," she said. "Only the dolmen was cleared, and there is no further reason for the scientists to come. So we can use it for a gate." She did something to a set of controls on the tube. "We have a rather special way of concealing entrances," she warned. "Do not be too astonished."

A dull light glowed from the lens. The tube hummed and quivered in her grip. A shiver went through the brambles, though there has no wind. Abruptly a circle of earth lifted.

Lifted—straight into the air—ten feet in diameter, twenty feet thick, a plug of turf and soil hung unsupported before Lockridge's eyes. He sprang aside with a yell.

"Quiet!" Storm rapped. "Get inside. Quick!"

Numbly, he advanced to the hole in the mound. A ramp led down out of sight. He swallowed. The fact that she watched him was what mostly drove him ahead. He went into the hill. She followed. Turning, she adjusted the tube in her hand. The cylinder of earth sank back. He heard a sigh of compression as it fitted itself into place with machined snugness. Simultaneously, a light came on—from no particular source, he saw in his bewilderment.

The ramp was simply the floor of a barrel-vaulted tunnel, a little wider than the door, which sloped before him around a curve. That bore was surfaced overall with a hard, smooth material from which the light poured, a chill white radiance whose shadowlessness made distances hard to judge. The air was fresh, moving, though he saw no ventilators.

He faced Storm and stammered. She put away the tube. Harshness left her. She glided to him, laid a hand on his arm, and smiled. "Poor Malcolm," she murmured. "You will have greater surprises."

"Judas!" he said weakly. "I hope not!" But her nearness and her touch were, even then, exhilarating. He began to recover his self-possession.

"How the deuce is that done?" he asked. Echoes bounced hollowly around his voice.

"Shh! Not so loud." Storm glanced at her color disc. "No one is here at present, but they may come from below, and sound carries damnably well in these tunnels."

She drew a breath. "If it will make you feel better, I shall explain the principle," she said. "The plug of earth is bound together by an energy web emanating from a network embedded in these walls. The same network blankets any effects that might occur in a metal detector, a sonic probe, or some other instrument that could otherwise detect this passage. It also refreshes and circulates the air through molecular porosities. The tube I used to lift the plug is merely a control; the actual power comes likewise from the network."

"But—" Lockridge shook his head. "Impossible. I know that much physics. I mean—well, maybe in theory—but no such gadget exists in practice."

"I told you this was a secret research project," Storm answered. "They achieved many things." Her lips bent upward—how close to his! "You are not frightened, are you, Malcolm?"

He squared his shoulders. "No. Let's move."

"Good man," she said, with a slight, blood-quickening emphasis on the second word. Releasing him, she led the way down.

"This is only the entrance," she said. "The corridor proper is more than a hundred feet below us."

They spiraled into the earth. Lockridge observed that his own stupefaction was gone. Alertness thrummed in him. Storm had done that. My God, he thought, what an adventure.

The passage debouched in a long room, featureless except at the farther wall. There stood a large box or cabinet of the same lustrous, self-closing metal as Storm's belt and a doorway some ten feet wide and twenty high. Curtained? No, as he neared, Lockridge saw that the veil which filled it, flickering with soft iridescence, every hue his eyes could see and (he suspected) many they could not, was immaterial: a shimmer in space, a mirage, a sheet of living light. The faintest hum came from it, and the air nearby smelled electric.

Storm paused there. Through her clothes he saw how the tall body tensed. His own pistol came out with hers. She glanced at him.

"The corridor is just beyond," she said in a whetted voice. "Now listen. I only hinted to you before that we might have to fight. But the enemy is everywhere. He may have learned of our place. His agents may even be on the other side of this gate. Are you ready, at my command, to shoot?"

He could only jerk his head up and then down.

"Very well. Follow me."

"No, wait, I'll go—"

"Follow, I said." She bounded through the curtain.

He came after. Crossing the threshold, he felt a brief, twisting shock, and stumbled. He caught himself and glared around.

Storm stood half crouched, peering from side to side. After a minute she glanced at her instrument, and the pistol sank in her hand. "No one," she breathed. "We are safe for the moment."

Lockridge drew a shaky lungful and tried to understand what sort of place he had entered.

The corridor was huge. Also hemicylindrical, with the same luminous surfacing, it must be a hundred feet in diameter. Arrow straight it ran, right and left, until the ends dwindled out of sight—why, it must go for miles, he realized. The humming noise and the lightning smell were more intense here, pervading his being, as if he were caught in some vast machine.

He looked back at the door through which he had come, and stiffened. "What the hell!"

On this side, though no higher, the portal was easily two hundred feet wide. A series of parallel black lines, several inches apart, extended from it, some distance across the corridor floor. At the head of each was a brief inscription, in no alphabet he could recognize. But every ten feet or so a number was added. He saw 4950, 4951, 4952. . . . Only the auroral curtain was the same.

"No time to waste." Storm tugged at his sleeve. "I shall explain later. Get aboard."

She gestured at a curve-fronted platform, not unlike a big metal toboggan with low sides, that hovered two feet off the floor. Several backless benches ran down its length. At the head was a panel where small lights glowed, red, green, blue, yellow— "Come *on!*"

He mounted with her. She took the front seat, laid her gun in her lap, and passed her hand across the lights. The sled swung around and started left down the corridor. It moved in total silence at a speed he guessed to be thirty miles an hour; but somehow the wind was screened off them.

"What the jumpin' blue blazes is this thing?" he choked.

"You have heard of hovercraft?" Storm said absently. Her eyes kept flickering from the emptiness ahead to the color disc in her fingers.

A grimness came upon Lockridge. "Yes, I have," he said, "and I know this is nothin' like them." He pointed to her instrument. "And what's that?"

She sighed. "A life indicator. And we are riding a gravity sled. Now be still and keep watch to our rear."

Lockridge felt almost too stiff to sit, but managed it. He set the rifle on the bench beside him. Sweat was clammy along his ribs, and he saw and heard with preternatural sharpness.

They glided by another portal, and another, and another. The gates came at variable intervals, averaging about half a mile, as near as Lockridge could gauge in this saturating cold illumination. Wild thoughts spun through his head. No Germans could ever have built this, no anti-Communist underground be using it. Beings from another planet, another star, somewhere out in the measureless darkness of the cosmos—

Three men came through a gate that the sled had just passed. Lockridge yelled at the same moment that Storm's indicator turned blood red. She twisted about and looked behind. Her mouth skinned back from her teeth. "So we fight," she said on a trumpet note, and fired aft.

A blinding beam sprang from her pistol. One of the men lurched and collapsed. Smoke roiled greasy from the hole in his breast. The other two had their guns unfastened before he was down. Storm's firebolt passed across them, broke in a coruscant many-colored fountain, and splashed the corridor

walls with vividness. The air crackled. Ozone stung Lockridge's nostrils.

She thumbed a switch on her weapon. The beam winked
out. A vague, hissing shimmer encompassed her and her companion. "Energy shielding," she said. "My entire output must
go to it, and even so, two beams striking the same spot could
break through. Shoot!"

Lockridge had no time to be appalled. He brought the rifle
to his cheek and sighted. The man he saw was big but dwindling with distance, only his close-fitting black garments and
golden-bronze Roman-like helmet could be made out, he was
a target with no face. Briefly there jagged across Lockridge's
memory the woods at home, green stillness and a squirrel in
branches above. . . . He shot. The bullet smote, the man fell
but picked himself up. Both of them sprang onto a gravity sled
such as was parked at every gate.

"The energy field slows material objects too," Storm said
bleakly. "Your bullet had too little residual velocity, at this
range."

The other sled got moving in pursuit. Its black-clad riders
hunched low under the bulwarks. Lockridge could just see the
tops of their helmets. "We got a lead on them," he said. "They
can't go any faster, can they?"

"No, but they will observe where we emerge, go back, and
tell Brann," Storm answered. "A mere identification of me will
be bad enough." Her eyes were ablaze, nose flared, breasts
rising and falling; but she spoke more coolly than he had
known men to do when they trained with live ammunition.
"We shall have to counterattack. Give me your pistol. When I
stand to draw their fire—no, be quiet, I will be shielded—you
shoot."

She whipped the sled about and sent it hurtling toward the
other one. The thing grew in Lockridge's vision with nightmare
slowness. And those were actual men he must kill. He kicked
away nausea. They were trying to kill him and Storm, weren't
they? He knelt beneath the sideshield and held his rifle ready.

The encounter exploded around him. Storm surged to her

feet, the energy gun in her left hand, the Webley barking in her right. Yards away, the other sled veered. Two firebeams struck at her, throwing sparks and sheets of radiance, moving toward convergence. And a slug whined from some noiseless, stubby-barreled weapon that one of the black-uniformed men also held.

Lockridge jumped up. In the corner of an eye he saw Storm, erect in a geyser of red, blue, yellow flame, hair tossed about her shoulders by thundering energies, shooting and laughing. He looked down upon the enemy, straight into a pale narrow countenance. The bullet gun swiveled toward him. He fired exactly twice.

The other sled passed by and on down the corridor.

Echoes died away. The air lost its sting. There was only the bone-deep song of unknown forces, the smell of them and the flimmer in a gateway.

Storm looked after the sprawled bodies as they departed, picked her life indicator off the bench, and nodded. "You got them," she whispered. "Oh, nobly shot!" She threw down the instrument, seized Lockridge and kissed him with bruising strength.

Before he could react, she let him go and turned the sled around. Her color was still high, but she spoke with utter coolness: "It would be a waste of time and charges to disintegrate them. The Rangers would still know quite well that they met their end at Warden hands. But no more than that should be obvious: provided we get out of the corridor before anyone else chances along."

Lockridge slumped onto a bench and tried to comprehend what had happened.

He didn't come out of his daze until Storm halted the sled and urged him off. She leaned over and activated the controls. It started away. "To its proper station," she explained briefly. "If Brann knew that the killers of his men had entered from 1964, and found an extra conveyance here, he would know the whole story. This way, now."

They approached the gate. Storm chose a line from the first

group, headed 1175. "Here you must be careful," she said. "We could easily get lost from each other. Walk exactly on this marker." She reached behind her and closed fingers on his. He was still too shocked to appreciate that contact as much as he knew, dimly, he would otherwise.

Following her, he passed through the curtain. She let him go, and he saw that they were in a room like the one from which they had entered. Storm opened the cabinet, consulted what he guessed might be a timepiece, and nodded in a satisfied way. Taking out a pair of bundles done up in a shaggy, coarse-woven blue material, she handed them to him and closed the cabinet. They went up the spiral ramp.

At the end, she opened another turf trapdoor with her control tube and closed it again behind them. The concealment was perfect.

Lockridge didn't notice. There was too much else.

The sun had still been well above the horizon when they entered the tunnel, and they couldn't have been inside more than half an hour. But here was night, with a nearly full moon high in the sky. By that wan radiance he saw how the moundside now covered the dolmen, up to the capstone, with a rude wooden door beneath. Around him, grasses nodded in a chill, moist breeze. No farmlands lay below; the knoll was surrounded by brush and young trees, a second-growth wilderness. To the south a ridge lifted that looked eerily familiar, but it was covered with forest. Old, those trees, incredibly, impossibly old, he had only seen oaks so big in the last untouched parts of America. Their tops were hoar in the moonlight, and shadows solid beneath.

An owl hooted. A wolf howled.

He raised his eyes again and saw this was not September. That sky belonged to the end of May.

4

"Yes, of course I lied to you," Storm said.

The campfire guttered high, sparks showered, light danced dull on smoke and picked her strong-boned features out of darkness in Rembrandt hints. Beyond and around, the night crowded close. Lockridge shivered and held his hands toward the coalbed.

"You would not have believed the truth before you saw," Storm went on. "Would you? At the very least, time would have been lost in explanation, and I had already been much too long in the twentieth century. Each hour multiplied my danger. If Brann had thought to guard that Danish gate— He must believe I was killed. There were several other women in my party, and some were mutilated beyond recognition in the fight with him. Nevertheless, he could have gotten wind of me."

Exhausted by reaction, Lockridge said merely, "You are from the future, then?"

She smiled. "So are you, now."

"My future, I mean. When?"

"About two thousand years after your era." Her humor faded, she sighed and looked into the gloom that lay back of him. "Though I have been in so many ages, I am woven into so much history, I sometimes wonder if any of my spirit remains in the year I was born."

"And—we're still in the same place as we entered the corridor, aren't we? But in the past. How far?"

"By your reckoning, the late spring of 1827 B.C. I checked the exact date on a calendar clock in the foreroom. Emergence cannot be precise, because the human body has a finite width equivalent to a couple of months. That was why we had to hold hands coming through—so we would not be separated by weeks." Briskly: "If such should ever happen, go back into the corridor and wait. Duration occurs there too, but on a different plane, so that we can rendezvous."

Nearly four thousand years, Lockridge thought. On this day Pharaoh sat the throne of Egypt, the sea king of Crete planned trade with Babylon, Mohenjodaro stood proud in the Indus valley, the General Grant Tree was a seedling. Bronze was known to the Mediterranean world but northern Europe was neolithic, and the dolmen of the knoll had been raised only a few generations ago by folk whose slash-and-burn agriculture exhausted the soil and forced them to move elsewhere. Eighteen hundred years before Christ, centuries before even Abraham, he sat camped in a Denmark which those people who called themselves Danes had yet to enter. The strangeness seeped through him like a physical cold. He fought back the sense and asked:

"What is that corridor, anyway? How does it work?"

"The physics would have no meaning to you," Storm said. "Think of it as a tube of force, whose length has been rotated onto the time axis. Entropy still increases inside; there is temporal flow. But from the viewpoint of one within, cosmic time —outside time—is frozen. By choosing the appropriate gate, one can step out into any corresponding era. The conversion factor—" she frowned in concentration, "—in your measurements, would be roughly thirty-five days per foot. Every few centuries there is a portal, twenty-five years wide. The intervals cannot be less than about two hundred years, or the weakened forcefield would collapse."

"Does it go clear up to your century?"

"No. This one extends from circa 4000 B.C. to A.D. 2000. It is not feasible to build them much longer. There are many corridors of varying lengths throughout the space-time of this planet. The gates are made to overlap in time, so that by going from one passage to another a traveler can find any specific year he wishes. For example, to go further pastward than 4000 B.C., we could take corridors I know of in England or China, whose gates also cover this year. To go futureward beyond the limits of this one, we would have to seek out still other places."

"When were they . . . invented?"

"A century or two before I was born. The struggle between Wardens and Rangers was already intense, so the original purpose of scientific research was largely shunted aside."

Wolves gave voice in the night. A heavy body went crashing through underbrush and a savage, yelping chorus took up pursuit. "You see," Storm said, "we cannot wage total war. That would cost us Earth, as it cost us Mars—a ring of radioactive fragments encircling the sun—I sometimes wonder if, at the last, engineers will not go back sixty million years and build great space fleets, for a battle that wiped out the dinosaurs and left eternal scars on the moon. . . ."

"You don't know your own future, then?" Lockridge asked with a crawling along his nerves.

The dark head shook. "No. When the, the activator is turned on to make a new corridor, it drives a shaft equally far in both directions. We ventured ahead of our era. There were guardians who turned us back, with weapons we did not understand. We no longer try. It was too terrible."

The knowledge of mysteries beyond mysteries was not to be endured. Lockridge fled to practicality.

"Okay," he said. "I seem to've enlisted in a war on your side. Do you mind tellin' me what the shootin's for? Who are your enemies?" He paused. "Who are you?"

"Let me continue to use the name I chose in your century," Storm said. "I believe it was a lucky one." She sat brooding a while. "I do not think you could really grasp the issue of my age. Too much history lies between you and us. Could a man from your past really feel what the basic difference is that divides East and West in your time?"

"I reckon not," Lockridge admitted. "In fact, quite a few of our own don't seem to see it."

"At that," Storm said, "the issue is the same. Because there has really only been one throughout man's existence—distorted, confused, hidden behind a thousand lesser motivations, and yet always in some fashion the clash between two philosophies, two ways of thought and life—of *being*—the question is forever: What is the nature of man?"

Lockridge waited. Storm brought her gaze back from the night, across the low fire to him, stabbingly intense.

"Life as it is imagined to be against life as it is," she said. "Plan against organic development. Control against freedom. Overriding rationalism against animal wholeness. The machine against the living flesh. If man and man's fate can be planned, organized, made to conform to some vision of ultimate perfection, is not man's duty to enforce the vision upon his fellow man, at whatever cost? That sounds familiar to you, no?

"But your country's great enemy is only one manifestation of a thing that was born before history: that spoke through the laws of Draco and Diocletian, the burning of the Confucian Willow Books, Torquemada, Calvin, Locke, Voltaire, Napoleon, Marx, Lenin, Arguellas, the Jovian Manifesto, and on and on. Oh, not clearly, not simply—there was no tyranny in the hearts of some who believed in supreme reason; and there was in others, like Nietzsche, who did not. To me, your industrial civilization, even in the countries that call themselves free, comes near to an ultimate horror; yet I use machines more powerful and subtle than you have dreamed. But in what spirit? There is the issue of battle!"

Her voice dropped. She looked into the forest walling this meadow. "I often think," she said slowly, "that the downward turn started in this very millennium, when the earth gods and their Mother were swept aside by those who worshipped skyward."

She shook herself, as if to be rid of something, and continued in a level tone, "Well, Malcolm, accept for now that the Wardens are keepers of life—life in its wholeness, boundedness, splendor, and tragedy—while the Rangers would make the world over in the machine's image. It is an oversimplification. I can perhaps explain better to you later on. But do you find my cause unworthy?"

Lockridge regarded her, where she rested like a young wildcat, and said with a surge that drove out all terror, remorse, and aloneness: "No. I'll go along. I already have."

"Thank you," she whispered. "If you knew what the token meant, not only in words but in your blood, I would leap over the fire to you for that."

What does it mean? he wanted to ask. Dizzyingly: A man might hope. But before he could speak, Storm grinned and said: "The next few months should be interesting for you."

"Good Lord, yes!" he realized. "Why, any anthropologist would give his right—uh—eye to be here. I still can't believe I am."

"There are dangers," she warned.

"So what is the situation, anyway? What do we have to do?"

"Let me begin at the first," Storm said. "As I told you, the struggle between Rangers and Wardens cannot be fought in our own time on any major scale. Instead, it has moved largely into the past. Bases are established at strategic points and—no matter now. I know the Rangers have a stronghold in Harald Bluetooth's reign. Though the Asa religion was already one of Sky Father, still, the introduction of Christianity was another advance for them, laying the foundation for centralized monarchy and the eventual rationalistic state. Thence came the men we met."

"Huh? Wait! You mean you people *change* the past?"

"Oh, no. Never. That is inherently impossible. If one tried, he would find events always frustrated him. What has been, is. We time travelers are ourselves part of the fabric. But let us say that we discover aspects of it which are useful to our respective causes, we get recruits, build up strength for the final contest.

"Well. In my time, the Rangers hold the western hemisphere, the Wardens the eastern. I led a party into the twentieth century and overseas to America. We could not build anything important by ourselves without being observed by enemy agents, who are much more numerous in your age than ours are. But our plan was to organize a company whose ostensible purpose was something unremarkable, to pose as ordinary citizens of the era. We picked yours because that was the first century in which such items as we needed—transistors, for instance—could be obtained locally and hence inconspicuously. In the guise of a mining enterprise in Colorado, we produced our underground installations, manufactured an activator, and drove a new passage.

"The plan was to strike through it, emerging in our own time, in the Rangers' heartland. But the moment the corridor was finished, Brann came down it with an overwhelmingly superior force. I do not know how he got word. Only I escaped. For more than a year, then, I wandered about in the United States, seeking a way of return. Every futureward corridor would be guarded, I knew, the Rangers being so strong in the Early Industrial civilization. Nowhere could I find a Warden."

"How'd you live?" Lockridge inquired.

"You would call it robbery," Storm said.

He started. She laughed. "This energy gun, which I had with me, can be set to do no more than stun. There was no problem in gathering some thousands of dollars, a few at a time. I was desperate. Can you blame me so very much?"

"I ought to." He looked at her in the firelight. "But I don't."

"I didn't think you would," she said softly. "You are such a one as I hardly dared hope I could find.

"You see, I needed a helper, a bodyguard, someone to make me appear otherwise than a woman traveling alone. That is too conspicuous in all past ages. And I had to go pastward.

"I ascertained there was no guard on this Danish corridor. It was the only one I dared attempt with a gate open on those decades. Even so, you saw how near we came to destruction.

"But now, here we are. There is a Warden base in Crete,

where the old faith is still strong. Unfortunately, I cannot simply call them to come fetch us. The Rangers are also active in this milieu—it is, as I said, a crucial one—and they might too likely intercept the message and find us before our friends can. But once we have reached Knossos, we can get an armed escort, from corridor to corridor until I have reached home. You will be dismissed in your own era." She shrugged. "I left a good many dollars hidden in the United States. You may as well have them for your trouble."

"Skip that," Lockridge said roughly. "How do we get to Crete?"

"By sea. There has long been trade between these parts and the Mediterranean. The Limfjord is not far away, and a ship from Iberia, which is under the religion of the megalith builders, should call sometime this summer. From Iberia we can transship. It should take no longer, and is less hazardous, than following the amber route overland."

"M-m-m . . . okay, sounds reasonable. And I suppose we have enough metal on us to buy passage. Or do we?"

Storm tossed her head. "If not," she said haughtily, "they will not refuse to carry Her Whom they worship."

"What?" Lockridge's mouth fell open. "You mean you can pose as—"

"No," she said. "I am the Goddess."

5

White sunrise mists rolled low across a drenched earth. Water dripped from a thousand leaves, glittered in the air and was lost in brush and bracken. The woods were clamorous with birdsong. High overhead wheeled an eagle, the young light like gold on its wings.

Lockridge woke to a hand shaking him and blinked sandy lids. "Huh? Whuh— No—" Yesterday had drained him, he was stiff and dull in the head, aching in his muscles. He looked into Storm's face and fumbled to recognize her, to know and accept what had happened.

"Rise," she said. "I have started the fire again. You will prepare breakfast."

Only then did he see that she was nude. He sat up in his sleeping bag with a choked-off oath of amazement, delight, and—awe was perhaps the word. He had not known the human body could be so beautiful.

Yet his instinctive reaction died at once. It was not only that she paid him no more attention than if he had been another woman, or a dog. One does not, cannot make passes at Nike of Samothrace.

And a remote bass bellow, thundering down the forest till a flock of capercailzie took flight with enough wings to blot out the sun, distracted him. "What's that?" he cried. "A bull?"

"An aurochs," Storm said. The fact that he was really here, now, personally, stabbed into him.

He scrambled from the bag, shivering in his pajamas. Storm paid the chill no heed, though dew lay heavy in her hair and gleamed down her flanks. Is she human? he wondered. After everything we've been through, everything we've got ahead of us, not a trace of strain—Superhuman. She made some mention of genetic control. They've created the man beyond man, off in the future. She wouldn't need much trickery to start the cult of the Labrys down in Crete, centuries ago. Only herself.

Storm squatted and opened one of the bundles from the cabinet. Lockridge took the opportunity to start changing behind her back. She glanced around. "We will need contemporary clothes," she said. "Our gear will excite sufficient gossip. Take the other costume."

He could not resent her ordering him about, but undid the package. The wrapping proved to be a short cloak of loosely woven wool, blue from some vegetable dye, with a thorn brooch. The main garment was a sleeveless bast tunic that he pulled over his head and belted with a thong. Sandals tied onto his feet and a birdskin fillet ornamented in a zigzag pattern went around his head. In addition he got a necklace, bear's claws alternating with shells, and a leafshaped dagger of flint so finely worked as to look almost metallic. The haft was wrapped in leather, the sheath was birchbark.

Storm surveyed him. He did the same to her. Female dress was no more than sandals, headband, necklace of raw amber, a foxskin purse slung from the shoulder, and a brief skirt decorated with feathers. But he scarcely noticed those details.

"You will do," she said. "Actually, we are an anachronism. We are dressed like well-to-do clanfolk of the Tenil Orugaray, the Sea People, the aborigines. But you have short hair and are clean-shaven, and my racial type—still, no matter. We will be travelers who have had to purchase our clothes locally when the old ones wore out. That practice is common. Besides, these primitives have small sense for logical consistency."

She pointed to a little box that had also been in the bundle. "Open that." He picked it up, but she had to show him how to squeeze to make the lid curl back. Within lay a transparent globule. "Put that in an ear," she said.

Throwing aside a midnight lock of hair, she demonstrated with a similar object. He remembered now the thing she wore in her own left ear, that he had taken for a hearing aid, and inserted his. It did not impair his perception of sound, but felt oddly cool, and a momentary tingle ran over his scalp and down his neck.

"Do you understand me?" Storm asked.

"Why, naturally—" He strangled on the words. They had not been in English.

Not in anything!

Storm laughed. "Take good care of your diaglossa. You will find it rather more valuable than a gun."

Lockridge wrenched his mind back to observation and reason. What had she actually said? *Gun* had been English and *diaglossa* didn't fit the pattern of the rest. Which was— Gradually, as he used the language, he would find it to be agglutinative, with a complex grammar and many fine distinctions unknown to civilized man. There were, for instance, some twenty different words for water, depending on what kind might be involved under what circumstances. On the other hand, he was unable to express in it such concepts as "mass," "government," or "monotheism": at least, not without the most elaborate circumlocutions. Only slowly, in the days that followed, would he notice how different from his own were notions like "cause," "time," "self," and "death."

"The device is a molecular encoder," Storm said in English. "It stores the important languages and basic customs of an era and an area—in this case, northern Europe from what will someday be Ireland to what will be Esthonia, plus some outside ones that might be encountered like Iberia and Crete. It draws energy from body heat, and meshes its output with the nerve flow of the brain. In effect, you have an artificial memory center added to your natural one."

"All that, in this cotton-pickin' little thing?" Lockridge asked weakly.

Storm's wide smooth shoulders lifted and fell. "A chromosome is smaller and carries more information. Make us some food."

Lockridge was downright glad to escape to the everydayness of camp cooking. Besides, he had gone to sleep supperless. The bundles included metal-sealed materials that he didn't recognize; but warmed up, the stuff was delicious. There were only a few meals' worth, and Storm told him impatiently to abandon the remnants. "We will live off hospitality," she said. "That one frying pan is so magnificent a gift as to warrant a year's keep, even at Pharaoh's court."

Lockridge discovered he was grinning. "Yeah, and what if some archeologist digs it up out of a kitchen midden, four thousand years from now?"

"It will be assumed a hoax, and ignored. Though in practice, sheet iron will scarcely last that long in this damp climate. Time is unchangeable. Now be still." Storm prowled the meadow, lost in her own thoughts, while he cooked. The long grass whispered about her ankles, dandelion blossoms lay at her feet like coins scattered before a conqueror.

Either there was some stimulant in the food, or motion worked the stiffness out of Lockridge. When he raked the fire wide and covered the ashes with dirt, and Storm said smiling, "Good, you know how to care for the land," he felt ready to fight bears.

She showed him how to operate the gate control tube and hid it in a hollow tree along with their twentieth-century clothes—though not the guns. Then they assembled their packs, put them on, and started.

"We are going to Avildaro," Storm said. "I have never been there myself, but it is a port of call, and if a ship does not happen by it this year, we will hear where else."

Lockridge knew, from the thing in his ear, that "Avildaro" was an elided form of a still older name which meant Sea Mother House; that She to Whom the village was dedicated was, in some way, an avatar of the Huntress Who stalked the forest at its back; that its people had dwelt there for uncounted centuries, descendants of the reindeer hunters who wandered in as the glaciers receded from Denmark and turned to the waters for their life when the herds followed the ice on into Sweden and Norway; that in this particular region they had begun to farm as well, a few generations ago, though not so much as the immigrants further inland from whom they had learned the art—for they still followed Her of the Wet Locks, Who had eaten the land across which their boats now ventured and Who likewise ate men, yet gave the shining fish, the oyster, the seal, and the porpoise to those who served Her; that of late the charioteers of Yuthoaz, who knew Her not but sacrificed to male gods, had troubled a long peace— He stopped summoning those ghostly memories that were not his. They blinded him to the day and the woman beside him.

The sun was well up now, the mists burned off and the sky clear overhead, with striding white clouds. At the edge of the primeval forest, Storm cast about. Beneath the oaks, underbrush made a nearly impenetrable wall. She took a while to find the trail north: dim, narrow, twisting in light flecks and green shadows among the great boles, beaten more by deer than by men.

"Have a care not to injure anything," she cautioned. "Woods are sacred. One must not hunt without sacrificing to Her, nor cut down a tree unless it is first propitiated."

But they entered no cathedral stillness. Life swarmed about, briar and bramble, fern and fungus, moss and mistletoe crowding under the oaks and burying every log. Anthills stood to a man's waist, butterflies splashed the air with saffron and dragonflies darted cobalt blue, squirrels ran among the branches like streaks of fire, a hundred kinds of bird were nesting. Song and chatter and wingbeat reverberated down the leafy arches; more distantly, grouse drummed, a wild pig grunted, the aurochs challenged all earth. Lockridge felt his spirit expand until it was one with the wilderness, drunk on sun and wind and the breath of flowers. Oh, yes, he thought, I've been out often enough to know this sort of existence can get pretty miserable. But the troubles are real ones—hunger, cold, wet, sickness, not academic infightin' and impertinent income tax forms —and I wonder if the rewards aren't the only real ones too. If Storm guards this, sure, I'm with her.

She said nothing for the next hour, and he felt no need himself to talk. That would have taken his mind off the sight of her, panther-gaited beside him, the light that was blue-black in her hair, malachite in her eyes, tawny down her skin until it lost itself in shadow between her breasts. Once there crossed his memory the myth of Actaeon, who saw Diana naked and was turned to a stag and torn apart by his own hounds. Well, he thought, I've escaped that—physically, anyhow—but I'd better not push my luck too hard.

This arm of the forest was not wide. They emerged by midmorning. Now north and west the land reached low, flat, to a shimmer on the horizon. Grasses rippled in a breeze, isolated copses soughed, light and shade ran beneath the clouds. The trail widened, grew muddy, and wound off past a bog.

At that place, abruptly, Storm halted. Reeds rustled around a pool, which was thick with lilypads where frogs jumped from a stork. The big white bird paid the humans no attention, and Lockridge's new memory told him storks were protected, taboo, bearers of luck and rebirth. A curiously shaped boulder had been rolled to the marge for a shrine. From the top, each year, the headman flung the finest tool that had been made in Avildaro, out to sink as a gift to Our Lady of the Ax. Today only a garland of marigolds lay there, offered by some young girl.

Storm's attention was elsewhere. The muscles stretched out in her belly and she dropped a hand to her pistol. Lockridge stooped with her. Wheel tracks and the marks of unshod hoofs remained in the damp ground. Someone, perhaps two days ago, had driven through these parts and—

"So they have come this far," the woman muttered.

"Who?" Lockridge asked.

"The Yuthoaz." She pronounced the name with an umlauted *u* and an *edh*. Lockridge was still mastering the technique of using a diaglossa, and could merely summon up now that this was what the local tribes of the Battle Ax culture called themselves. And the Ax of those sun-worshipping invaders was not the tree-felling Labrys: it was a tomahawk.

Storm rose, tugged her chin, and scowled. "The available information is too scanty," she complained. "No one thought this station important enough to scout out intensively. We don't know what is going to happen here this year."

After a moment, musingly: "However, reconnaissance certainly established that no large-scale use of energy devices occurred in this area during this entire millennium. That is one reason I chose to go so far back, rather than leave the corridor at a later date when the Wardens are also operating. I *know* the Rangers are not coming here. Thus I dared leave the corridor in the first year of this gate; it will be accessible for a quarter century. And—yes, another datum, a report recorded from a survey party out of Ireland, whose time portals are a century out of phase with Denmark's—Avildaro still stands, has even grown to importance, a hundred years hence." She shifted her pack and resumed walking. "So we have little to fear. At most, we may find ourselves involved in a skirmish between two Stone Age bands."

Lockridge fell into step with her. A couple of miles went by in footfalls through the blowing grass, among the scattered groves. Save for an occasional giant, spared because it was holy, these coastal trees were not oak but ash, elm, pine, and especially beech, another tall invader that had begun to encroach on Jutland.

As the trail rounded such a stand, Lockridge saw a goat flock some distance off. Two preadolescent boys, naked, sun-darkened, with shocks of bleached hair, were keeping watch. One played a bone flute, another dangled his legs from a branch. But when they spied the newcomers, a yell rose from them. The first boy pelted down the trail, the second rocketed up the tree and vanished in leafage.

Storm nodded. "Yes, they have some reason to fear trouble. Matters were not so before."

Lockridge pseudo-remembered what life had been for the Tenil Orugaray: peace, hospitality, bouts of hard work separated by long easy intervals when one practiced the arts of amber shaping, music, dance, love, the chase, and simple idleness; only the friendliest rivalry between the fisher settlements scattered along this coast, whose people were all intricately related anyway; only contact for trade with the full-time farmers inland. Not that these folk were weaklings. They hunted wisent, bear, and wild boar, broke new ground with pointed sticks, dragged rocks cross-country to build their dolmens and the still bigger, more modern passage graves; they survived winters when gales drove sleet and snow and the sea itself out of the west against them; their skin boats pursued seal and porpoise beyond the bay, which was open in this era, and often crossed the North Sea to trade in England or Flanders. But nothing like war—hardly ever even murder—had been known until the chariot drivers arrived.

"Storm," he asked slowly, "did you start the cult of the Goddess to get the idea of peace into men?"

Her nostrils dilated and she spoke almost in scorn. "The Goddess is triune: Maiden, Mother, and Queen of Death." Jarred, he heard the rest dimly. "Life has its terrible side. How well do you think those weak-tea-and-social-work clubs you call Protestant churches will survive what lies ahead for your age? In the bull dance of Crete, those who die are considered sacrifices to the Powers. The megalith builders of Denmark—not here, where the faith has entered a still older culture, but elsewhere—kill and eat a man each year." She observed his shock, smiled, and patted his hand. "Don't take it so hard, Malcolm. I had to use what human material there was. And war for abstractions like power, plunder, glory, that *is* alien to Her."

He could not argue, could do no more than accept, when she addressed him thus. But he remained silent for the next half hour.

By that time they were among fields. Guarded by thorn fences, emmer, spelt, and barley had just begun to sprout, misty green over the dark earth. Just a few score acres were under cultivation—communally, as the sheep, goats, and wood-

ranging pigs, though not the oxen, were kept—and the women
who might ordinarily have been out weeding were not in sight.
Otherwise, unfenced pastures reached on either hand. Ahead
blinked the bright sheet of the Limfjord. A grove hid the village, but smoke rose above.

Several men jogtrotted thence. They were big-boned and
fair, clad similarly to Lockridge, their hair braided and beards
haggled short. Some had wicker shields, vividly painted. Their
weapons were flint-tipped spears, bows, daggers, and slings.

Storm halted and raised empty hands. Lockridge did likewise. Seeing the gesture and the dress, the village men eased
off noticeably. But as they approached, an uncertainty came
over them. They shuffled their feet, dropped their eyes, and
finally stopped.

They don't know exactly who or what she is, Lockridge
thought, but there's always that about her.

"In every name of Her," Storm said, "we come friends."

The leader gathered courage and advanced. He was a
heavy-set, grizzled man, face weathered and eyes crow-footed
by a lifetime at sea. His necklace included a pair of walrus
tusks, and a bracelet of trade copper gleamed on one burly
wrist. "Then in Her names," he rumbled, "and in mine, Echegon whose mother was Ularu and who leads in council, be you
welcome."

Thus jogged, Lockridge's new memory sent him off into a
professional analysis of what had been implied. The names
given were genuine—no secret was made of the real ones for
fear of magic—and came from an interpretation by Avildaro's
Wise Woman of whatever dreams one had during the puberty
rites. "Welcome" meant more than formal politeness: the
guest was sacred and could ask for anything short of participa-
tion in the special clan rituals. But of course he kept his de-
mands within reason, if only because he might be host next
time around.

With a fraction of his awareness, Lockridge listened to
Storm's explanation as the party walked shoreward. She and
her companion were travelers from the South (the far-off ex-

otic South whence all wonders came—but about which the shrewder men were surprisingly well-informed) who had gotten separated from their party. They wished to abide in Avildaro until they could get passage home. Once established, she hinted, they would make rich gifts.

The fishermen relaxed still more. If these were a goddess and her attendant wandering incognito, at least they proposed to act like ordinary human beings. And their stories would enliven many an evening; envious visitors would come from miles around, to hear and see and bring home the importance of Avildaro; their presence might influence the Yuthoaz, whose scouts had lately been observed, to keep away. The group entered the village with much boisterous talk and merriment.

6

Auri, whose name meant Flower Feather, had said: "Do you truly wish to see the fowl marshes? I could be your guide."

Lockridge had rubbed his chin, where the bristles were now a short beard, and glanced at Echegon. He expected anything from shocked disapproval to an indulgent chuckle. Instead, the headman fairly leaped at the chance, almost pathetically eager to send his daughter on a picnic with his guest. Lockridge wasn't sure why.

Storm refused an invitation to join them, to Auri's evident relief. The girl was more than a little frightened of the dark woman who held herself so aloof and spent so much time alone in the forest. Storm admitted to Lockridge that this was as much to confirm her own *mana* in the eyes of the tribe as for any other reason; but she seemed to have withdrawn from him too, he hadn't seen a lot of her during the week and a half they had dwelt in Avildaro. Though he was too fascinated by what he experienced to feel deeply hurt, it had nonetheless reminded him what a gulf there was between them.

Now, as the sun declined, he dug in his paddle and sent the canoe homeward.

This was not one of the big skin coracles which went outside the Limfjord. He had already been on a seal hunt in one of those, a breakneck, bloody affair with a crew that whooped and sang and made horseplay amidst the long gray waves. Awkward with a bone-tipped harpoon, he got back respect when they hoisted the felt sail; steersmanship was not hard for one who had used the much trickier fore-and-aft rig of a twentieth-century racer. His canoe today was merely a light dugout with wicker bulwarks, calling for no more care than a green branch tied at the bow to keep the gods of the wet under control.

Still, reedy, but aswarm with ducks, geese, swans, storks, herons, the marsh fell behind. Lockridge paralleled the southern bayshore, which sloped in a greenness turned gold by the long light. On his left, the water shimmered to the horizon, disturbed only by a few circling gulls and the occasional leap of a fish. So quiet was the air that those remote sounds came almost as clear as the swirl and drip from his paddle. He caught a mingled smell of earth and salt, forest and kelp. The sky arched cloudless, deeply blue, darkening toward evening above Auri's head where she sat in the bows.

Whoof! Lockridge thought. A nice day, but am I glad to be out of those mosquitoes! They didn't bother her any . . . well, I reckon these natives are bitten so often they develop immunity.

His itches weren't too bad, though, not even the unsatisfiable itch for a cigarette; and what he felt was compensated for by the sense of water turned alive by his strokes and the rubbery resurgence in his muscles. Also, of course, by having a pretty girl along.

"Did you find pleasure in the day?" she asked shyly.

"Oh, yes," he said. "Thanks so much for taking me."

She looked astonished, and he recalled that the Tenil Orugaray, like the Navajo, spoke thanks only for very great favors. Everyday helpfulness was taken for granted. The diaglossa made him fluent in their language but didn't override long-established habits.

Color stained her face and throat and bare young bosom. She dropped her eyes and murmured, "No, I must thank you."

He considered her. They didn't keep track of birthdays here, but Auri was so slim, with such an endearing coltishness in her movements, that he supposed she was about fifteen. At that, he wondered why she was still a virgin. Other girls, wedded or not, enjoyed even younger a Samoan sort of liberty.

Naturally, he wouldn't dream of jeopardizing his position here by getting forward with the sole surviving female child in his host's house. More important yet was honor—and inhibition, no doubt. He'd already refused the advances of some he felt were too young; they had plenty of older sisters. Auri's innocence came to him like a breeze from the hawthorns flowering behind her home.

He must admit being a wee bit tempted. She was cute: immense blue eyes, freckle-dusted snub nose, soft mouth, the unbound hair of a maiden flowing in flaxen waves from under a garland of primroses and down her back. And she hung around him in the village to a downright embarrassing extent. However.

"You have nothing to thank me for, Auri," Lockridge said. "You and yours have shown me more kindness than I deserve."

"No, but much!" she protested. "You bless me."

"How so? I have done nothing."

Her fingers twisted together and she looked into her lap. It was so difficult for her to explain that he wished he hadn't asked, but he couldn't think of a way to stop her.

The story was simple. Among the Tenil Orugaray a maiden was sacred, inviolable. But when she herself felt the time had come, she named a man to initiate her at the spring sowing festival, a tender and awesome rite. Auri's chosen had drowned at sea a few days before their moment. Clearly the Powers were angry, and the Wise Woman decided that, in addition to being purified, she must remain alone until the curse was somehow removed. That was more than a year ago.

It was a serious matter for her father (or, at least, the head of her household; paternity was anyone's guess in this culture) —and, he being headman, for the tribe. While no women who were not grandmothers sat in council, the sexes had essentially equal rights, and descent was matrilineal. If Auri died childless, what became of the inheritance? As for herself, she was not precisely shunned, but there had been a bitter year of being left out of almost everything.

When the strangers came, bearing unheard-of marvels and bestowing some as gifts, that appeared to be a sign. The Wise Woman cast beech chips in the darkness of her hut and told Echegon that this was indeed so. Great and unknown Powers indwelt in The Storm and her (Her?) attendant Malcolm. By favoring Echegon's house, they drew off evil. Today, when Malcolm himself had not scorned to go out on the ever-treacherous water with Auri—

"You could not stay?" she pleaded. "If you honored me next spring, I would be . . . more than a woman. The curse would change to a blessing upon me."

His cheeks burned. "I'm sorry," he said, as kindly as might be. "We cannot wait, but must be gone with the first ship."

She bent her head and caught her lip between white teeth.

"But I shall certainly see that the ban is removed," he promised. "Tomorrow I will confer with the Wise Woman. Between us, she and I can doubtless find a way."

Auri wiped away some tears and gave him an uncertain smile. "Thank you. I still wish you could remain—or come back in spring? But if you give me my life again—" She gulped. "There are no words to thank you for that."

How cheaply one became a god.

Trying to put her at ease, he turned the talk to matters that were commonplace for her. She was so surprised that he should ask about potterymaking, which was woman's work, that she quite forgot her troubles, especially since she was reckoned good at fashioning the handsome ware he had admired. It led her to remember the amber harvest: "When we go out after a storm," she said breathlessly, eyes alight, "the whole people, out on the dunes to gather what has washed ashore . . . oh, then is a merry time, and the fish and oysters we bake! Why do you not raise a storm while you are here, Malcolm, so you may have the fun too? I will show you a place I know where the gulls come to your hand for food, and we will swim in the breakers after floating chunks, and, and everything!"

"I fear the weather is beyond my control," he said. "I am only a man, Auri. I have some powers, yes, but they are not really great."

"I think you can do everything."

"Uh . . . um . . . this amber. You gather it mostly for trade, do you not?"

The bright head nodded. "The inlanders want it, and the folk beyond the westward sea, and the ship people from the South."

"Do you also trade flint?" He knew the answer, having spent hours watching a master at work: chips flew from his stone anvil, against his leather apron, with sparks and sulfury smell and deep-toned ring of blows, and a thing of beauty grew beneath the gnarled old hands. But Lockridge wanted to keep the talk light. Auri's laugh was so good to hear.

"Yes, tools we sell too, though only inland," she said. "If the ship calls somewhere else than Avildaro, may I go with you to see it?"

"Well . . . surely, if no one objects."

"I would like to go with you to the South," she said wistfully.

He thought of her in a Cretan slave market, or puzzled and lost in his own world of machines, and sighed. "No, that cannot be. I'm sorry."

"I knew it." Her tone was quiet, with no trace of self-pity. One learned in the Neolithic to accept what was. Even her long isolation in the shadow of wrath had not broken her capacity for joy.

He looked at her, where she sat supple and sun-browned with one hand trailing in the clucking water, and wondered what her destiny was. History would forget the Tenil Orugaray, they would be no more than a few relics dredged out of bogs; before then, she would be down in dust, and when her grandchildren perished—if she lived long enough to have any, in this world of wild beasts and wilder men, storm, flood, uncurable sicknesses and implacable gods—the last memory of her gentleness would flicker out forever.

He saw her few years of youth, when she could outrun deer and spend the whole light summer night giving and getting kisses; the children that would come and come and come, because so many died that every woman must bear the utmost she was able lest the tribe itself die; the middle years, when she was honored as the matron of the headman's house, watched sons and daughters grow up and her own strength fade; age, when she gave the council what wisdom she had reaped, while the world closed in with blindness, deafness, toothlessness, rheumatism, arthritis, and the only time left her was in the half-remembered past; the final sight of her, grown small and strange, down into the passage grave through the roofhole that meant birth; and for some years, sacrifices before the tomb and shudders at night when the wind whimpered outside the house, for it might be her ghost returning; and darkness.

He saw her four thousand years hence and four thousand miles westward: cramped over a school desk; dragging out an adolescence bored, useless, titillated and frustrated; marrying a man, or a series of men, whose work was to sell what nobody needed or really wanted—marrying also a mortgage and a commuter's iron schedule; sacrificing all but two weeks a year of carefully measured freedom in order to buy the silly gadgets and pay the vindictive taxes; breathing smoke and dust and poison; sitting in a car, at a bridge table, in a beauty parlor, before a television, the spring gone from her body and the teeth rotten in her mouth before she was twenty; living in the heartland of liberty, the strongest nation earth had yet known, while it crawled from the march of the tyrants and the barbarians; living in horror of cancer, heart failure, mental disease, and the final nuclear flame.

Lockridge cut off the vision. He was being unjust to his own age, he knew—and to this one as well. Life was physically harder in some places, harder on the spirit in others, and sometimes it destroyed both. At most, the gods gave only a little happiness; the rest was merely existence. Taken altogether, he

didn't think they were less generous here and now than they
had been to him. And here was where Auri belonged.

"You think much," she said timidly.

He started and missed a stroke. Clear drops showered from
the paddle, agleam in the level light. "Why, no," he said. "I was
only wandering."

Again he had misused the idiom. The spirit that wandered,
in thought or in dream, could enter strange realms. She regarded him with reverence. After a while when nothing but
the canoe's passage and the far-off cries of homing geese broke
the stillness, she asked low, "May I call you Lynx?"

He blinked.

"I do not understand your name Malcolm," she explained.
"So it is a strong magic, too strong for me. But you are like a big
golden lynx."

"Why—why—" However childish, the gesture touched him.
"If you want. But I don't think Flower Feather could be bet-
tered."

Auri flushed and looked away. They continued in silence.

And the silence lengthened. Gradually Lockridge grew
aware of that. Ordinarily, this near the village, there was plenty
of noise: children shouting at their games, fishermen hailing
the shore as they approached, housewives gossiping, perhaps
the triumphant song of hunters who had bagged an elk. But
he turned right and paddled up the cove between narrowing
wooded banks, and no human voice reached him. He glanced
at Auri. Maybe she knew what was afoot. She sat chin in hand,
gazing at him, oblivious to everything else. He hadn't the heart
to speak. Instead, he sent the canoe forward as fast as he was
able.

Avildaro came in sight. Under the ancient shaw at its back,
it was a cluster of sod-roofed wattle huts around the Long
House of ceremony, which was a more elaborate half-timbered
peat structure. Boats were drawn onto the beach, where nets
dried on poles. Several hundred yards off stood the kitchen
midden. The Tenil Orugaray no longer lived at the very foot
of that mound of oyster shells, bones, and other trash, as their

ancestors had done; but they carried the offal there, for the half-tame pigs to eat, and the site was veiled with flies.

Auri came out of her trance. The clear brow wrinkled. "But no one is about!" she said.

"There must be someone in the Long House," Lockridge answered. Smoke curled from the venthole in its roof. "We had better go see." He was glad of the Webley at his hip.

He pulled the canoe ashore, with the girl's help, and made fast. Her hand stole into his as they entered the village. Shadows darkened the dusty paths between huts, and the air seemed suddenly cold. "What does this mean?" she begged of him.

"If you don't know—" He lengthened his stride.

Noise certainly buzzed from the hall. Two young men stood guard outside. "Here they come!" one of them shouted. Both dipped their spears to Lockridge.

He went through the skin-curtained door with Auri. His eyes needed a while to adapt to the gloom within; there were no windows, and the smoke that didn't escape stung. The fire in the central pit was holy, never allowed to go out. (Like most primitive customs, that had a practical basis. Fires were never easy to start before matches were invented, and anyone might come here to light a brand.) It had been stoked up until the flames danced and crackled, throwing uneasy flickers across sooted walls and pillars roughly hewn with magical symbols. The whole population was crowded in: some four hundred men, women, and children squatting on the dirt floor, mumbling to each other.

Echegon and his chief councilors stood near the fire with Storm. When Lockridge saw her, tall and arrogant, he forgot about Auri and went to her. "What's wrong?" he asked.

"The Yuthoaz are coming," she said.

He spent a minute assimilating what the diaglossa associated with that name. The Battle Ax people; the northward-thrusting edge of that huge wave, more cultural than racial, of Indo-European-speaking warriors which had been spreading from southern Russia in the past century or two. Elsewhere they were destined to topple civilizations: India, Crete, Hatti, Greece would go down in ruin before them, and their languages and religions and ways of life would shape all Europe. But hitherto, in sparsely populated Scandinavia, there had not been great conflict between the native hunters, fishers, and farmers, and the chariot-driving immigrant herdsmen.

Still, Avildaro had heard of bloody clashes to the east.

Echegon hugged Auri to him for a moment before he said: "I had not too much fear for you under Malcolm's protection. But I thank Her that you are back." The strong, bearded visage turned to Lockridge. "Today," he said, "men hunting southward hastened home with word that the Yuthoaz are moving against us and will be here tomorrow. They are plainly a war band, nothing but armed men, and Avildaro is the first village on their way. What have we done to offend them or the gods?"

Lockridge glanced at Storm. "Well," he said in English, "I kind of hate to use our weapons on those poor devils, but if we've got to—"

She shook her head. "No. The energies might be detected. Or, at least, the story might reach Ranger agents and alert them to us. Best that you and I take refuge elsewhere."

"What? But—but—"

"Remember," she said, "time is immutable. Since this place survives a hundred years from now, quite likely the natives will repel the attack tomorrow."

He could not break free of her eyes; but Auri's were on him too, and Echegon's, and his boatmates' and girl friends' and the flintsmith's and everyone's. He squared his shoulders. "Maybe they didn't, either," he said. "Maybe they're conquered underlings in the future, or would be except for us. I'm stayin'."

"You dare—" Storm checked herself. A moment she stood taut and still. Then she smiled, reached out and stroked his cheek. "I might have known," she said. "Very well, I shall stay too."

7

They came west across the meadows, the oak forest on their left, and the men of Avildaro stood to meet them. They numbered perhaps a hundred in all, with ten chariots, the rest loping on foot: no more than their opponents. When first he squinted through the brilliant noontide, Lockridge could hardly believe that these were the dreaded men of the Battle Ax.

As they neared, he studied one who was typical. In body the warrior was not very different from the Tenil Orugaray: somewhat shorter and stockier, his brown hair twisted into a queue and his beard into a fork, his countenance more Central European than Russian in its beak-nosed harshness. He wore a jerkin and knee-length skirt of leather, a clan symbol burned in, carried a round bullhide shield painted with the fylfot, and had for weapons a flint dagger and a beautifully fashioned stone ax. His lips were drawn wide in carnivore anticipation.

The chariot he followed, evidently his chieftain's, was a light two-wheeled affair of wood and wicker, pulled by four shaggy little horses. A young boy, unarmed and clad merely in a loincloth, guided them. Behind him stood the master: bigger than most, wielding an ax so long and heavy it was a halberd, with two spears racked ready to hand. The chief had a helmet, corselet, and greaves of reinforced leather; a short bronze sword hung at his waist, a faded cloak of linen from the South fluttered off his shoulders, and a necklace of massy gold flashed beneath his shaggy chin.

Such were the Yuthoaz. When they saw the uneven line of fishermen, they slowed their pace. Then the lead charioteer winded a bison horn, the troop howled wolfish war cries, and the horses thudded into gallop. After them banged the wagons, leaped the yelping footmen, boomed the axes on drumhead shields.

Echegon's gaze pleaded with Storm and Lockridge. "Now?" he asked.

"A little longer. Let them get close." Storm shaded her eyes and peered. "Something about him in the rear—the others block my view—"

Lockridge could sense the tension at his back: sighs and mutters, feet that shifted, the acrid stink of sweat. Those were not cowards who waited to guard their homes. But the enemy was equipped and trained for war; and even to him, who had known tanks, the charge of the chariots grew terrifying as they swelled before his eyes.

He brought up his rifle. The stock was cool and hard along his cheek. Storm had grudgingly agreed to let the twentieth-century guns be used today. And perhaps the fact they were about to witness lightnings, even on their own behalf, stretched thin the courage of the Tenil Orugaray.

"Better let me start shootin'," he said in English.

"Not yet!" Storm spoke so sharply, above the racket, that he gave her a glance. The feline eyes were narrowed, the teeth revealed, and a hand rested on the energy pistol she had said she would not employ. "I have to see that one man first."

The charioteer in the van lifted his ax and swept it down again. Archers and slingers at the rear of the Yuthoaz halted, their weapons leaped clear, stones and flintheaded arrows whistled toward the seafolk.

"Shoot!" Echegon bellowed. He need not have done so. A snarl of defiance and a ragged volley lifted from his line.

At this range, no harm was done. Lockridge saw a missile or two thunk against a shield. But the Yuthoaz were in full career.

They'd be on him in another minute. He could make out the flared nostrils and white-rimmed eyes of the nearest horses, blowing manes, flickering whips, a beardless driver and the savage grin that split the beard behind, an ax upraised whose stone gleamed like metal. "To hell with this!" he cried. "I want 'em to know what hit 'em!"

He got that chieftain in his sights and squeezed trigger. The gun kicked back with a solidity that strengthened his soul. Its bang was lost in yells, hoofbeats, squeal of axles and rattle of wheels. But the target flung his arms wide and fell to earth. The halberd soared through an arc. The grass hid man and weapon alike.

The boy reined in, drop-jawed and scared. Lockridge realized at once that he needn't kill humans, swung around and went for the next team of horses. *Crack! Crack!* One animal per bunch would do, to put a wagon out of commission. A stone glanced off the gun barrel, which rang. But the second chariot went over, harness tangled, tongue snapped across, left wheel demolished in the wreck. The live horses reared and neighed their fear.

Lockridge saw the charge waver. Two or three more of those battle cars stopped, and the invaders would bolt. He stepped forward to be in plain sight, his blood too much athrum for him to care about arrows, and let the sun flash off his metal.

The sun itself struck him.

Thunder exploded in his skull. Blinded, shattered, he whirled into night.

Awareness returned with a hurricane of anguish. Light-spots still clouded his vision. Through screams, whinnies, rumbling and booming, he heard the shout: *"Forward, Yuthoaz! Forward with Sky Father!"*

It was in a language the diaglossa knew, but not the Tenil Orugaray.

He groped to hands and knees. The first thing he saw was his rifle, half melted on the ground. That destruction had absorbed most of the energy beam. The cartridges had not gone off in the clip, nor had he himself suffered worse than a vicious burn on face and chest. But fire was in his skin. He could not think for the torment.

A dead man lay nearby. Little remained of the features except charred meat and bone. The copper band on one arm identified Echegon.

Storm stood close by. Her own weapon was out to make a shield. Brief rainbow fountains of flame played around her. The enemy beam passed on, to sickle down three young men who had gone sealing with Lockridge.

The Yuthoaz roared! In one tide, they swept over the villagers. Lockridge saw a son of Echegon—unmistakable, that countenance and that doggedness—ground his spear as if the horses earthquaking down upon him were a wild boar. Their driver swerved them. The chariot clattered past. The warrior who stood in it swung his ax with dreadful skill. Brains spurted. Echegon's son fell by his father. The Yutho hooted mirth, chopped on the other side at someone Lockridge couldn't see, hurled a spear at an archer, and was gone by.

Elsewhere, the village men were in flight. Panic had them, and they wailed as they ran into the forest. Pursuit ended there. The Yuthoaz, whose patron gods were in the sky, did not like those rustling twilit reaches. They turned back to dispatch and scalp any wounded of their enemy.

One chariot rushed toward Storm. Her energy shield made her lioness form shimmer; in Lockridge's delirium it was as if he watched a myth. He had the Webley too. He fumbled for it, but consciousness left him before he got the weapon loose. His last sight was of the one who stood back of the driver—no Yutho—a man beardless and white-skinned, immensely tall, in a hooded black cloak that flapped after him like wings—

Lockridge awoke slowly. For a while he was content to lie on the earth and know he was free from pain.

Piece by piece, there came to him what had happened. When he heard a woman scream, he opened his eyes and sat bolt upright.

The sun was down, but through the doorway of the hut

where he was, past the shore and the bloodily shining Limfjord, he glimpsed clouds still lit. The single room here had
been stripped of its poor possessions and the entrance was
barred with branches lashed together and fastened to the door-
posts by thongs. Beyond, two Yuthoaz stood guard. One kept
glancing inside and fingering a sprig of mistletoe against
witchcraft. His mate's eyes rested enviously on a pair of warriors who drove several cows along the beach. Elsewhere was
tumult, deep-throated male shouts and guffaws, tramp of
horses and clatter of wheels, while the conquered keened their
grief.

"How are you, Malcolm?"

Lockridge twisted his head around. Storm Darroway knelt
beside him. He could see her as little more than another
shadow in the murky cabin, but he caught the fragrance of
her hair, her hands moved softly across him, and she sounded
more anxious than he had ever heard her before.

"Alive . . . I reckon." He touched fingers to face and breast,
where some grease had been smeared. "Doesn't hurt. I—I actually feel rested."

"You were lucky that Brann had antishock drug and enzy-
matic ointment with him, and decided to save you," Storm
said. "Your burns will be healed by tomorrow." She paused,
then—her tone might almost have been Auri's: "So I am also
lucky."

"What's goin' on out there?"

"The Yuthoaz are plundering Avildaro."

"Women—kids—no!" Lockridge struggled to stand.

She pulled him down. "Save your strength."

"But those devils—"

She said with a touch of her old sharpness: "At the moment,
your female friends do not suffer greatly. Remember the local
mores." Empathy returned. "But of course they mourn for those
they love, dead or fled, and they will be slaves. . . . No, wait.
This isn't the South. A barbarian's slave does not live so very
differently from the barbarian himself. She suffers—unfreedom,
yes, homesickness, the fact that no woman whatsoever has the

respect among the Indo-Europeans that she had in this place.
But spare your pity for later. You and I are in worse trouble
than your little companion of yesterday."

"M-m-m, okay." He subsided. "What went wrong?"

She moved around to sit on the floor in front of him, hugged
her knees, and let the breath whistle out between her lips. "I
was a *slogg*," she said bitterly. "I never imagined Brann was
in this age. He organized the attack, that is obvious."

He felt the shaken self-accusation in her, reached out and
said, "You couldn't have known."

Her fingers hugged his. They went limp again, and she said
in a winter voice: "There are no excuses for a Warden who
fails. There is only the failure."

Because that was the code of the service whose uniform he
had worn, he thought suddenly that he understood her and
they had become one. He drew her to him as he might have
drawn his sister in her sorrow, and she laid her head on his
shoulder and clung tight.

After a while, when darkness was nigh absolute, she pulled
herself gently free and breathed, "Thank you." They sat side
by side now, hands clasped.

She said low and fast: "You must realize the numbers in this
war through time are not large. With powers such as a single
person may wield, they cannot be. Brann is—you have no word.
A crucial figure. Though he must take the field himself, because so few are able, he is a commander, a maker of planet-
shaking decisions, a . . . king. And I am as great a prize. And
he has me.

"I do not know how he learned where and when I was. I
cannot imagine. If he could not find me in your century, how
could he hound me down to this forgotten moment? It fright-
ens me, Malcolm." Her clasp was cold and close around his.
"What contortion in time itself has he made?

"He is here alone. But no more were needed. I think he must
have come out of the tunnel under the dolmen earlier than we
did, sought the Battle Ax people, and made himself their god.
That would not be hard to do. This whole inwandering of the

Indo-Europeans—Dyaush Pitar's, Sky Father's, the sun's worshippers, herdsmen, weaponmakers, charioteers, warriors, the men of clever hands and limitless dreams, whose wives are underlings and whose children are property—this was engineered by the Rangers. Do you understand? The invaders are the destroyers of the old civilizations, the old faith; they are the ancestors of the machine people. The Yuthoaz *belong* to Brann. He need but appear among them, as I need but appear in Avildaro or Crete, and in their dim way they will know what he is and he will know how to control them.

"Somehow he learned we were here. He could have brought his full force against us. But that might have warned our agents, who are still strong in this millennium, and led to uncontrollable events. Instead, he told the Yuthoaz to fall on Avildaro, swore the sun and the lightning would fight with them, and swore truly.

"Having won—" Lockridge felt her shudder—"he will send for a certain few of his people, and what else he needs, to work on me."

He held her close. Her whisper was frantic in his ear: "Listen. You may get a chance to escape. Who knows? The book of time was written when first the universe exploded outward; but we have not yet turned over the next leaf. Brann will take you for a mere hireling. He may see no danger in you. If you can—if you can—go up the corridor. Seek out Herr Jesper Fledelius in Viborg, at the Inn of the Golden Lion, on an All Hallows Eve in the years from 1521 to 1541. Can you remember that? He is one of us. Can you but reach him, perhaps, perhaps—"

"Yes. Sure. If." Lockridge did not want to speak further. In an hour or two she could explain. But right now she was so alone. He reached around with his free hand to clasp her shoulder. She moved to make his palm slip downward, and laid her mouth on his.

"Not much life is left me," she choked. "Use what I have. Comfort me, Malcolm."

Stunned, he could only think: Storm, oh, Storm. He gave her back the kiss, he drowned in the waves of her hair, there was nothing but darkness and her.

And a torch flared through the bars. A spear gestured, a voice barked, "Come. You, the man. He wants you."

8

Brann of the Rangers sat alone in the Long House. The holy fire had gone out, but radiance from a crystalline globe sheened off the bearskin on his dais. The warriors who led Lockridge to him bent their knees with awe.

"God among us," said their burly redhaired leader, "we have fetched the wizard as you commanded."

Brann nodded. "That is well. Wait in a corner."

The four men touched tomahawk to brow and withdrew beyond the circle of illumination. Their torch sputtered red and yellow, light barely touching the weatherbeaten faces. Silence stretched.

"Be seated, if you wish," Brann said mildly, in English. "We have much to talk about, Malcolm Lockridge."

How did he know the complete name?

The American remained on his feet, because otherwise he would have had to sit by Brann, and looked at him. So this was the enemy.

The Ranger had removed his cloak, to show a lean, long-muscled body almost seven feet tall, clad in the form-fitting black Lockridge remembered from the corridor. His skin was very white, the hands delicately tapered, the face . . . beautiful, you could say, narrow, straight-nosed, a cold perfection of line. There was no trace of beard; the hair was dense and closely cut, like a sable cap. His eyes were iron gray.

He smiled. "Well, stand, then." He pointed to a bottle and

two glasses, slim lovely shapes beside him. "Will you drink? The wine is Bourgogne 2012. That was a wonderful year."

"No," Lockridge said.

Brann shrugged, poured for himself, and sipped. "I do not necessarily mean you harm," he said.

"You've done enough already," Lockridge spat.

"Regrettable, to be sure. Still, if one has lived with the concept of time as unchangeable, unappeasable—has seen much worse than today, over and over and over, and risked the same for himself—what use in sentimentalism? For that matter, Lockridge, today you killed a man whose wives and children will mourn him."

"He was fixin' to kill me, wasn't he?"

"True. But he was not a bad man. He guided his kin and dependents as well as he was able, treated his friends honorably and did not go out of his way to be horrible to his enemies. You passed through the village on your way here. Be honest. You saw no slaughter, no torture, no mutilation, no arson—did you? On the whole, in centuries to come, this latest wave of immigrants will blend in rather peacefully. The affray here was somewhat exceptional. Far oftener, in northern Europe if not in the South or East, the newcomers will dominate simply because their ways are better suited to the coming age of bronze. They are more mobile, have wider horizons, can better defend themselves; on that account, the aborigines will imitate them. You yourself have been shaped by them, and so has much you hold dear."

"Words," Lockridge said. "The fact is, you got 'em to attack us. You killed friends of mine."

Brann shook his head. "No. The Koriach did."

"Who?"

"The woman. What did she call herself to you?"

Lockridge hesitated. But he could see no gain in being stubborn about trifles. "Storm Darroway."

Brann laughed without sound. "That fits. Her pattern was always flamboyant. Very well, if you like, we shall call her Storm." He set his glass down and leaned forward. The long features grew stern. "She brought this trouble on the villagers, by coming to them. And she knew the risk. Do you seriously believe she cared one atom what might happen, to them or to you? No, no, my friend, you were all only counters in a very large and very old game. She has molded whole civilizations, and cast them aside when they no longer served her purpose, as calmly as you might discard a broken tool. What are a handful of Stone Age savages to her?"

Lockridge clenched his fists. "Shut up!" he shouted.

A stir and a growl came from the Yuthoaz in the shadows. Brann waved them back, though he kept a hand near the energy pistol at his broad coppery belt. "She does make a rather overwhelming impression, does she not?" he murmured. "No doubt she told you that her Wardens stand for absolute good and we Rangers for absolute evil. You would have no way of disproof. But think, man. When was such a thing ever true?"

"In my own time," Lockridge retorted. "Like the Nazis." Brann cocked an eyebrow with such sardonicism that he must add, feebly, "I don't claim the Allies were saints. But damn it, the choice was clear."

"Where is your evidence, other than Storm's word, that the situation in the time war is analogous?" Brann asked.

Lockridge swallowed. The night seemed to close in, with murk and damp and remote indifferent forest sounds. He felt his aloneness, and tightened sinews against it till his jaws ached.

"Listen," Brann said earnestly. "I do not, myself, maintain that we Rangers are models of virtue. This is as ruthless a war as was ever fought, a war between philosophies, whose two sides shape the very past that brought them into being. I ask you, though, to consider. Is the science that sends men beyond the moon, liberates them from toil and famine, saves a child from strangling with diphtheria—is it evil? Is the Constitution of the United States evil? Is it wrong for man to use his reason, the one thing that makes him more than an animal, and to harness the animal within him? Well, if not, where do these things come from? What view of life, what kind of life, must there be to create them?

"Not the Wardens' way! Do you seriously think this earthward-looking, magic-muttering, instinct-bound, orgiastic faith of the Goddess can ever rise above itself? Would you like to see it return in the future? It has done so, you know, in my age. And then, like the worm that bites its own tail, it has gone back to cozen and terrify men in this twilight past, until they crawl before Her. Oh, they can be happy, in a fashion; the influence is diluted. But wait until you see the horror of the Wardens' real reign!

"Think—one small archeological item—the aborigines here bury their dead in communal graves. But the Battle Ax culture gives each his own. Does that suggest anything to you?"

Lockridge had a fleeting odd recollection of his grandfather telling him about the Indian wars. He'd always sympathized with the Indians; and yet, if he could rewrite their history, would he?

He thrust the disturbing thought away, straightened, and said, "I chose Storm Darroway's side. I'm not about to change."

"Or did she choose you?" Brann replied softly. "How did you happen to meet?"

Lockridge had not meant to reveal a word. God alone knew what enemy purpose that would serve. But—well—Brann didn't act like a villain. And if he could be mollified, he might go easier on Storm. And anyhow, what importance did the details of Lockridge's recruitment have? He explained curtly. Brann asked some questions. Before Lockridge quite knew what had happened, he was seated by the Ranger, a glass in his hand, and had told the entire story.

"Ah, so," Brann nodded. "A curious affair. Though not untypical. Both sides use natives in their operations. That is one of the practical reasons for all this juggling of cultures and religions. You seem unusually able, however. I would like to have you for my ally."

"You won't," Lockridge said, less violently than he had intended.

Brann gave him a sidewise glance. "No? Perhaps not. But tell me again, how did Storm Darroway finance herself in your era?"

"Robbery," Lockridge was forced to confess. "She set her energy pistol to stun. Didn't have any choice. *You* waged war."

Brann freed his gun and toyed with it. "You may be interested to know," he said idly, "that these weapons cannot be set at less than lethal force."

Lockridge sprang up. The glass fell from his grasp. It did not shatter, but the wine ran across the floor like blood.

"They can, though, disintegrate a corpse," Brann said.

Lockridge's fist leaped at the talking mouth. Brann wasn't there to meet the blow. He had flicked aside, risen, and covered the other man with his pistol. "Easy," he warned.

"You're lyin'," Lockridge gasped. The world rocked around him.

"If and when I can trust you, you will be welcome to test a gun for yourself," Brann said. "Meanwhile, use your brain. I know somewhat of the twentieth century, not only through this diaglossa but the months I spent hunting my opponent—for I did know she had escaped alive. From your account—easy, I said!—from your account, Lockridge, she had thousands of dollars. How many passersby must she have stunned, to rifle their wallets, before she got that sum together? Would such a wave of robberies, where person after person awakened from a mysterious swoon, not have been the sensation of the year? Would it not? But you read never a word.

"On the other hand, disappearances are quite common, and if the one who vanishes is obscure, the story only makes a back page of the local newspaper. . . . Wait. I did not say she never used her gun to burgle an empty place at night, and set a fire to cover her traces; though it is queer that she did not tell you this was her *modus operandi*. But I do offer you evidence that she is—perhaps not consciously evil, perhaps merely without mercy. After all, she is a goddess. What are mortals to her, who is immortal?"

Lockridge heaved air into his lungs. An uncontrollable trembling ran through him, his skin was cold and his mouth dry. Somehow he was able to speak: "You got the drop on me. But I'm goin'. I don't have to listen to any more."

"No," Brann agreed. "I think best you be shown the truth gradually. You are a loyal sort of man. Which makes me think you will prove valuable, once you have decided where your true loyalty lies."

Lockridge turned on his heel with a snarl and strode for the door. The Yuthoaz hurried to surround him.

Brann's voice came in pursuit: "For your information, you *will* change sides. How do you think I learned of the Warden corridor in America, and of Storm's flight to this milieu? How do you even think I know your name? You came to my own time and place, Lockridge, and warned me!"

"You lie!" he screamed, and fled the house.

Hard hands dragged him to a stop. He stood cursing for a long while.

When finally a measure of calm returned, he looked around as if in search of a foundation for his universe. Avildaro lay empty and still. Those women and children who had not escaped to the wilderness with the old, whom the invaders had contemptuously let go, were herded at the campfires which twinkled in the meadows. Thence came a sad lowing of seized cattle; more distantly, frogs croaked. The huts were shaggy-topped blots of blackness. Before them shimmered the water, behind them rustled the grove under a sky splendid with stars. The air was cool and moist.

"Not easy, talking with a god, aye?" said the redhaired leader with some compassion.

Lockridge snorted and began to walk toward the cabin where Storm was. The Yutho stopped him. "Hold, wizard. The god has told us you can't see her again, or you might cook trouble." In his tumult, Lockridge had not heard that. "He told us also that he's taken away your power to work spells," the warrior added. "So why not be a man like any other? We have to keep you guarded, but we mean you no ill."

Storm! Lockridge cried within himself. But there was no

choice save to leave her alone in the dark. The torch, held by a young man with an oddly pleasant freckled countenance, threw its restless dim light on tomahawks held at the ready.

He surrendered and fell in step with his captors. The chief walked beside him. "My name is Withucar, Hronach's son," he said affably. With a god for boss, he felt no terror of the wizard. "My sign is the wolf. Who are you, and whence came you?"

Lockridge looked into the candid, eager blue eyes and could not hate him. "Call me Malcolm," he answered dully. "I'm from America, a long way off across the sea."

Withucar grimaced. "A wet way, and not mine."

Yet, Lockridge remembered, the Danes—all Europeans— would eventually sail the seas of the whole world. So some spirit of Crete and the Tenil Orugaray was to endure. Brann had spoken truly, as far as he went: the Battle Ax people were not fiends but plain immigrants. More warlike, of course, than the folk older in this land; more individualistic, in spite of being governed by a chariot-driving aristocracy; holding a simpler religion, whose gods ruled the cosmos as a father among their worshippers ruled his family; but men of courage, honor, and a certain rough kindliness. It was not their fault that black-clad creatures had come through time and used them.

As if reading his mind, Withucar continued, "Understand, I have naught ill to say of the sea and woods tribes. They are brave, and—" he sketched a sign in the air, "I pay due respect to the gods they follow. We'd not have moved against you today, had not our god commanded us. But he told us this place was sheltering a witch who was his enemy. And, now we're here, we'll take our reward. For myself, I'd as lief have traded. Maybe, in time, gotten a wife from them. That's profitable, if she comes of a big house. They inherit in the female line, you see, which means I'd have raked in her mother's goods. However, as things are, I suppose we'll extend our grazing range hither, now that we have the land. But we're not so many that we can be forever at war with the other villages hereabouts, so if we can't make terms, we may just take our booty and go home." He shrugged. "The chiefs will hold council about that."

A dreamy part of Lockridge, four thousand years removed, analyzed the word for "chief." It meant simply "patriarch," man of considerable property, head of his sons, retainers, and the ambitious young men who had sworn him service. In that capacity, he also officiated at the sacrifices; but there was nothing like a priesthood, or like the tradition which fixed a man of the Tenil Orugaray in his status before he was born. For that matter, religion was not so binding on the Yuthoaz—fewer taboos, less ritual, less horror of the unknown, a clean faith in sun, wind, rain, fire. The darker elements of Nordic paganism would enter later from the old earth cults.

He shoved that thought aside and concentrated almost frantically on the language. No such thing as an Indo-European tongue existed: only a set of concepts, reflected in grammar and vocabulary, that influenced aboriginal speech as Norman French was to influence English. (Daughter = *dohitar* = milker of cows, which was man's work in Avildaro.) Less than half the words Withucar used went back to the Black Sea steppes. He himself had probably been born in Poland, Germany, or—

"Here we are," the Yutho said. "I'm sorry we must bind you for the night. That's no way to treat a man. But the god ordered us. And wouldn't you rather sleep in the open than in one of those filthy huts?"

Lockridge scarcely heard. He stopped in his tracks with an oath.

The campfire burned high, blotting out the Great Bear in smoke, dancing with flames that picked forth Withucar's chariot and his hobbled horses where they grazed. Another half dozen men lounged around it, weapons close to hand but eyes sleepy and sated. One—a boy of perhaps seventeen, square-shouldered in his leather, a downy cheek puckered by an old battle scar—held a thong. The other end was tied around Auri's wrist.

"By all the Maruts!" Withucar exclaimed. "What's this?"

The girl had lain huddled in hopelessness. When she saw Lockridge, she sprang up with a cry. Her hair was matted, grime on her face was streaked by wept-out tears, a bruise on her thigh stood red and purpling.

The boy grinned. "We heard someone slink about not long ago. I was the one who found and caught her. Pretty, aye?"

"Lynx!" Auri wailed in her own speech. She stumbled toward him. The young warrior jerked her leash. She fell onto her knees.

"Lynx, I escaped to the forest, but I had to come back and see if you—" She could talk no more.

Lockridge stood gripped in nightmare.

"Well, well," Withucar smiled. "The gods must like you, Thuno."

"I waited until you came back, chieftain," the boy said, a little smugly. "May I take her away now?"

Withucar nodded. Thuno rose, grabbed a handful of Auri's hair, and forced her to her feet. "Come along, you," he said. His lips, half parted, glistened.

She screamed and tried to pull free. He cuffed her so her head rocked. "Lynx!" she sobbed: a grisly, grinding noise, despair that clawed for words. "I must not!"

The paralysis broke from Lockridge. He knew what she meant. Until the ban on her was lifted, it was death and more than death for her to lie with a man. Never mind about superstition; how would his own sister have felt? "No!" he yelled.

"Ha?" Withucar said.

"I know her." His appeal tumbled from Lockridge. He shook the chief by the shoulders. "She's holy, not to be touched—there's the worst of curses for anyone who does."

The men about the fire, who had watched in amusement, sprang erect and bristled. Withucar looked dismayed. But Thuno, aroused as he was, snapped, "He lies!"

"I'll swear by anything you like," Lockridge said.

"What are a wizard's oaths worth?" Thuno sneered. "If he means she's a maiden, well, what harm's that ever done us! And she can't be anything else. They don't have sacred women here, except for one old crone who's whelped many a time while young."

Withucar's gaze flickered back and forth. He tugged his beard and said in unease, "Right . . . right . . . but still, best you be safe."

"I am a free man," Thuno said harshly. "On my head be whatever happens." He laughed. "I know the first thing that'll happen. Come!"

"You're the chief," Lockridge raved to Withucar. "Stop him!"

The Yutho sighed. "I cannot. As he said, he is a free man." He regarded the American shrewdly. "I've seen those who came under the terror of the gods. You haven't that look. Maybe you want her for yourself?"

Auri raked fingernails at Thuno's grinning face. He got her by the arm and twisted. She stumbled before him.

And her father and her brother lay out for ravens to eat—Lockridge exploded into motion.

9

Withucar stood next to him. Lockridge whirled and drove a fist into the leader's belly, just below the rib cage. Tough muscle resisted his knuckles, bruisingly, but the man lurched and went to the ground.

The freckled lad who held the torch dropped it and whipped up his ax. Lockridge's Marine training responded. One step brought him close. He chopped at the throat with the edge of his hand. The Yutho uttered a croak, crumpled, and lay still.

Before he could grab the other's weapon, Lockridge sensed a body at his back. Reflex brought his wrists to his neck. Arms closed around it. He felt their hairiness, snapped his wrists apart again, and broke the stranglehold. Turning, he put a leg behind the warrior's ankles and shoved. One more down!

The men around the fire howled and surged against him. Lockridge swept the torch off the earth. A comet's tail of fire blazed when he swept it at the nearest pair of eyes. That attacker stumbled back before he should be blinded. Two others fell over him in a tangle of limbs and curses.

Lockridge leaped over the fire. Thuno stood there alone, gaping. But as the American came upon him, he let go Auri's leash. His own ax was not quickly reachable, but he yanked out his flint dagger and rushed in with an overhand stab.

Lockridge blocked that with one wrist. The sharp edge slithered along his forearm. Blood ran from the gash it left. Lockridge didn't notice. He brought his knee up. Thuno shrieked and reeled away.

"Run, Auri!" Lockridge bellowed.

He had only disabled two out of ten. The rest charged around the fire. He couldn't win over so many, but he could gain her time. He pelted off. A hurled spear smote the ground beside him.

He stopped, pulled the weapon free, and faced the attack. Don't try to stab with this thing, he thought amidst the hammering in his temples. Got better uses for a long straight shaft. He held it in both hands near the middle, balanced on his toes, and waited.

The mass poured upon him. He went into a rage of quarterstaff play. Wood smote solidly on a head, broke fingers that held an ax, rammed a solar plexus, darted between legs to trip, whirred and clattered and thudded home. The night turned into blows, grunts, shouts, where firelight made teeth and eyeballs flash.

Suddenly, fantastically, Lockridge stood alone. Three Yuthoaz writhed groaning in the shadows that wove about his feet. The rest had scattered. They panted and glared at him from near the fire. He saw their hides gleam with sweat.

"Maruts snatch you off!" Withucar roared. "He's only a man!" Still his four hale followers remained at bay. They did not even string a bow.

With his wind back, the chieftain advanced by himself. Lockridge swung the stick at him. Squint-eyed, Withucar had been watching for that. He parried with his tomahawk. The violence rang through Lockridge's bones. His weapon fell from numbed hands. Withucar kicked it out of reach, bawled victory, and trod close. And now, from other camps, others who had heard the racket came running.

Lockridge jumped to meet the Yutho. Again he blocked a downward blow. His shoulder thrust against Withucar. Dimly, he felt a beard bristle cross his skin. He got an arm lock. A heave, cruelly deft—bone snapped with a pistol crack—Withucar floundered off, wheezing through tight-held jaws.

A big man from another fire was almost upon Lockridge, ax aloft. He wore a tunic. Lockridge braced himself, swerved from the attack, took its impact on his hip; his fingers grabbed coarse cloth and a single judo maneuver turned motion into flight. The big man crashed six feet away.

The night burst with howls. Men drew back, shadows in shadow. Lockridge seized Withucar's tomahawk, whirled it on high, and let loose a rebel yell.

Like lightning, he realized what had happened. However total their victory, the invaders were inwardly shaken by the forces they had seen today. Now one man had beaten half a dozen in as many minutes. Darkness and confusion made it impossible to see that he had simply used tactics unknown to this era. He was a troll broken free, and terror seized them.

They didn't run, but they milled beyond his edge of clear vision. The diaglossa hinted what to cry: "I will eat the next man who touches me!" Their horror winded through the night. Sky Father's worshippers still feared the earth gods, for whom, further inland, a human being was devoured every harvest.

Slowly, Lockridge turned and walked off. His back ached with the tension of awaiting a spear, an arrow, a skull-crushing ax blow . . . and not looking behind. He saw the world through a haze, and his heart kept sickeningly missing beats.

An oak reared gnarly before him. The leaves whispered. Somewhere a nightjar echoed them. Lockridge passed into the dark of the far side.

A hand plucked at him. He recoiled and struck out. His fist brushed softness. "Lynx," quivered her voice, "wait for me."

He must husk several times before he could speak, dry-mouthed: "Auri, you should have run off."

"I did. I stopped here to see what befell you. Come." She pressed close, and the universe was no longer a fever dream. "I know ways to the forest," she said.

"That is well." Self-possession returned to him, like a series of bolts snicking home. He could think again. Peering around the tree bole, he saw fires scattered wide across the fields, figures that flitted among them, a rare gleam of polished stone or copper. The bass babble was just too distant for him to make out words.

"They will soon get back their courage," he said, "especially after Brann is told what happened and reassures them. The woods are not close, and they will search for us. Can we stay hidden?"

"She of the Earth will help us," Auri said.

She urged him out into the open and went on all fours. Weasel slim and supple, she traced a winding path where the grass grew tallest. Lockridge followed her more clumsily. But he had stalked this way before, ages ago, in that unborn future when he was a boy.

Beyond enemy view, they rose and loped south. Neither spoke; breath was too precious. Lockridge's pupils expanded until he could see how the grass rippled in a breeze and how the copses stood pale on top, solidly black below, under the high constellations. Through foot-thuds, he heard a fox bark, a hare scutter, frogs chorus. Auri was a moving slenderness beside him, her mane white in the star-glow.

Then a wolf howled from the woods that began to show darkling ahead. As if it were a signal, the bison horns moaned, and he heard men yelp in pursuit of him.

The rest of the flight was a blur. He would never have escaped without Auri. Running, twisting, dodging, she led him through every dip of ground and patch of shadow that her Goddess afforded them. Once they lay behind a boulder and heard men go past, a yard away; once they got up a tree just before spears went bobbing underneath. When finally the forest enclosed him, he fell and lay like one whose bones had been sucked out.

Awareness returned in pieces. First he noticed glimmers of sky overhead, where the leaves left small open spaces. Otherwise he was nearly blind in the night. Bracken rustled and brushed his limbs with harsh fronds, but the ground was soft damp mould, pungent to smell. He tingled and throbbed. Yet Auri was curled against him, he felt her warmth and breath and caught the faint woodsmoke odor of her hair. Everything had grown most quiet.

He forced himself to sit up. She awakened when he moved. "Did we really get away?" he mumbled.

"Yes," the girl said, her tone more level than his. "If they follow, we will know them by their trampling—" a note of scorn for all clumsy heathdwellers "—and find concealment." She hugged him. "Oh, Lynx!"

"Easy. Easy." He disengaged her and groped for the ax. Wonder touched him. "I never expected we both would escape."

"No, surely you knew what you did. You can do anything."

"Uh—" Lockridge shook his head, trying to clear it. For the first time, he understood what had gone on. He really hadn't planned events. Auri's plight triggered the rage pent in him; thereafter, drilled-in habits had carried him along. Unless, of course, the Tenil Orugaray were right in believing that a man could be possessed by Those who walked this wilderness.

"Why did you come back?" he asked.

"To seek you, who would lift the ban on me," Auri said naively.

That made sense, though it dashed his ego a little. She'd acted in what seemed her own self-interest. And maybe not too recklessly, even, judging by how she had given the Yuthoaz the slip afterward. Only by pure bad luck had she been heard and captured; then pure good luck brought Lockridge to the very band that had seized her.

Luck? Time could turn on itself. There was indeed such a thing as destiny. Though it might be blind—Lockridge remembered Brann's final word. "You came to me . . . and warned me!" An ugly thrill went down his nerves. No! he spat at the night. That was a lie!

Defiance brought decision. He paid Auri scant heed, while his plan and the somber sense of fate grew within him, but he heard her talking:

"Many got from Avildaro into the forest. I know where some

are hidden, those I left to return to you. We can seek them out, and afterward another village of the Tenil Orugaray."

Lockridge braced himself. "You shall," he said. "But I have a different place to go."

"What? Where? Beneath the sea?"

"No, ashore. And at once, before Brann thinks to send men there. A forsaken dolmen, half a morning's walk to the south. Do you know it?"

Auri shivered. "Yes." Her voice grew thin. "The House of the Old Dead. Once the Tenil Vaskulan lived in that place and buried their great folk; now only ghosts. Must you indeed? And after sunset?"

"Yes. Have no fears."

She gulped. "Not—not if you say so."

"Come, then. Guide me."

They began to walk, through choked brush and down deer trails saturated with murk, he stumbling and swearing, she slipping sprite-like along. "You see," he explained when they stopped to rest, "my, uh, my friend, The Storm, is still in Brann's hands. I must try to get help for her rescue."

"That witch?" He heard a whisper of tangled locks as Auri tossed her head, and a sniff that actually made him chuckle. "Can she not look after herself?"

"Well, the rescue party should also be able to chase the Yuthoaz home."

"So you will come back!" she exclaimed in a rush of gladness. Somehow he didn't think it was selfish. And had her return to Avildaro been entirely so? He felt uncomfortable.

Little else was said. Progress was too difficult. The slow hours passed; and the night, short in this season near midsummer, began to wane. Stars paled, a grayness crept between the trees, the first twitter of birds came faint and clear.

Lockridge thought that now he could recognize the path he had followed with Storm. Not far to go—

Auri stiffened. Her eyes, luminous in the small dimly seen face, widened. "Hold!" she breathed.

"What?" Lockridge gripped the ax till his palm hurt.

"Do you not hear?"

He didn't. She led him forward, turning her head right and left, parting withes with enormous caution. Presently the sound reached him too: a crackle in the brush, far behind but ever more near.

His gullet tightened. "Animals?" he hoped foolishly.

"Men," Auri told him. "Bound our way."

So Brann had dispatched a patrol to guard the time gate. Had the Yuthoaz been as woodscrafty as this girl, they would have been waiting there for him. As matters stood, he had a chance.

"Fast!" he ordered. "Never mind silence. We must reach the dolmen ahead of them."

Auri sprinted. He came behind. In the misty twilight, he stumbled over a log and into a stand of saplings. They caught at his garments and cried out in wooden voices. Shouts lifted from the glades at his back.

"They heard," Auri warned. "Swiftly!"

Over the trail they fled. Trees crawled past with horrible slowness. And the light strengthened.

When they emerged on the meadow, it lay aglitter with dew under a sky flushed rose. The hillock loomed before them. Breath raw in his lungs, knifed by his spleen, Lockridge made for the hollow tree where Storm had hidden the entrance control.

He fumbled within. Auri screamed. Lockridge drew forth the metal tube and looked about. A score of warriors were at the edge of the clearing.

They roared when they saw him and bounded forward. Lockridge staggered with Auri, up the knoll, above a second-growth tangle into plain view. An arrow went *whoo-oo* past his ear.

"No, you dolt!" called the Yutho leader. "The god said to take him alive!"

Lockridge twisted studs on the tube. A man broke through the young trees at the foot of the mound, poised, and waved his fellows on. Lockridge saw with unnatural sharpness: braided hair, leather kilt, muscular torso and the long toma- hawk—Brann must have nerved this gang up to face almost anything.

The tube glowed and trembled in his grasp. Other Yuthoaz joined the first and plowed through grass and briars, on to do battle. Lockridge threw Withucar's ax. The lead man dodged and barked laughter. His followers rioted behind him.

The earth moved.

Auri wailed, went to her knees, and clutched Lockridge's waist. The Yuthoaz stopped cold. After an instant, they scam- pered with yells into the thicket below. There they halted. Glimpsewise through leaves, Lockridge saw them in their con- fusion. He heard their captain bay, "The god swore we couldn't be hurt by any magic! Come on, you sons of rabbits!"

The downramp shone white. The Yuthoaz advanced again. Auri couldn't be left here. Lockridge seized the girl's arm and flung her into the entrance.

The leader was almost upon him. He tumbled through the hole, fell flat, and twisted the controls. The hovering plug of earth moved down, blotted out the sky, hissed into place.

Silence closed like fingers.

Auri broke it in a shriek that rose swiftly toward hysteria. Lockridge collected himself and slapped her. She sat where she was, dumbstricken, staring at him with eyes from which humanity was gone.

"I'm sorry," Lockridge said. And he was as he watched the red blotch appear on her cheek. "But you must not run wild. We are safe now."

"W-w-w-w—" She fought for breath. Her gaze dashed back and forth, around the icily lit walls that enclosed her; she groveled on the floor and whimpered, "We are in the House of the Old Dead."

Lockridge shook her and snapped, "There is nothing to fear. They have no powers against me. Believe!"

He had not expected will to mount so fast in her. She drank several sobs, her body stiffened and shaking, but after a minute of regarding him she said, "I believe you, Lynx," and the craziness departed.

That gave him back his own strength, together with a bleak alertness. "I did not mean for you to come here," he said, "but we had no choice if you were not to be caught. Now you will see strange things. Do not let them frighten you." A satiric part recalled how Storm had given him much the same advice. Had he indeed come to accept this eldritch world of passage between the ages so soon? His home century seemed a half-forgotten dream.

But that was doubtless because of present urgency. "We have to move," he said. "The Yuthoaz cannot follow us in here, but they will tell their master, and he can. Or we may meet—well, never mind." If they, unarmed, encountered Rangers in the corridor, that was the end of the affair. "This way."

She followed him mutely, down to the foreroom. The auroral curtain in the gate drew a gasp from her, and she held his hand with a child's tightness. He rummaged through the locker but found nothing except outfits appropriate to this milieu. Time travelers must carry their own advanced gear. Damn!

It was a gruesome effort to step through the gate, when anything might lie beyond. But the corridor stretched in humming whiteness, empty as far as he could see. He let the wind out of his chest and collapsed weakly onto the gravity sled.

They couldn't linger, though. At any moment, someone might enter through some other gate and spy them. (Just what did that mean, here in this time which ran outside of time? He'd think about it later.) Moving his hands experimentally to cover the control lights, he found how to operate the vehicle and sent it gliding futureward.

Auri sat close beside him. She clutched the bench hard, but panic was gone and she even showed a trace of bright-eyed curiosity. There was less amazement in her than he had felt. But then, to her all these wonders were equally wonderful, and, in fact, no more mysterious than rain, wind, birth, death, and the wheel of the seasons.

"So what to do?" Lockridge puzzled aloud. "I could go on

to 1964, and we might try just to disappear. But I don't reckon
that'd work. Too damn many Rangers there, and too damn
easy for 'em to trace a man, especially when you'd make us
sort of conspicuous, kid. And if Storm herself couldn't make
contact with any Wardens then, I sure can't." He realized he
had spoken in English. Doubtless Auri took his words for an
incantation.

What had Storm told him?

Instantly, overwhelmingly, he was back in the prison hut,
and she was with him, and his mouth knew her kiss. For a
while he forgot everything else.

Sense came back. The corridor encompassed him with blind
radiance, with hollowness and strangeness. Storm was far away
—centuries away. But he could return to her. And would, by
heaven!

Might he dash clear up to her age? No. This shaft didn't
reach that far. And too risky, in any event. The sooner they
got out and vanished in the world, the better. But she had
spoken of a Herr Jesper Fledelius, in Viborg of the Reformation era. Yes, his best bet. And, too, a feeling of destiny still
drove him.

He slowed the sled and paid attention to the gate markers.
He couldn't read their alphabet, but Arabic numerals were
recognizable. Pretty clearly, years were counted from the
"lower" end of the passage. So, if 1827 B.C. equalled 1175. . . .

When the numbers 45—— appeared, he stopped the sled and
sent it back. Auri waited while he forced himself to study the
layout and think. Blast that uncertainty factor! He wanted to
come out a few days in advance of All Hallows, to allow time
to reach Viborg, but not so far in advance that Brann's hounds
could get on his track.

As best he could, he selected a line in the set corresponding
to Anno Domini 1535. Auri linked fingers with him and followed him trustingly through the curtain.

Again the long, still room, and the locker. But the clothes
stored here were something else from the Neolithic. A variety
of costumes was available, peasant, gentleman, priest, soldier,

and more. He didn't know which was best. What the hell had gone on in Denmark of the sixteenth century? Hell indeed, if the time war were involved.

Well, here was a purse of gold, silver, and copper money—Auri exclaimed at the sight of all that metal—and cash was always useful. But a lower-class person who carried so much would be suspected of robbery. Thus Lockridge chose what he imagined was a prosperous man's traveling garb: linen under-clothes and shirt, satin doublet, crimson trunk hose, high boots, floppy-brimmed cap, blue cloak trimmed with fur, sword and knife (the latter doubtless mainly for eating purposes), and miscellaneous gear that he could only guess about. Diaglossas, of course, for him and Auri; and then he knew that there were so many wigs because men today wore their hair long. He donned a yellow one. It seemed briefly to writhe, as if alive, and settled onto his head with a firmness that gave a perfect illusion of nature.

Auri stripped off her skirt and ornaments, innocent beneath his eyes, and fumbled with the long gray gown and hooded cloak he picked for her. "The seafarers from the South do not dress more queerly than those who dwell below the earth," she said.

"We are bound up again," Lockridge told her. "Into a very different land. Now, this thing I have put in your ear will guide you in speech and behavior. But best hold yourself as meek and quiet as you can. Let me take the lead. We will tell people you are my wife."

She frowned, turning the implications over in her head. Her sense of wonder was stunned, she accepted everything as it came to her, though she kept a fox's alertness: an attitude that Zen masters might envy. But the Danish word *hustru* held a universe of concepts about the relationship between the sexes that the Yuthoaz would have taken for granted but that were new to her.

Abruptly she flushed. Her passivity vanished in joy, she threw her arms about him and cried: "Then the curse is gone? Oh, Lynx, I am yours!"

"Whoa, there. Whoa!" He fended her off. His own ears burned. "Not so fast. The month, uh, won't be spring here."

Nor was it. When they emerged on the moundside and closed the door, he found night again—a cold, autumnal night where the half moon flew between ragged clouds and the wind whined in sere grasses. Naked and empty stood the dolmen above. The forest where once the Goddess walked was gone; only a few scrubby elms swayed in the north. Beyond them, bone-white, gleamed encroaching sand dunes that the future had yet to drive back.

But there had been cultivation around the hillock. Had been. Traces of furrows remained among weeds, and the clay chimney of a burned cottage reared jagged on the southern ridge. War had passed through these parts, less than a year ago.

10

In awe, the Neolithic girl asked, "Is the Knossos they tell of as great as that?"

Despite weariness and unease, Lockridge had to grin. To his eyes, sixteenth-century Viborg was like the crossroads town where his parents used to shop. Much prettier, though, especially after two days of heathland. And it promised snugness, now when the last sunlight speared through rainclouds rising blue-black on a wind that flapped his cloak and whistled of winter.

Past the lake, he glimpsed through an oak grove (the beeches had still not driven the king tree out of Denmark) the warm brick hue of an abandoned monastery. Hard by, the city walls retained some green in the grass that covered their lower embankments. The same tinge was given by moss to such of the high-peaked thatch roofs as he could see. Spare and graceful, the cathedral's twin towers reached for heaven.

"I think Knossos may be a little bigger," he said.

His smile faded. Thirty-three hundred years, he thought, and every hope which had then blossomed so brightly was dust, not even remembered. And other hopes had sprung, and died, until today—

The diaglossa gave basic information but was silent about historical events. So had it been in Auri's age and, he suspected, in every year of earth's existence on which a time gate opened. He had a guess at the reason. Rangers and Wardens recruited native auxiliaries; but who could remain steady if he knew what must befall his people?

Denmark lay in evil days. He and Auri had kept to the lesser roads, little more than cartwheel tracks that wound through forest and heather; they lived off rations from the supply bundle and slept out, wrapped together in their cloaks, when exhaustion forced a halt more than darkness did. But they saw farmsteads and folk; they stopped to drink at wells; and though every peasant was sullen, frightened, short-spoken, one was bound to learn a few things. A song was in the land:

> *"All the small birds that are in the woods,*
> *Complain of the hawk the sorest;*
> *He rips from off them both plumes and down,*
> *He'd hunt them out of the forest.*
>
> *Off then flew the eagle old,*
> *All with his children too;*
> *The other small birds, they grew then wild,*
> *They knew never what to do—"*

Four hundred years hence lay the happy country Lockridge had seen. That was cold comfort, on this gray cold evening. How long would its moment be?

"Come," he said. "We'd best hurry. They close the gates at sunset."

He led the way by the lakeside, till the path joined the highroad. According to the boy who had opened a little toward him, even sung him the ballad (which was of the great noblemen, loosed upon the common folk now that King Kristiern II who had been their friend lay captive in Sønderborg Castle), tomorrow was the Eve of All Hallows. His timing had been close; he wanted to get settled in town and acquire some feel of things before seeking out Jesper Fledelius.

The highway was also dirt, muddy and deeply rutted. No traffic moved on it. North Jutland was still a ghostly country after last year's revolt, broken by the cannon of Johan Rantzau. The wind shrilled through leafless branches.

Half a dozen men stood guard at the portal. They were German Landsknechts, in soiled blue uniforms whose sleeves puffed out around the corselets. Two-handed swords, five feet long, were slung on their backs. A pair of halberds clashed together to bar the way, a third slanted toward Lockridge's breast. "*Halt!*" snapped the leader. "*Wer gehts da?*"

The American wet his lips. These mercenaries didn't look impressive. They were shorter than he by several inches— most people were in this undernourished age, as they had not been in his time or in Auri's—and faces under the tall helmets were scarred by smallpox. But they could kill him with no trouble.

He had cobbled together a story. "I am an English merchant, traveling with my wife," he said in their own language. "Our ship was wrecked on the west coast." So desolate had that been, what he saw of it, that he didn't think anyone would give him the lie. The diaglossa informed him that marine disasters were not uncommon. "We made our way here overland."

The sergeant looked skeptical. His men tautened. "At this time of year? And you were the only ones saved?"

"No, no, everyone got ashore without harm," Lockridge said. "The ship is aground and damaged, but not broken apart." Travel-stained though he was, he had obviously not been through salt water. "The master chose to keep the men there, lest the goods be plundered. As I had business in Viborg that will scarcely wait, I offered to carry word and ask for help." Such an expedition would take at least three days to arrive and find nothing, an equal time to get back. By then he should be gone.

"English, ha?" The little eyes narrowed. "I never heard an Englander speak as if born in Mecklenburg."

Lockridge swore at himself. He should have used what fragments of German he remembered from college, not been seduced by the instrument in his ear. "But I was," he said. "My father was a factor there for many years. Believe me, I am respectable." He dipped into his purse, brought out a couple of gold nobles, and jingled them suggestively. "See, I can afford to ask honest men to drink my health."

"Friedrich! Fetch the Junker!" A Landsknecht sloped off through the tunnel-like gate. His spear butt rattled on cobblestones. Lockridge backed away. "Stay where you are, outlander!" Edged steel thrust forward.

Auri caught at Lockridge's arm. The sergeant twisted his mustache. "Yonder's no wife to a rich merchant," he pounced. "She's been in the sun as much as any serf wench." He wiped his nose with the back of one hairy hand and stood pondering. "Yet she walks like a lady," he muttered. "What *are* you two, anyhow?"

Lockridge saw fear give way in Auri's eyes to something she had not known before: shame, at the way the Landsknechts leered. His fingers itched for a gun. "Watch yourselves," he barked. "Else I'll have you whipped."

The sergeant snickered. "Or I'll see you on the gallows, other side of town—spy! The crows'll welcome you. They've long picked clean the peasants we dangled up for them."

Lockridge choked. He hadn't expected trouble. What had gone wrong?

His glance flickered about, seeking escape. There was none. Arquebuses were racked with smoldering matches, ready to shoot, and he heard iron-shod hoofs clatter near.

The rider came into view, clad in half armor, his long face cast in arrogant lines. He must be one of the Danish aristocrats, Lockridge thought, in charge of this watch, of this foreign garrison set among his own people. The Germans saluted clumsily. "Here's Junker Erik Ulfeld," the sergeant announced. "Tell him your tale."

Blond brows lifted. "What have you to say?" Ulfeld drawled, also in German.

Lockridge gave his right name—might as well—and repeated his yarn in more detail. Ulfeld stroked his chin. He was what passed for clean-shaven, which with contemporary razors meant that his palm went over a skin like sandpaper.

"What proof have you?"

"No documents, my lord," Lockridge said. Sweat trickled from his armpits, down his ribs. The horseman loomed mountainous over him, against a roiling cloud mass; sunlight had taken on a brazen storm tinge which made the world stand out stark, and the wind moaned louder. "Those were lost in the shipwreck."

"Do you know anyone here, then?" Ulfeld snapped.

"Yes, at the Inn of the Golden Lion—" Lockridge's voice jerked to a stop. Ulfeld had laid hand to hilt. Lockridge understood, and cursed his diaglossa. The question had been in Danish; unthinkingly, he had answered likewise.

"An Englishman who speaks two foreign languages so well?" Ulfeld murmured. His pale eyes flared. "Or a man of Count Kristoffer's?"

"God's bones, my lord!" blurted the sergeant. "A murderburner!"

Weapons rammed closer. The knowledge came too late into Lockridge. Because they had gunpowder, and the earth had been circumnavigated, and Copernicus was alive, he hadn't stopped to examine just how different this period really was from his own. With wooden houses, straw roofs, no more water than could be drawn in a bucket, hardly a town escaped repeated devastation by fire. Today's fear of enemy arsonists was akin to the fear he remembered of atomic rockets.

"No!" he cried. "Listen to me! I've lived in Denmark and the German cities—"

"Beyond a doubt," said Ulfeld dryly, "in Lübeck."

Through the lurching of his wits, a curious, detached chain of logic zigzagged in Lockridge. Lübeck was a Hanseatic town, evidently leagued with Kristoffer, the count whose doomed war on behalf of the old king still raged in the islands, from what little that poor peasant boy had known to tell. Ulfeld's conclusion was much too natural.

"But you said a good burgher could identify you," the Dane went on. "Who is he?"

"They call him Jesper Fledelius," Auri ventured.

"What the pox!" Ulfeld's calm broke. His horse snorted and curvetted, mane aflutter in the wind. The sergeant gestured to his Landsknechts, who closed around the strangers.

Oh, Lord, Lockridge groaned to himself, weren't we in deep enough? I was goin' to stall if I could, till I found out if that name meant anything. He hardly noticed when he was relieved of sword and knife, nor even how rudely Auri was frisked.

Ulfeld got back his mask of remoteness. "At the Inn of the Golden Lion, did you say?" he asked.

Lockridge could only go ahead. "Yes, my lord. So I was told. Though he may not be there yet. But I haven't been in Denmark for years. I know little of what's happened here. In fact, I have never met this Jesper. My company of merchant adventurers only gave me his name as one who . . . who could help us arrange trade. If I were an enemy agent, my lord, would I come as I have done?"

"If you were a true merchant," Ulfeld retorted, "would you not have known you could not come here to trade, as freely as if we were Indian savages with no laws governing who may do so?"

"He has a full purse, Junker," the sergeant said smugly. "He tried to buy his way past us." Lockridge wanted to smash the man's teeth. He almost enjoyed hearing Ulfeld say curtly:

"That would have been a dear gift for you." The nobleman sat his horse a while, expertly curbing its restlessness. Auri shrank from the beast, it was so much bigger than the ponies she knew and never had she heard of riding one.

Decision came. "Fetch me a squad," Ulfeld ordered.

"I'll come too, my lord," the sergeant said.

Ulfeld's mouth bent upward. "No doubt you smell reward money. Indeed there is a price on Herr Jesper's head. But keep your post."

The Landsknechts muttered in their whiskers. Ulfeld gave them a look. They fell to a sort of attention; there was that gallows behind the city.

"We shall go to the inn," Ulfeld said, "and see what there is to see, and afterward put some questions." His gaze brooded on Auri. She straightened and glared back. "A wench from the Ditmarsh, I'll be bound. No other baseborn folk dare hold themselves so high. My father died there in King Hans' day, when they opened the sluices on our army. Perhaps tonight—"

Sickness filled Lockridge's throat.

Several more foot soldiers appeared. Ulfeld told them to bring the prisoners along, and rode on through the gate.

Viborg within was less attractive than from a distance. The streets were lanes where pigs rooted in ripe offal above which the stepping stones down the middle scarcely rose. With dusk setting in, few people were abroad. Lockridge saw a work-man in his smock, bent from a lifetime's toil; a serving maid with a basketful of bread; a leper who shook his rattle in warn-ing as he tottered near; a laden ox-drawn wagon with great wooden wheels. They faded rapidly into the gloom that waxed between high-gabled houses already barred and shuttered against night robbers. The first spatters of rain stung his cheeks.

Then a sound broke through wind, foot-splash, hoof-clop, a high and striding peal. "Oh!" Auri exclaimed. "The Goddess' voice!"

"Church bells," Lockridge said. In all his desperation, he had to admit the sound was lovely; and so was the sight of the cathedral, dim across a market square. . . . The wind shifted and filled his nose with graveyard stench.

Not far beyond, Ulfeld drew rein. A wooden sign creaked as it swayed. By light leaking yellow through door and shutters, into the now heavy dusk, Lockridge could just make out a crudely painted lion rampant. The Landsknechts grounded their pikes with a bang. One hastened to hold the nobleman's stirrup while he dismounted. Dully sheening in his breastplate and helmet, Junker Erik waited with drawn sword and let a soldier beat on the door.

"Open, you swine!" the German shouted.

The door groaned ajar. A stout little man peered out and said angrily, "We want none of your trade in an honest place—Herr Knight! I beg forgiveness!"

Ulfeld shoved him aside. Lockridge and Auri were hustled after.

The room was small. A twentieth-century man would bump his head on the sooty rafters if he stood erect, and the walls closed narrowly in. The floor was dirt, strewn with rushes. Lamps flickered on shelves to throw a dull light and many hulking shadows. A stove built of clay pots, in whose mouths a frozen hand or foot might be warmed, gave some heat; its crude vent gave more smoke, until Lockridge's eyes smarted. A trestle table had not yet been taken down for the night. One man sat there with a pot of beer.

"Who else is guesting?" Ulfeld demanded.

"None, my lord." It was unpleasant how the innkeeper cringed. "We get scant custom these days, you know."

Ulfeld jerked his head. "Search." He advanced on the lone patron, who remained benched. "Who are you?"

"Herr Torben Jensen Sverdrup, of Vendsyssel." The gravelly bass was amiable, as from much drink. "Pardon me if I do not rise. I've carried Swedish iron in my leg for long years. Seek you someone?"

Ulfeld glowered at him. The man was big, he would have been big in any century, with ox shoulders above an impressive paunch. His face was made ugly by pockmarks and flattened nose, but the eyes were light and cheerful. Grizzled dark hair and beard fell unkempt to a doublet equally greasy. "Have you proof who you are?" Ulfeld asked.

"Oh, indeed, indeed. I am on lawful business, trying to get the beef trade started again, now it's back where it belongs in well-born hands." Sverdrup belched. "Will you drink with me? I think I can even spare a few pennies to treat your men."

Ulfeld aimed his sword at the throat of the other. "Jesper Fledelius!"

"Ha? Who's that? Never heard of him."

A frightened feminine squeal from the rooms to the rear was followed by German laughter. "Ah, yes," Sverdrup grinned, "mine host has a pretty daughter." He peered at

Lockridge and Auri. "That's another nice little partridge you have with you, Herr. What's the meaning?"

"I have heard—" Ulfeld's look speared Sverdrup and the landlord— "that the traitor Fledelius is in this house."

Sverdrup took a giant's draught from his pot. "One hears many things. Are you not satisfied to have Skipper Klement in Viborg?"

"There's a cell next his, and a headsman's ax, for Fledelius. These strangers tell of an appointment with him. I must ask for letters that prove who you are."

Sverdrup blinked at the prisoners. "I might well wish to be Fledelius, if so fair a lady craves to see him. But alas, no, I am only a poor old squire from the Skaw." He fumbled in his clothes, dislodging a substantial colony of fleas. "Here. I trust your schooling is less rusty than mine."

Ulfeld scowled at the parchment. His men came back. "None but the landlord's family, Herr," one reported.

"So, so, did I not tell you?" the innkeeper chattered. "Herr Torben has guested the Golden Lion in former years, my lord. He is known to me, and I have always had a good name, ask the burgomaster if Mikkel Mortensen is not an honest loyal man."

Ulfeld tossed the letter on the table. "We will keep a watch," he decided. "The outlaw may still show himself. But give him no chance of a warning. You two—" He pointed at a couple of his mercenaries. "Remain here for the time. Guard each door and arrest any who enter. Let no one leave. You others, follow me."

"Will you not even have a pot with a lonely old man?" Sverdrup urged.

"No. I must see these prisoners questioned."

If need be, with rack and pincers and the bone-crushing boot. For Auri— Through a mist that swirled, Lockridge stared at the man behind the table. "No, wait," he croaked. "Help."

The pouched eyes drooped. "I am sorry, little maiden," Sverdrup mumbled. "But so many are dead, so many more soon to die." He traced a cross.

A hand thrust Lockridge toward the door. He dug in his heels. The butt of a pike cracked across one knee. Pain lanced through him, he stumbled and cursed. Auri's hood had fallen back, and a soldier snatched her by a lock of hair.

"No!" the girl screamed. "We belong to Her!"

Sverdrup's mug banged down on the board. Auri drew a sign in the air. Lockridge couldn't make it out, something of her own ritual, dead and forgotten, a blind cry—

The big man reached under the table and climbed stiffly to his feet. From the cloak that had covered it on the floor, a crossbow looked forth, cocked and loaded.

"Not so hasty, my lord," he puffed. "Not quite so hasty, I beg you."

Ulfeld spun on his heel. The sword gleamed up. German spears poised amidst obscene oaths.

If a bear could grin, it would look like the man who must be Jesper Fledelius. "Calmly, now, calmly," he said. "One move, one least of little moves, and my lord the knight will not be so handsome any longer. We do not wish to distress the ladies of Viborg, do we?"

"They'll kill you!" the tavernkeeper wailed. "Jesus have mercy on us!"

"Well, they might try, after this lady I embrace has said her one sharp word," Fledelius nodded. "But here is also my sword. It's made meals off a good many Swedes, and Holsteiners, and even Danes. Naught is so tasty as a Dane who's foresworn the old eagle—unless maybe a German hireling. We might have a most interesting discussion, we several. However, you, Herr Knight, would unhappily be forced to a spectator's seat, and even though you would doubtless be given one befitting your rank in Hell, nevertheless, any of these lads who outlived the night would not be thanked for losing a life so precious. They might even be asked to dance on a rope's end, eh? So do let us try to settle our dispute by peaceful, scholastic means, as is seemly for Christian men."

A silence closed in that made Lockridge's breath more loud in his ears than the wind and thickening rain outside.

"Mikkel, my good man," said Jesper Fledelius, "you must have somewhere a length of rope. With that we may bind these excellent fellows, rather than cut them down like Turks. Of course, it is a Turkish fate to lie in a tavern and have no means of drawing beer. But someone will happen along to-morrow. Men are always thirsty. A symbol of the Evangelicum, think you not?—beer laving the throat as salvation laves the sin-parched soul." He beamed at Auri. "Scripture speaks truly of wisdom in innocence, little maiden. Words might not have moved this cowardly old carcass of mine, for words are cheap and crafty. But you showed me Her token, which does not lie. I thank you."

The landlord began to sob. A woman and a couple of children stuck terrified faces out from the back entrance. "Be of good cheer, Mikkel," the outlaw said. "Plainly, you and yours must leave this town with us. A pity, to let this fine hostel fall into the oafish hands of Junker bailiffs. But the Coven will feed and shelter you." The gross face flashed momentarily with utter love. "And when She returns, you shall be rewarded."

He gestured with his chin at Lockridge. "Herr, be so kind as to remove the weapons from these—" the expression was shocking in that cool tone— "and get them secured. We must be off as fast as God allows. Our Lady's business does not wait."

11

Rain roared on the hut. It was a shepherd's huddling place, alone on the heath, deserted in this season: a thing of peat where a man might rest, so crude and poor that the Tenil Orugaray would have disdained it. But Auri slept, curled on the ground, head pillowed in Lockridge's lap.

Mikkel Mortensen crouched outside with his wife and brood. The American felt humiliated by that, still more so by their unresentfulness of him, whom they took for an *Adelsmand*, resting somewhat dry. Fledelius had insisted. "We've secret matters to talk of, you and I, and these creaky bones will not let me do more than wheeze along when we go afoot tomorrow."

There had been no way to get horses through the smugglers' tunnel that went under the walls of Viborg. The fugitives were not far from the town. But outside reigned an emptiness and a blackness broken only by an occasional lightning flare. Then every twig of heather, every hurtling drop of rain and runnel of water across soaked earth stood forth briefly and blindingly white.

Fireless, the inside of the hut was thick with night and cold. Lockridge's drenched garments were worse than useless, he had stripped to his hose like Fledelius, hugged his ribs and tried to keep the teeth quiet in his head. Auri lay naked and unbothered. He ought to have taken in one of the tavernkeeper's children, rather than her; but she needed his presence, in this world of iron and cruelty, more than they needed the roof.

Another bolt clove the sky. Thunder crashed in its wake. For an instant, Jesper Fledelius' battered countenance made a gargoyle in the doorway. Sightlessness returned. The wind yammered.

"Understand," the Dane said earnestly, "I am a good Christian man. I'll have naught to do with that Lutheran heresy the Junkers and their toy king are foisting on the realm, and surely not with the heathendom of the witches. Yet there is white magic as well as black. Is there not? And it was ever old custom to leave offerings for the unseen ones. They do not really invoke Satan, those poor ignorant peasants who gather on May Eve and tomorrow. Nor yet the false gods you may read of in the chronicles of Saxo Grammaticus. Viborg was once *Vebjörg,* Holy Mount. Where the cathedral now stands was a sanctuary ancient before Odin led his folk in from the East. Spirits of earth and water—may not a man appeal to them without grave sin? These days, the peasant has often none else to turn to." He shifted on the damp dirt. "However, I myself am only in touch with the Coven, I do not belong to it."

"I understand," Lockridge said.

He believed he spoke truth, and saw more than he uttered. Dim and enormous, the pattern had begun to grow before him.

Man's history was the history of religion.

What Auri had, who slept so peacefully here among thunders, and Auri's people, and the Indians he had seen in Yucatán, and every primitive race he knew of whose culture had not taken a completely perverted turn—was wholeness of spirit. It was purely a question of taste whether that made up for all they lacked. The fact remained, they were one with earth and sky and sea in a way that those who set the gods apart from themselves, or who denied any gods, could never be. When the Indo-Europeans brought their patriarchal pantheon to a land, they brought much that was good; but they created a new and lonely kind of man.

There was no sharp dichotomy. The old ones endured. After a time, they blended with the aliens, transfigured them, un-

til ageless forms stood clear again and only names had
changed. Dyaush Pitar, with his sun chariot and battle ax, became Thor, whose car was drawn by honest earthy goats and
whose hammer brought the rain which was life. No blood was
offered the Redbeard; he was himself a yeoman. And when
Odin, one-eyed wolf god to whom the warlords gave men, fell
before Christ and lived in memory as no more than a troll—
Thor called himself St. Olaf, Frey was St. Erik whose wagon
was drawn out each spring to bless the fields, and She took on
the blue mantle of the Virgin Mary. And always and forever
there were the little gods, sprites, hobgoblins, leprechauns,
mermaids, so much in the world that they were not even called
gods, whom men made into signs of help and harm, love and
fear, every wonderful mystery and fickleness which was life.

Lockridge was agnostic himself (child of a sad, brain-heavy
and gut-light time which he now saw must not have long to
live) and passed no opinions on the objective truths involved.
As far as he knew, Mary might be the actual Queen of Heaven,
the Triple Goddess only an early intuition of her. A sensible
man like Jesper Fledelius could believe that. Or both might
be shadows cast by some ultimate reality; or both might be
myth. What mattered in history was not what men thought
but what they felt.

And into this great slow conflict and interweaving of two
world-views the time war had entered. Rangers engineered the
march of the warmaking tribes and their militant gods; Wardens found secret ways to keep what was old and make the invaders over into its image. Rangers urged on the tomahawk
people, who obliterated the cult of the passage grave; but Neolithic herdsmen became Bronze Age farmers and seafarers, and
the sun was no longer a fire spirit but earth's guardian and
fructifying husband. Christendom entered, with books and
logic and the first god who ever punished incorrect beliefs
about his own nature—and erelong the people's hearts belonged to Mary. The Reformation brought back Jehovah,
armed with a terrible weapon against instinct—the printing
press—but religion itself was subtly divided, discredited, emas-

culated, until the world five or six hundred years hence felt its own barrenness and yearned for a faith which went deeper than words. Lockridge looked into the century after his own and did not see science triumphant; he saw men gathered on hills in the name of a new god or of an ancient one reborn.

Or a goddess?

"How did she come to you?" he asked.

"Well, now." Fledelius' voice rumbled hoarse, coarse, and reverent. "The story is a bit long. You must know, I am—was— the squire near Lemvig, as my fathers before me since the first Valdemar. That's a poor district, we Fledeliuses were never of the high haughty houses, we were close to our peasants; and in Jutland to this day the commons are more free than in the islands, where serfs may be bought and sold. On my grounds there is a *kæmpehøj—*" I know that dolmen, Lockridge thought in eeriness— "where folk were wont to make little offerings. They spoke of wonders glimpsed from time to time, strange comings and goings, I know not what. But if the priest said naught, who was I to meddle with old usage? Bad luck comes from such. The Lutherans will learn that, to the land's sorrow.

"So. I fought in the wars. Let me say naught against my lord King Kristiern. Sweden was his by right going back to Queen Margrete, and I call Sten Sture a traitor that he raised the realm against Danish rule. Yet . . . I am no milksop, understand, I've split my share of pates . . . yet when we entered Stockholm, pledges of amnesty had been given; and still bodies were piled high and headless, like cordwood, those freezing days. So with some heartsickness I returned home and vowed I'd stay on my own sandy acres. My wife died too—well, she was a good old mare, she was, and our only son studying in Paris and no doubt looking down on me who can scarcely write my name.

"And then one summer eve, when I walked the fields by that curious dolmen, She came forth."

From his clumsy words, as he struggled to describe her, Lockridge knew Storm Darroway again.

"Witch or saint or eternal spirit of the land, I cannot say

what She is. Belike She put a spell on me. What of that? She sought not to lure me from Christian practice, rather She told of matters I'd not known about, like the Coven, and warned of troublous times to come. And She showed me wonders. This poor old brain cannot well grasp Her notion about traveling from past to future and back; but are not all things possible under God? She gave me gold, which I had sore need of after being so long in the wars with so little plunder. But chiefly I serve for Her own sake and the hope of one day seeing Her anew.

"My duty is light. I am to be at the Inn of the Golden Lion each All Hallows Eve for twenty years. You see, She is in a war. Her friends and Her enemies alike flit about, even through the air; they may be anywhere, any time. The warlocks—not the commons, who come only for a bit of heathendom, but their leaders who can command them—the warlocks are Hers, part of Her net of spies and agents. But they cannot show themselves in respectable places as I might. If any came, like you, needing aid, I was to be there, and direct them to the Sabbath where they might find strong arms and magical engines. Another man was chosen for May Eve, but he is dead now. Easy service for much gold, not so?"

The equinoctial nights, Lockridge thought; those belonged to the earth gods. Summer and winter solstice were the sun's —the Rangers'.

Fledelius' words roughened yet more. "No doubt She thought that in my embitterment I would stay neutral, and thus safe, in the struggle She must have foreseen. But I failed Her. Far too often, I could not be there. Do you think any died on that account?"

"No," Lockridge said. "*We* found you. Remember, the war is worldwide and agewide. Yours is only one outpost."

He wondered, chillingly, how many there were. No one could oversee every part of space and time. Storm would have had to establish such small half-comprehending alliances: like a pagan cult, born of despair, founded on immemorial symbols that she furnished and interpreted. Other eras had other secrecies. All were created just to be there in case of need.

And the need was very great now. She lay bound at Brann's triumph, thirty-three hundred years ago; when his technicians arrived, they would suck her dry of what she knew and cast the husk aside; and more and more, Lockridge saw what a keystone she must be of her whole cause. If this one band of Jutes could help her, it would—maybe—justify the thousands upon thousands throughout Europe who were caught and burnt alive by the witch hunters of the Reformation.

He didn't want to pursue that thought. Instead, he speculated on what enclaves the Rangers maintained. In Akhnaton's court? Caesar's? Mohammed's? The Manhattan Project?

"You see," Fledelius pleaded, "after the king fled to Holland —well, I'd forgiven him Stockholm, when he gave so many rights to the people—why, even sorcerers were only to be flogged out of a city—I went with Søren Norby to fight the usurper. And afterward I sailed with Skipper Klement, and stood at Aalborg last year when they finally broke us. Hence I am outlaw. But I did find a priest who would forge for me a letter and seal by which to enter Viborg. And mine host Mikkel knows me of old, and belongs to the Coven himself. So I was on hand when you came. Is that not so?"

"Indeed so," Lockridge replied most gently.

Fledelius slapped his sheathed sword. Doubts and guilts departed; he became again the man who had gibed at Junker Erik. "God be praised! Now your turn, friend. Who's it our task to send to the devil?"

As nearly as language and concepts allowed, Lockridge told him.

On a hill in the wastes burned the witchfire. Light flickered red off a high boulder to which Auri made obeisance. It had been an altar in her own time. Overhead the stars of All Hallows Eve glittered many and remote. The land was still, the air frosty.

Lockridge paid little attention to the worshippers. They were a handful: shaggy peasants in smocks and woolen caps, villagers in patched jerkin and hose, their teen-aged children, an incongruous bawd from Viborg whose finery was pathetic in this skyey dark. They had stolen from hut and house and trudged across miles for an hour's release, reassurance, appeasement of the land's ancient Powers, and a little, little courage to meet their masters next day. Lockridge hoped he could remove Auri hence before anything started. Not that the orgy would shock her as such; but he didn't want her to see what must be a degraded remnant of her own joyous mysteries.

His look and mind went back to the Master.

Tall and lean stood Marcus Nielsen, his alien features shadowed by the cowl of a tattered Dominican habit. In this age they knew him as a hedge priest. Unlike England, where he called himself Mark of Salisbury, Denmark did not persecute Catholics; but magicians were once more in danger of their lives. He was born Mareth the Warden, two thousand years after Lockridge, and he flitted the byways of Reformation Europe to serve Storm Darroway his queen.

"You bear evil tidings," he said. The diaglossa gave him French to use with the American, incomprehensible to his flock or to stolid Fledelius, and he had ordered Auri to stand beyond earshot.

He paused, then: "You may not know how critical she and Brann are. So few are capable on either side. They become like primitive kings, leading their troops into battle. You and I are nothing, but her capture is a disaster."

"Well," Lockridge said brusquely, "you've been warned now. I suppose you have access to the future. Organize a rescue party."

"Matters are not that simple," Mareth answered. "In the whole period of history from Luther to—beyond your time— the Rangers are ascendant. Warden forces are concentrated elsewhen. We maintain only a few agents like myself in this century." He twisted his fingers together and frowned at them. "In fact, frankly, we seem to be cut off. As nearly as our intelligence can learn, every gate through which one might go very far futureward is watched. She should have told you to seek a point of Danish time when the Wardens are better established. Frodhi's reign, for instance. However, she was personally involving in setting up this watchpost, because the milieu *is* so difficult and dangerous. So I imagine it was what first crossed her mind, in the short while you had to talk."

Again Lockridge saw her, felt her. He clutched the other man's robe. "Hell take it, you're supposed to handle problems! There must be something we can do!"

"Yes, yes." Annoyed, Mareth brushed him off. "We must certainly act. But not precipitately. You have not experienced the oneness of time. Respect those who have."

"Look, if I could come up the local corridor, we can all go back down it. We can even arrive in the Neolithic before Brann does, and be waiting for him."

"No." Mareth shook his head with needless violence. "Time is immutable." He drew a breath and continued more calmly. "The attempt would be foredoomed. We would be certain to encounter something, like a superior enemy force within the corridor, that would frustrate us. Anyhow, I see no point in using the Danish shaft at all. We have nothing here to help us except these." His gesture at the Coveners, kneeling frightened on the rim of firelight, was contemptuous. "True, we could try to go down it by ourselves and get reinforcements from the pre-Viking era. But why do so—or why take the risk of crossing the world to seek our Oriental and African bases —when better help is so much closer to hand?"

"Huh?" Lockridge gaped at him.

The Warden's academic manner slipped off. He paced back and forth, thinking aloud, a war chief in friar's gown.

"Brann came alone, since he knew the Koriach—she—was also alone, and he has no more forces to spare than we do. But having caught her, he will summon men to consolidate his gains. We have to reckon with that. The uncertainty of emergence, you remember. Since we did not appear to save her that night, we will not. Therefore, the chances are that we will not appear—will not have appeared—until after he has a number of Rangers with him. And, obviously, they will post a guard on the corridor gate.

"But in this present century, Denmark is not where our real European strength lies. Rather we are concentrated in Britain. King Henry has forsaken the Roman Church; but we saw to it that he did not go over to Lutheranism either, and for us his kingdom is pivotal. What you know as the episode of the two Queen Marys is a time of gain for the Wardens; the Rangers will resurge with Cromwell, but we will drive them out at the Restoration.

"I know. You are wondering why anyone would wage a campaign whose outcome is known beforehand. Well, for one thing, in the course of waging it, casualties are inflicted on the enemy. More important, each milieu which is firmly held is a source of strength, of recruits, of power to call on, another weight thrown in the scalepans of the future when the final decision, whose nature we do not know, is reached.

"But to continue. I have a flock in England too; and there I am not the pagan ritemaster of a few starveling peasants, but a preacher to knights and strong yeomen, urging them to stand by the Holy Catholic Faith. And . . . we have a corridor there whose existence the Rangers do not suspect, with its own gate on the Neolithic. That gate opens pastward of the Danish one, but there is a few months' overlap, in the exact year we must reach."

He seized Lockridge's shoulders. His visage blazed. "Man, are you with me? For her?"

12

"Hai-ee-ee! *Hingst, Hest, og Plag faar flygte Dag! Kommer, kommer, kommer!*"

The witchmaster's robe flapped about him like wings. As his arms and face turned heavenward, a whirlwind unseen, unfelt, unheard, lifted him and his chosen. Upward they fled until they were lost among cold constellations. The balefire flared from its coals, threw spark and flame after its lord, and sank again. The folk of the Coven shuddered and departed.

Auri bit back a cry, shut her eyes, clung to Lockridge's hand. Jesper Fledelius rattled a string of foul oaths, then felt himself safe after all and whooped like a boy. The American shared some of that excitement. He'd flown before, but never at the end of a gravity beam.

There was no airblast. The force that streamed from the belt under Mareth's habit deflected it. One went bat silent, several hundred feet above ground, and speed mounted into the hundreds of miles per hour.

Darkling rolled the heath; Viborg was a blot seen for an instant and lost; the Limfjord shimmered; the western dunes fell behind, and the North Sea ran in waves touched with icy gleams by a sickle moon rising ahead of dawn. Lost in night and wonder, Lockridge was startled when England bulked into view—so soon?

Across the flatlands of East Anglia they went. Thatch-roofed villages lay among stubblefields, a castle raised battlements above a river, it was a dream and impossible that he, prosaic he, should follow a wizard through the sky on the same night as King Henry snored beside Anne Boleyn . . . poor Anne whose head would fly from the ax in less than a year, and none to warn her. But her daughter lay cradled in that same palace and was named Elizabeth. The strangeness possessed Lockridge like a vision: not merely his own fate, but the mystery that was every man's.

Cultivation gave way to a wilderness where islands crowded among meres and marshy streams, the Lincolnshire Fens. Mareth swooped downward. The last withered leafage parted before him, he came to rest and deftly drew in the others. By the paling sky Lockridge saw a wattle hut.

"This is my English base," the Warden told him. "The time gate lies beneath. You will remain here while I gather men."

Behind that primitive façade, the cabin was almost luxurious, with hardwood floors and wainscoting, ample furniture and a good store of books. Food stocks and other supplies from the future were hidden behind sliding panels; nothing showed that would have been too foreign to this century. An intruder might have noticed how the interior kept warm and dry in every season. However, none ventured here. The peasants had their superstitions, the gentry were indifferent.

The three from Mareth's past were only too glad of a respite. They were ordinary humans, not masterworks of an age that could shape heredity in any desired pattern, and their nerves were stretched near breaking. The next two days were an interlude of sleep and hazy half wakefulness.

On the third morning, though, Auri sought Lockridge. He was seated on a bench outside the door, enjoying a smoke. While not an addict, he had rather missed tobacco, and it was thoughtful, if slightly anachronistic, of the Wardens to keep some on hand along with clay pipes. And the weather had turned pleasant. Sunlight spilled wan between the naked willows. A belated flock of geese made a southward V far overhead, their honking drifted down to him through a great quietness, far and lonely wander-song. Then he heard her feet patter close, looked up and was struck by beauty.

There had been no time, before he tumbled into this drowsy interlude, to think of her as much except a child that needed what small protection he could spare. But on this morning she had gone out in a marsh almost like the one at home, clad in no more than her waist-long cornsilk hair, and was renewed. She scampered toward him with a deer's grace, eyes blue and huge in the pert countenance. He saw laughter and marvel on her lips and stood up with his pulse begun to race.

"Oh, come look," she cried, "I've found the most wonderful boat!"

"Good Lord!" Lockridge choked. "Get some clothes on, girl."

"Why? The air is warm." She danced before him. "Lynx, we can go out on the water and fish, the whole day is ours and the Goddess is happy and you must be rested now, come along, do!"

"Well—" Well, why not? "Yes. You get dressed, though, understand?"

"If you wish." Puzzled but obedient, she fetched a shift from the cabin, where Fledelius was still noisily asleep among strewn ale jugs, and darted through the woods ahead of Lockridge.

The skiff, tied to a stump, looked simple to him. But of course Auri's boats were coracles, or dugouts with bulwarks secured by pegs and withes. This one used nails of real metal! And she gasped to see him row, instead of punt or paddle. "Surely this came from Crete," she breathed.

He hadn't the heart to tell her Crete lay impoverished and oppressed under the Venetians, awaiting next century's Turkish conquest. "Maybe." He slid the boat among reeds and osiers until he reached an open stretch of shallow water. Here the island was hidden by brush and the mere blinked bright and still. Auri had taken fishing tackle as well as her garment. She baited a hook and cast skilfully toward a lurking place under a log. He sprawled back and got his pipe started afresh.

"That's a strange rite you do," Auri said.

"Only for pleasure."

"Can I try? Please?"

She wheedled him into it, with the expected results. Gulping and sputtering, she handed back the pipe. "Whoo-ah!" She wiped her eyes. "No, too strong for the likes of me."

Lockridge chuckled. "I warned you, young one."

"I should have listened. You are never wrong."

"Now, wait—"

"But I wish you wouldn't speak to me as to a child." She flushed. The long lashes quivered downward. "I am ready to become a woman whenever you want me."

The blood mounted in Lockridge too. "I've promised to take the spell off you," he mumbled. The idea occurred to him that he might die in the coming battle. "In fact, it is off. You need no further magic. Uh . . . passage through the underworld, you know . . . rebirth. Do you see?"

Gladness leaped in her. She moved toward him.

"No, no, no!" he said desperately. "I can't—myself—"

"Why not?"

"Look, uh, look around you, this isn't springtime."

"Does that matter? Everything else has changed. And Lynx, you are so very dear to me."

She pressed against him, warm, round, and eager. Her mouth and hands had an enchanting awkwardness. He thought, in the cloud of her tresses and herself, Why, my own grandfather would've called her husband high. . . . No, God damn it!

"I'll have to leave you, Auri—"

"Then leave me with your child. I w-w-won't think past that, not today."

Strictness was beyond him. He could only hit on one thing to do. He let himself be pushed too far to one side, and the skiff capsized.

By the time they had righted it and bailed it out, matters were under control. Auri accepted the sign of godly displeasure without fear, for she had spent her life among such omens, nor even with overmuch disappointment, for the heart was too sunny in her. She peeled off the wet shift in a fit of giggles at Lockridge's refusal to do likewise.

"At least I may look at you," she said when a soberer mood came. "There will be other times, after you have set Avildaro free."

A glumness had settled on him. "The village you knew won't come again," he said. "Remember who fell."

"I know," she answered gravely. "Echegon, who was always kind, and Vurowa the merry, and so many more." But everything that had passed since had blurred her grief. Besides, the Tenil Orugaray were not given to mourning a loss as keenly as those who came after them. They had learned too well to accept what was.

"And you'll still have the Yuthoaz to reckon with," Lockridge said. "We may push this one band out, this one time. But there are others, strong and land-hungry. They will return."

"Why must you always fret so, Lynx?" Auri cocked her head. "We do have this day . . . and whee, a fish!"

He wished he could join her in more than a pretense of merriment. But his own dead were too much with him: nations, kings, and the unremembered humble, through all the ages of the time war—yes, even that kid he'd killed in his own land, four hundred years hence. He saw now that his self-righteousness had been a cover for blood guilt. Oh, o' course *I never meant the thing to happen,* he told himself wearily, *but it did happen . . . it will happen . . . and I'd turn time inside out if I could, to undo it.*

They were lunching off their catch, *sashimi* style, when a horn blew. Lockridge started. This fast? He rowed hard to get back.

Mareth was indeed there, with six other Wardens. They had abandoned the disguises of priest, knight, merchant, yeoman, beggar for a uniform skin-tight like the Rangers', but forest green and with iridescent cloaks cataracting from their shoulders. Under the bronzy helmets, long dark eyes in faces eerily akin to Storm's looked aloofly upon their helpers.

"We have one more agent in the British Isles," Mareth said.

"He will bring our army after dark. Meanwhile, we have preparations to make."

Lockridge, Auri, and Fledelius found themselves working on tasks they did not understand. Because this corridor was secret from the enemy, and this gate opened on a vital period, the anteroom was stocked with engines of war and the exits were broad enough to admit them. The American could identify some things in a general way, vehicles, guns; but what was the crystalline globe in which a night swirled studded with starlike points? What was the helix of yellow fire that felt cold to the touch? His questions were rebuffed.

Even Fledelius bristled. "I'm no serf of theirs," he growled to Lockridge.

The American checked his own annoyance. "You know how often underlings like to throw their weight around. When we get to the queen, she'll be different."

"Yes, true. For Her I'll swallow pride. . . . Throw their weight around. Haw, haw! You've a rare wit, lad." Fledelius guffawed and slapped Lockridge's back so he staggered.

Dusk fell, and dark. Down the sky there whirled the men of Harry's England.

They were a wild, tough crew, a hundred in number: discharged soldiers, sailors half buccaneer, fortune-hunting younger sons, highwaymen, tinkers, rebellious Welshmen, Lowland cattle rustlers, gathered together from Dover to Lands End, from the Cheviot Hills to the London alleys. Lockridge could only guess how each had been recruited. Some for religion, some for money, some for refuge from the hangman—one by one, the Wardens found them and drew them into a secret league, and now the hour was on hand to use them.

Torchlight picked faces out of the mass that seethed and grumbled on the island. Lockridge stood next to a squat, pigtailed seaman in ragged shirt and trousers, barefoot, earringed, scarred by old fights. "Where are you from, friend?" he asked.

"A Devon man, I be." Lockridge could just understand him; even a Londoner still treated his vowels like a Dutchman, and this fellow added a dialect thick enough to cut. "But I were in Mother Colley's stew in Southampton when the summons came." He smacked his lips. "Ah, there were a rare bouncetail trull! Had I had one hour the longer, not soon 'ud she forget Ned Brown. But when the medallion spoke, God's bones, I've stood 'neath French gunfire and piked Caribals when they howled up the sides of our galleon, yet never 'ud I dare leave yon summons unheeded."

"The, uh, medallion?"

Brown tapped a disc hung about his neck, stamped with the image of the Virgin. Lockridge noticed the same thing on several other hairy breasts. "What, thou wert not gi'en this token? Well, it whispers when they've need o' thee, in such a way that none may hear save thyself, and tells whither thou must hie. *He* met me there and flitted me to a meeting ground in the wilds, thence hither. . . . I knew not the service numbered this many."

Mareth stood forth at the cabin door. His voice rose, not loudly, but the turbulence was hushed. "Men," he said, "long have most of you been in the Fellowship, and no few will remember times when it saved you from dungeon or death. You know you are enlisted in the cause of white magicians, who by their arts aid the Holy Catholic Faith against paynim and heretic. This night you are called to redeem your pledge. Far and strangely shall you fare, to battle against wild men while we your masters engage the wizards they serve. Go you bravely forward, in God's name, and those who outlive the day shall have rich reward, while those who fall shall be yet more highly rewarded in Heaven. Kneel, now, and receive absolution."

Lockridge went through the ritual with a bad taste in his mouth. Was this much cynicism necessary?

Well—to save Storm Darroway. I'll be seein' her again, he thought, and the heart fluttered in him.

More hushed and serious than he would have believed possible, the English filed through the cabin door and down the ramp. In the anteroom, before the curtain of rainbow, they got their weapons: sword, pike, ax, crossbow. Gunpowder would be useless against the Rangers, needless against the Yuthoaz. But Mareth beckoned to Lockridge. "You had best stay with me, for a guide," he said, and laid an energy pistol in the American's hand. "Here, you come from a sufficiently sophisticated era to operate this. The controls are simple."

"I know how," Lockridge snapped.

Mareth dropped his hauteur. "Yes, she singled you out, did she not?" he murmured. "You are no ordinary man."

Auri struggled through the press. "Lynx," she pleaded. The terror was back to gnaw at her. "Stay near me."

"Have her wait here," Mareth ordered.

"No," Lockridge said. "She comes along if she wants to."

Mareth shrugged. "Keep her out of the way, then."

"I have to be in the forefront," Lockridge told her. She shivered between his palms. He must give her a kiss . . . mustn't he?

"Come, lass," Jesper Fledelius laid a gorilla arm across her shoulders. "Stay near me. We Danes should hang together, amidst these English louts." They slipped off into the crowd.

During the day, Lockridge had helped manhandle several flyers through the gate. They were sheening ovoids, transparent, not of matter but of forces he did not comprehend. Each could hold twenty. He shoved into the lead one with Mareth. The men already there breathed heavily, whispered prayers or curses, and flicked their eyes about like trapped animals. "Will they not be too panicky to fight?" Lockridge wondered in Danish.

"No, I know them," Mareth said. "Besides, the initiation ceremonies involve unconscious conditioning. Their fear will turn to fury."

The machine rose without sound and started down the cold-white, humming bore. A Warden at every console, the others followed. "Since you've got this passage," Lockridge asked, "why didn't you get still more reinforcements from other periods?"

"None are available," Mareth said. He spoke absently, hands moving over the control lights, features taut with concentration. "The corridor was built chiefly for access to this very era. Its future end terminates in the eighteenth century, when we have another strong point in India. The Rangers are especially active in England between the Norman Conquest and the Wars of the Roses, so we have no gates there opening on the Middle Ages at all—nor many in earlier epochs, when the critical regions, the theaters of major conflict, are elsewhere. In fact, gates throughout the Neolithic and Bronze Age North serve as little more than transfer points. It is largely a fortunate coincidence that we do have one here with a temporal overlap on the one in Denmark."

Lockridge wanted to inquire further. But the flyer, remorselessly swift, was already at the year they sought.

Mareth guided it out. He left for a glance at the calendar clock in the locker. "Good!" he said fiercely when he returned. "We were lucky. No need to wait. This is night, with sunrise due soon, and must be quite near the moment when she was captured."

Force beams had kept the fleet together while they crossed the time threshold. They swept up the entry, which opened for them and closed again behind. Mareth set his controls for low flight eastward.

Lockridge stared out. Under the Stone Age moonlight, the Fens lay yet bigger and wilder. But beyond them, on the coast, he spied fisher villages that might almost have been Avildaro.

That was no accident. Before the North Sea came into being, men had walked from Denmark to England; the Maglemose culture was one. Afterward their boats crossed the waters, and Her missionaries came from the South to both lands. The diaglossa in his left ear told him that if they spoke slowly, the tribes of eastern England and western Jutland could still understand each other.

Such kinship faded with inland miles. Northern England was dominated by the hunters and axmakers who centered at Langdale Pike but traded from end to end of the island. The Thames valley had been settled, peacefully enough, by recent immigrants from across the Channel; and the farmers of the south downs were giving up those grim rites which formerly made them shunned. That might be due to the influence of a powerful, progressive confederation in the southwest, which had even started a little tin mining to draw merchants from the civilized lands. Chief among those were the Beaker People, who traveled in small companies and dealt in bronze and beer. An old era was dying in Denmark, a new one being born in England: this westland lay nearer to the future. Looking back, Lockridge saw rivers and illimitable forests; as if from a dream, he knew how birds winged in their millions and elk shook their great horns and men were happy. It came to him with a pang that here was where he belonged.

No. The sea rolled beneath him. He was bound home to Storm.

Mareth went at a dawdler's pace, waiting for the sky to lighten. Even so, only a couple of hours had passed when the Limfjord slipped into view.

"Stand by!"

The flyers snarled downward. Water flashed steely, dew glittered on the grass and leaves of a young summer suddenly reborn, Avildaro's roofs sprang from behind her sacred grove. Lockridge saw that the Battle Ax men were still encamped in the fields further on. He glimpsed a sentry, wide-eyed by a dying watchfire, shouting men out of their blankets.

Another shimmery vessel whipped up from before the Long House. So Brann had had time to call in his people. Lightnings crackled under the waning stars, dazzling bright, thunder at their heels.

Mareth rattled a string of commands in an unknown language. A pair of flyers converged on the Rangers' one. Flame raved, and that bubble was no longer. Black-clad forms tumbled through the air to spatter horribly on the ground.

"Down we go," Mareth said to Lockridge. "They didn't expect attack, so there aren't many here. But if they call for help— We have to take control fast."

He skimmed the flyer along the bay, struck earth, and made the force-field vanish. "Get out!" he yelled.

Lockridge was first. The English poured after him. Another flyer landed beside his. Jesper Fledelius led the wave from it. His sword flared aloft. "God and King Kristiern!" he roared. The other vehicles had descended some ways off, in the meadows where the Yuthoaz were. They rose again after their men were out. Cool and detached, the Warden pilots oversaw the battle, spoke commands through the amulets, made each man of theirs a chess piece.

Metal clanged against stone. Lockridge dashed for the hut he recalled. It was empty. With a curse, he whirled and sped to the Long House.

A dozen Yuthoaz were on guard. Gallant in the face of supernatural dread, they stood fast with axes lifted. Brann trod forth.

His long visage was drawn into a disquieting grin. An energy pistol flashed in his hand. Lockridge's own gun was set to protect him. He plunged through the fire geyser and hurled his body at the Ranger. They went over in the dust. Their weapons skittered free and they sought each other's throats.

Fledelius' sword rose and fell. An axman tumbled in blood. Another smote, the Dane countered, his English followers arrived and combat erupted.

From the corner of an eye, Lockridge glimpsed two more black-clad forms, spouts and crackles where beams played on shields. He himself had all he could do, fighting Brann. The Ranger was inhumanly strong and skilled. But suddenly he saw who Lockridge was, face to face. Horror stretched his mouth open. He let go and made a fending motion. Lockridge chopped him in the larynx, got on top, and banged his head on the earth till he went limp.

Not stopping to wonder what had happened inside that long skull, the American sprang up. Elsewhere, Fledelius and his men pursued Yutho sentries. The other Rangers lay scorched before Mareth and his Warden companions. Lockridge ignored them. He burst through the doorway of the Long House.

Gloom filled the interior. He groped forward. "Storm," he called shakenly, "Storm, are you there?"

Shadow among shadows, she lay bound on a dais. He felt sweat chill on her naked skin, ripped the wires from her head, drew her to him and sobbed. There was a moment beyond time when she did not move and he thought her dead. Then, "You came," she whispered, and kissed him.

13

Word rang through the forest, the refugees returned home, and joy dwelt in Avildaro.

The feast was not less wild and merry for being a funeral of the slain as well as a triumph. The strangers whose metal weapons had driven out the Yuthoaz were welcomed into the frolic. They had no comprehensible language, but what did that matter? A roasting pig spoke to them with its savor, a man with his grin, a woman with herself.

Only the Long House was avoided. For there stayed the green gods who had delivered their people. Meat and drink were brought to the door, and every adult male vied for the honor of standing by as servant or messenger. On the second noon of celebration, one sought out Lockridge, where he watched the dancers in a meadow, and said he was summoned.

He left with thumping eagerness. Worry about Storm had prevented him from taking much part in the sport. Now he was told that She of the Moon commanded his presence.

Sunlight, smells of woodland and smoke and salt water, distant shouts and songs, vanished from his consciousness when he entered the house. Not yet had the holy fire been rekindled; a promise was given that She would perform that rite in Her good time. Luminous globes made the interior radiant, rafters and columns stood forth rugged against sooty walls, the strewn furs glowed as if alive. Seven Wardens on the daises waited for their queen. They didn't condescend to greet Lockridge.

But all rose when Storm appeared. The rear end of the house was now blocked off, not by a material screen but by a force curtain which drank down light. She came through it. Next to such blackness she seemed to burn.

Or no . . . she shone, Lockridge thought dizzily, like that sea which was also the Goddess'. The three days and nights of her ordeal in the mind machine still marked her, high cheekbones stood sharply forth and the eyes smoldered feverish green. But she carried herself spear straight, and blue-black hair swept sheening past the tawniness of face and throat. From the gate of King Frodhi there had been brought her garb befitting her time and station. In blue translucence the robe descended to the copper belt of power; thence it broadened and rippled to the ankles, darkening toward purple, with argent emblems inwoven that were at once foam and serpents. A brooch shaped like the Labrys upheld a cloak whose lining was white as a summer cloud but which outside was gray for thunderheads and mare's-tails. Her shoes were gold sparked with diamond dust. A crescent of hammered silver crowned her brow.

Mareth accompanied her. He was saying something in the Warden language. Storm's gesture chopped off his words. "Speak so Malcolm can understand you," she ordered in the Orugaray.

He looked shocked. "This hog-tongue, brilliance?"

"Cretan, then. It's subtle enough."

"But brilliance, I was about to report on—"

"He needs to know." Storm let him swallow his humiliation while she advanced to Lockridge. She smiled. He bent unskilfully to kiss the hand she offered.

"I've not yet thanked you for what you did," Storm said. "But no words would serve. It was more than saving me. You struck a mighty blow for our whole cause."

"I—I'm glad," he gulped.

"Be seated, if you wish." Cat lithe, she turned from him and began to pace. He did not hear her footfalls on the dirt. Weak in the knees, he sank down beside a Warden, who nodded to him with instant deference.

Vibrancy played over Storm's features. "We have Brann alive," she said. The soft Cretan speech clanged in her throat. "With what we are learning from him, we have a chance to win the upper hand in Europe for the next thousand years. Mareth, proceed."

He who was priest and warlock had stayed on his feet. "I cannot understand how you endured, brilliance," he said. "Already Brann cracks. The trickle of his secrets will soon be a flood."

"He got the same from me," Storm said grimly. "Had he been able to use the information—no, I don't want to be reminded."

Lockridge glanced at the dark veil, and away in haste. His stomach writhed. Behind lay Brann.

He didn't know just what was being done. Not torture, surely. Storm wouldn't stoop to that, and anyhow it was crude, probably even useless against the nerves bred and trained, the unshakable will, of the future's lords. Storm had been drugged; currents of force had roiled her brain to its inmost depths. They would not let her die, but overrode the ego and compelled a ghastly automatism of thought, so that inch by inch everything she had ever known and done, everything she dreamed and was, came to the surface and was coldly marked into the molecules of a wire.

No living creature should have to go through that.

The hell not! Lockridge boiled. Brann's eatin' his own medicine, after he got my friends killed who'd never hurt him any. This is a war.

Mareth collected his dignity. "So," he began. "We have learned the immediate situation, that being in the focus of his attention. When Lockridge escaped up the corridor, Brann had naturally no idea of the help available in England. But the possibility that Lockridge might somehow get news to the Wardens was worrisome. Thus Brann informed his agents throughout Danish history. They are, ah, still searching for our man, no doubt, and for any indications of a Warden rescue party being organized.

"Meanwhile, he had to balance the risks of transporting your brilliance elsewhere and elsewhen, or keeping you here. Since he had some reason to believe Lockridge would not, after all, betray him to us, he decided to stay, at least temporarily. This is a distant and seldom visited milieu. If he brought in only a few Rangers, and kept the Battle Ax people on hand as his principal auxiliaries, he should be fairly safe from detection.

"But as a result, we now have him, and unbeknownst to his organization. When we have completed his processing, we will have the information needful to mount surprise assaults on Ranger positions throughout time, ambush individual agents, break up enclaves—deal them the worst setback of the whole war."

Storm nodded. "Yes. I have been thinking about that," she said. "We can decoy the enemy into believing we have promptly moved away ourselves, while actually remaining. Brann was quite right about this being a good place to operate from. Attention is all on Crete, Anatolia, India. The Rangers think the destruction of those civilizations will hurt us severely. Well, let them continue to think so. Let them spend themselves in helping along an Indo-European conquest that is foredoomed to happen. Both sides have tended to forget the North."

Her cloak swirled as she strode. She smote fist into palm and cried: "Yes! Piece by piece, we'll withdraw forces hither. We can quietly organize this part of the world just as we please. There is no proof that we never did; the possibility stands gate-open. How much word will ever reach the South about the doings of barbarians in these far hinterlands? When the Bronze Age comes, it will bear *our* shape, furnish *us* men and goods, guard *Warden* bases. The final great futureward thrust may well be pivoted here!"

In a blaze of energy, she turned to them and snapped forth orders. "As soon as may be, we shall have to develop native armed forces, strong enough to inhibit cultural meddling.

Jusquo, consider ways and means and give me some suggestions tomorrow. Sparian, pull those Britishers out of their swinishness and organize them as a guard. But they're too conspicuous; we must not keep them any longer than need be. The gate in their country is unmanned, isn't it? Urio, pick a few of them and flit across; train them to stand sentry for the weeks it will yet remain open. We might need such a bolthole. We certainly have to let Crete know we are here and arrange a consultation. Radio and mindwave are too risky. Zarech and Nygis, prepare to flit there in person after dark. Chilon, start a program of acquiring detailed information about this entire region. Mareth, you may continue to oversee the work on Brann."

Something in their expressions spoke to her. She said impatiently, "Yes, yes, I know you have your places in the sixteenth century and don't feel competent here. Well, you must learn to feel otherwise. The Cretan base has all it can do. They can't spare us anyone until reorganization is well under way. If we stop to squeal for help, we give the enemy too much chance to discover what is happening."

The eighth Warden lifted his hand. "Yes, Hu?" Storm said.

"Are we not to inform our own era, brilliance?" the man asked deferentially.

"Of course. That news can go from Crete." The jade eyes narrowed. She laid fingers to chin and spoke softly. "You yourself will go home by a different route—with Malcolm."

"Huh?" Lockridge exclaimed.

"Don't you remember?" Mareth said. His lips writhed. "We have it recorded that he told you. You came and betrayed her to him."

"I—I—" Lockridge's mind whirred.

Storm moved near. He rose. She laid a hand on his shoulder and said: "Perhaps I've no right to demand this. But the fact cannot be evaded. One way or another, you will seek Brann in his own land and tell him whither I fled. And thus you will begin the chain of events that leads to his defeat. Be proud. It is not granted many to be destiny."

"But I don't know—I'm only a savage, next to him—or you—"

"One link in the chain is myself, bound in blindness," Storm whispered. "The scars will never leave my soul. Do you think I would not wish otherwise? But we have only the one road, and walk it we must. This is the last thing I ask of you, Malcolm, and the greatest. Afterward you may go to your own country. And I shall always remember you."

He clenched his fists. "Okay, Storm," he got out in English. "On your account."

Her smile, gentle and the least bit sad, was more thanks than he felt he deserved.

"Go out to the revels," she said. "Be happy while you can."

He bowed and stumbled away.

The sun dazzled him. He didn't want to join the fun, there was too much that had to be faced down. Instead he wandered off along the shore. Presently a hill was between him and the village. He stood alone and stared across the bay. Wavelets lapped the turf, gulls skimmed white across blueness, a thrush whistled from the oak tree at his back.

"Lynx."

He turned. Auri walked toward him. Again she wore the garb of her people, bast skirt, foxskin purse, necklace of amber. Thereto had been added in honor the copper bracelet which was Echegon the headman's, wound tight to fit her wrist; and a dandelion garland made gold across the blowing sun-whitened hair. But her mouth was unsteady and tears blurred the sky-colored eyes.

"Why, what's the matter, little one? Why aren't you at the feast?"

She stopped beside him. Her head drooped. "I wanted to find you."

"I was around, except for when I was talking to The Storm. But you—" Now that he thought back, Lockridge realized that Auri had not danced or sung or gone with anyone to the greenwood. Instead, she hung about the fringes like a small disconsolate shadow. "What's wrong? I told everyone the curse was off you. Don't they believe me?"

"They do," she sighed. "After what has happened, they find me blessed. I didn't know a blessing could be so heavy."

Perhaps only because he didn't want to dwell on his own troubles, Lockridge sat down and let her cry on his breast. The story came out in broken words. Quite simply, her journey through the underworld had filled her with *mana*. She had become a vessel of unknown Powers. The Goddess must have singled her out for who could tell what. So who dared meddle with her? She wasn't shunned, or any such thing. Rather, she was reverenced. They would do whatever she asked, on the spot, except treat her like one of themselves.

"It . . . isn't . . . that they won't . . . love me. I could wait . . . for you . . . or someone else, if you really won't. But . . . when they see me . . . they stop laughing!"

"Poor kid," Lockridge murmured in the language of his mother. "Poor tyke. What a hell of a reward you got."

"Are you afraid of me, Lynx?"

"No, of course not. We've been through too much together."

Auri hugged him close. Face buried on his shoulder, she stammered, "If I were yours, they, they, they would know that was right. They would know this was the Goddess' will which had been fulfilled. I would have a place among them again. Would I not?"

He dared not confess she was entirely correct. She would always have a special standing. But once her now unguessable destiny was no longer potential but actual, for the whole world to see, awe would be lost in ordinariness and she be granted plain, easy friendship.

"I don't think any other man will ever dare touch me," Auri said. "But that's best. I don't want anyone but you."

Damnation, you idiot! Lockridge raged at himself. Forget her age. She's no American highschooler. She's seen birth and love and death her whole life, she's run free in woods where there are wolves and paddled skin boats through storms, she's ground grain with stones and dressed skins with her teeth, she's outlived sickness, North Sea winters, a war, a trip that'd have had most grown men gibberin'. Girls younger than she is

—and she's older than Shakespeare's Juliet—are already mothers. Can't you set aside your stupid inhibitions and do her this one kindness?

No. That day in the skiff, he had come very close to surrender. Now he faced dreadfulness. He could only hold to his course by keeping his mind filled with Storm. If he came back alive, he would demand as his payment that she let him forsake all else and follow her. He knew she was indifferent to what he might do with any chance-met female. But he no longer was. He couldn't be.

"Auri," he said, cursing his own gaucherie, "my work is not done. I must depart soon, on Her business, and I don't know if I will ever return."

She gasped, clutched herself to him and wept until both their bodies shook. "Take me with you! Take me with you!"

A shadow fell across them. Lockridge looked up. Storm stood watching. She carried the Wise Woman's staff, wreathed with hawthorn; she must have gone forth to bless the people now hers. Dark hair, dress of ocean, cloak of rain, fluttered in a sudden gust, around the tall form.

Her smile was unreadable, but not like the one she had bestowed on him in the Long House. "I think," she said with an edge to her tone, "I shall grant the child her wish."

14

Hu the Warden did not expect trouble on his way home. Lockridge was certain to reach Brann, during the interval between Storm's departure for the twentieth century and her enemy's devastating counterblow. That fact was in the structure of the universe.

However, details were unknown. (Like the aftermath, Lockridge thought bleakly. Did he or did he not get back alive? The margin of error in a gate made it unfeasible to check that in advance.) If nothing else, Ranger agents who observed Hu's party might deduce too much. He proceeded with caution.

Even by daylight, unpursued, in the company of a hero and a god, Auri was terrified of the tomb entrance to the corridor. Lockridge saw how forlornly she stiffened her back and said, "Be brave this one more time, as you were before."

She gave him a shaken, grateful smile.

He had protested Storm's decree. But the Warden queen dropped her imperiousness and said mildly, "We have to get accurate data on this culture. Not mere anthropological notes; the psyche must be understood in depth, or we can make some terrible mistakes in dealing with them as closely as I now plan to. Skilled specialists can learn much by observing a typical member of a primitive society exposed to civilization. So why not herself? She can't be more hurt than she has been. Would you put someone else in her anomalous position?" He couldn't argue.

The earth opened. The three descended.

They met no one on their trip futureward. But Hu took them out in the seventh century A.D. "At this gate, Frodhi rules the Danish islands," he explained. "Also here on the mainland is peace, and the Vanir—the older gods of earth and water—are still at least coequal with the Aesir. A little further on, the Rangers will drive us back and the Vikings begin to sail. We are too likely to encounter enemy agents in that part of the bore."

Remembering those he had fought, Lockridge grimaced.

Winter lay on the world outside, snow crusted between the bare trees of a forest still enormous, the sky cold and feature-lessly gray. "We can move at once," Hu decided, "safe from ground observation. Not that it matters if some native spies us. However—" He touched the controls of his gravity belt. They lifted.

"Lynx, where are we?" Auri exclaimed. "There cannot be so much beauty!"

Lockridge, used to the spectacle of clouds seen like blue-shadowed white mountains from above, had more interest in why they flew warm through this frigid air. Some radiant-heating gimmick? But watching the girl's eyes grow bright, Lockridge envied her a little. And the rebirth of her laugh heartened him.

Denmark fell behind. Germany, frontier land of Christen-dom, was hidden by the same vapor mass until, after an hour, the Alps stood forth sharp on the world's rim. Hu got his bear-ings and presently took his followers down below the overcast. Lockridge glimpsed a village, sod-roofed timber cabins within a stockade in the middle of an otherwise empty winterscape. The ground was hilly, rivers ran black across a thin snow blanket, ice rimmed every lake. One day this would be called Bavaria.

Hu went as quickly as he could, on a slant toward a certain high ridge. When they were down, he gusted a quite human sigh of relief. "Home!" he said.

Lockridge looked about. Craggy and gloomy, the wilderness pressed in on him. "Well, everyone to his own taste."

Hu's chiseled features reflected annoyance. "This is the Koriach's land: an estate of hers in the future, and therefore hers throughout the whole of time. No fewer than seven corridors were established hereabouts. One has a gate on this quarter century."

"But not on my own period, eh? So she couldn't have gone to Germany from America. I wonder, though, why she didn't figure to head back from Neolithic Denmark by this route, instead of via Crete."

"Use your brain!" Hu snapped. "After meeting those Rangers in that corridor—you were there, you should know—she estimated too great a probability of doing so again. Only now, when we have Brann, is this a reasonably safe course to follow." He walked off. Lockridge and Auri came after, the girl shivering. Her bare feet made the frozen ground creak.

"Hey, that's not good," Lockridge said. "Here." He picked her up. She snuggled happily against him.

They hadn't far to go. Within a shallow cave, Hu opened the ground. Light from a ramp mingled with the dull dayglow.

They rode to tomorrow in a silence that made the throb of energies seem the louder. Once they transferred, passing through a gate into a tunnel which, physically, existed in the twenty-third century, and so through another gate into the corridor Hu wanted. Lockridge's pulse accelerated and his palate went dry.

At the end, beyond the threshold, he found an anteroom more spacious than any other he had seen. The floor was richly carpeted; red drapes hung between multitudinous lockers. Four guards in green brought guns to brows, a salute, when Hu appeared. They were unlike him but curiously similar to each other: short, squat, flat-nosed and heavy-jawed.

Hu ignored them, searched in a cabinet, and extended two diaglossas. Lockridge removed his from the Reformation period, to make room in that ear. "I will take it," Hu said.

"No, I'll hang on to it," Lockridge replied. "I'll want to talk with my buddy Jesper again."

"Do you understand me?" Hu said. "I gave you an order." The guards moved near.

Lockridge lost his temper. "You know what you can do with your orders," he said. "If you understand *me*. I'm her man—nobody else's."

Almost, the Warden came to attention. His face blanked. "As you wish."

Lockridge pursued his little victory. "You can also furnish me a pair of pants. This Neolithic rig hasn't got pockets."

"You will receive a pouchbelt. Come along . . . please."

The guards had not followed the exchange, which was in Cretan. But it was disturbing how they sensed what had happened and shrank back. Lockridge inserted the new diaglossa and activated his mind in the way he had somewhat mastered to bring forth specific information.

Languages: two major ones, Eastern and Western, Warden and Ranger; others survived among the lower classes of either hegemony. Religion: here a mystical, ritualistic pantheism, with Her the symbol and embodiment of all that was divine; among the enemy, only a harsh materialistic theory of history. Government: he was sickened by the rush of data on Ranger lands, underlings made into flesh-and-blood machines for the use of a few overlords. Not much came to him concerning the Wardens. This was clearly not a democracy, but he got the impression of a benevolent hierarchical structure, its law derived rather from tradition than from formal innovation, power divided among aristocrats who were at one with their people, more like priests or parents than masters. Priestesses, mothers, mistresses? Women dominated. At the apex were the Koriachs, who were—well—something in between a Pope and a Dalai Lama? No, not that either. Odd, how sketchy the account was. Maybe because visitors got the local scene explained to them *viva voce*.

The palace opened before Lockridge and he forgot his doubts.

They hadn't taken the ramp, but floated up a shaft to emerge high in the great building. A floor bluish green, where inlaid patterns of bird, fish, serpent, and flower seemed nearly alive, shone acre-wide. It was warm and soft underfoot. Columns built from jade and coral soared to a height he could scarcely believe. Their capitals exploded in a riot of jeweled foliage. But no less lovely were the plants that grew between them and around a central fountain. He recognized little in those crimson, purple, golden, sweet-scented banks; a science two thousand years beyond his had created new joy. The vaulted roof was colored transparency, the whole rainbow melted into a *mandala* that caught the eye and bespoke infinitude, no cathedral window had been so grave and gorgeous. The walls were clear. He saw through them to a landscape of gardens, terraces, orchards, parks, the hills were aglow with summer. And . . . what was that enormous curve-tusked majesty, walking out from among the trees, dwarfing the deer herd . . . a mammoth, brought across twenty millennia for a sign of Her awesomeness?

Seven youths and seven maidens, alike as twins, slim and beautiful in their nudity, bent the knee to Hu. "Welcome," they chorused. "Welcome, you who serve the Mystery."

Only one evening dared the Wardens grant Lockridge before he went on his mission. Too many spies were about, they explained.

Luxuriously robed, he sat with Auri in a thing neither chair nor couch, that fitted itself to every changeable contour of their bodies, and feasted on foods unknown to him, untellably delicious. The wine was as rare, and turned the world into dreamlike happiness. "Is this drugged?" he asked, and Hu said, "Dismiss your prejudices. Why should one not use a harmless euphoriac?" The Warden went on to speak of potions and incenses that opened the door to a sense of Her veritable presence in everything which existed. "But those are kept for the most solemn rites. Man is too weak to endure long the godhead in him."

"Woman may do so oftener," said the Lady Yuria.

She was high in Storm's councils, fair-haired, violet-eyed, but with her cousinship plain to see in the Diana face and figure. More women than men were at the board, and took clear precedence. A family resemblance marked them all, both sexes handsome, vital, ageless. Their conversation was a glittering interplay in which Lockridge was soon lost; he gave up trying to participate, leaned back and enjoyed it as he would music. Afterward he had no firm idea of what had actually been said.

They retired to another hall where colors shifted in hypnotic rhythm through floor and walls. Servants catfooted about with trays of refreshment, but there was no visible source for the melodies to which they danced. His diaglossa taught Lockridge the intricate measures, and the Warden ladies were supple in his arms, blending their movements with his until two bodies became one. Though the scale was strange to him, he was more deeply moved by this music than by most else he had known in his life.

"I think you must have subsonics along with the notes," he ventured.

Yuria nodded. "Naturally. But why must you have a name and an explanation? Is not the reality enough?"

"Sorry. I'm just a barbarian."

She smiled and drew closer in the figure they were treading. "Not 'just.' I begin to see why you found favor with the Koriach. Few of us here—certainly not myself—could be such adventurers as she and you."

"Uh . . . thanks."

"I am supposed to care for your young friend—look, she has fallen asleep—she won't need me this night. Would you care to spend it with me?"

Lockridge had thought he wanted only Storm, but Yuria was so much like her that every desire in him shouted Yes! He needed his whole will to explain that he must get rested for tomorrow. "When you get back, then?" Yuria invited.

"I shall be honored." Between the wine, the music, and the woman, he had no doubt of his return.

The Lady Tareth danced by with Hu and called gaily, "Keep some time for me, warrior." Her partner grinned without resentment. Marriage was a forgotten institution. Storm had remarked once, with some anger, that free people had no property rights in each other.

Lockridge went to bed early and happy. He slept as he had not done since he was newborn.

Morning was less cheerful. Hu insisted he take another euphoriac. "You need a mind unclouded by fear," the Warden said. "This will be difficult and dangerous at best."

They went out for some practice with the devices the American would be using, to make real for him the knowledge imparted by the diaglossa. High they flew over endless parkland. Near the limit of their trip, Lockridge spied a dove-gray tower. At the fifteen hundred foot summit, two wings reached out beneath a golden wheel, to make the ankh which signifies life. "Is that on the edge of a city?" he asked.

Hu spat. "Don't speak to me of cities. The Rangers build such vile warrens. We let men live next to the earth their mother. That's an industrial plant. None but technicians are quartered there. Automatic machinery can do without sunlight."

They returned to the palace. From outside, its roofs and spires made one immense subtly colored waterfall. Hu conducted Lockridge to a small room where several others waited. They were men; war, like engineering, was still largely a male provenance, short of that ultimate level on which Storm operated.

The briefing was long. "We can get you within several miles of Niyorek." Hu pointed to a spot on the map before him, the east coast of a strangely altered North America. "After that, you must make your own way. With your beard shaven off, a Ranger uniform, your diaglossa and what additional information we can supply, you should be able to reach Brann's headquarters. We have ascertained he is there at this moment, and of course we know that you will see him."

The drug did not keep Lockridge's belly muscles from tightening. "What else do you know?" he asked slowly.

"That you got away again. It was reported to him—it will be reported—that you escaped to a time corridor." Hu's gaze became hooded. "Best I say no more. You would be too handicapped by a sense of being a puppet in an unchangeable drama."

"Or by knowing they killed me?" Lockridge barked.

"They did not," Hu said. "You must simply take my word. I could be lying. I would lie, if necessary. But I tell you as plain truth, you will not be captured or killed by the Rangers. Unless possibly at some later date . . . because Brann himself never found out what became of you. With luck, however, you should emerge from the corridor through another, pastward gate, slip out of the city, and cross the ocean to this place. There you will know how to get back to the present. I hope to greet you within this month."

The bitterness faded in Lockridge. "Okay," he said. "Let's get down to details."

15

There was no full-dress fighting in this era, or there would have been no Earth. Somewhere, sometime, when one side or the other believed it had grown strong enough, the great onslaught would be launched; but its nature was unguessable by the combatants themselves. Meanwhile the hemispheres were fortresses and skirmishes were incessant.

The Warden spaceship screamed on a long curve, westward and downward across an ocean where a storm had been generated for this night. At the end of that trajectory, a voice said, "Now," and Lockridge's capsule was ejected. Meteor-like, it streaked through wind and rain, aflame with the violence of its transit. The ship came about and raked for altitude.

Lockridge lay amidst incandescence. Heat buffeted him; his skull rang with vibration. Then the weakened pod burst open and he cast himself free on his gravity belt.

So fast was he still going that the force field was barely able to shield him from a stream that would have torn him asunder. The hurricane raved about his screen, blackness, lightning, and a wall of rain. Waves grabbed upward at him, spindrift smoking off their crests. As his speed dropped below the sonic, he heard the wind skirl, thunder crash, waters roar. A blue-white flare cut through the weather and left him dazzled for minutes. The explosion that followed struck his ears like a hammer. So they detected us, he thought stunned, and shot a firebolt at the ship. I wonder if she got away.

I wonder if I will.

But so small an object as a man was engulfed by the tempest. Nor were the Rangers likely to be on the alert for him. They would only expect their enemies to take this much trouble for a major operation and could not know that the sending of a single agent was indeed one.

History said he was going to reach Brann's castle.

Climate control fields pushed the storm away from the coast. Lockridge broke into clear air and saw Niyorek.

Monstrous it gloomed on the shore, and inland farther than his vision went. Maps and diaglossa had told of an America webbed from end to end with megalopolis. Little broke that mass of concrete, steel, energy, ten billion slaves jammed together, save here and there a desert which had once been green countryside. The gutting of his land seemed so vast a crime that he needed no drug to cast out fear. Oh, Indian summers along the Smokies, he thought, I'm comin' to get revenge for you.

North, south, and ahead, the city raised ramparts where nothing but a few wan lamps, and the spout from a hundred furnaces, relieved the lower murk. A sound came over the sea, humming, throbbing, sometimes shrilling so high it was pain to hear: the voice of the machines. On the upper levels, individual towers lifted a mile or more, the first dawn-glow pallid on their windowless sides. Cables, tubes, elevated ways meshed them together. The spectacle had a certain grandeur. They were not small-minded, the men who dreamed those vertical caverns into the sky. But the outlines were brutal, bespeaking a spirit whose highest wish was the unrestrained exercise of unlimited power, forever.

Lockridge's helmet vibrated with a call. "Who comes yonder?" Black-uniformed like himself, two sentries stooped on him. Below, rafted weapons raised their snouts.

He had been schooled. "Guardsmaster Darvast, household troops of Director Brann, returning from a special mission." The Ranger language was harsh on his tongue. He must admit its grammar and semantics were closer to English than the

Warden speech, in which he could not even say some things
with any precision. But here, the closest word to "freedom"
meant "ability to accomplish," and there was none for "love" at
all.

Since he was going to identify himself to Brann anyway, he
had suggested doing so at the start. But Hu vetoed the idea.
"You would have to go through too many layers of bureau-
cracy." Perforce, that last phrase was a Ranger one. "While
you would reach him eventually, the interrogation processes
would reveal too much to them, and leave you too crippled."

"Land at Gate 43 for identification," the radio voice commanded.

Lockridge obeyed, setting down on a flange that jutted over
the water. It was naked metal, as was the immense portal in
the wall before him. A guard stepped from an emplacement.
"Your ego pattern," he said.

Warden agents had done their job well. Against a day of
need, an identity had been planted in that machine which
recorded the life of each person in the hemisphere. Lockridge
went to the mind scanner and thought a code word. The cir-
cuits took it for the entire biogram of Darvast 05-874-623-189,
bred thirty years ago, educated in Crèche 935 and the Acad-
emy of War, special service appointee to Director Brann, polit-
ically reliable and holder of several decorations for hazardous
assignments successfully carried out. The guard saluted with
an arm laid across his breast. "Pass, master."

The gates opened, eerily quiet for such ponderosity. The
city's pulse came through, and a gust of foul air. Lockridge
went in.

There had been no time to give him more than a general
idea of the layout; he must concentrate on learning what was
known about the castle. Play by ear, he thought. I've got my
direction, more or less.

Brann's tower had been unmistakable, sheathed in steel and
topped by a ball of blue flame. It must be a couple of miles
from here. Lockridge began walking.

He found he had entered at the bottom of human habitation. The city went deep below ground, but only machines housed there, with a few armored engineers and a million convict attendants who did not live long amidst the fumes and radiation. Here, walls, rusted and grimed, enclosed a narrow pedestrian passageway. High overhead, girders and upper-level structures shut out the sky. The air throbbed and stank. Around him pullulated the half-skilled, the useless, the un-caught criminals, with sleazy clothes over fish-belly skins. No one looked hungry—machine-produced food was issued free at one's assigned refectory—but Lockridge felt as if his lungs were being contaminated by the smell of unwashed bodies. Raucousness:

"So I said to him, I said, you can't do this to me, I said, I know the apartment proctor personal, I said, and—"

"—where y' can get the real thing, yuh, 's true, a real happy-jolt right 'n y' head—"

"Better leave him alone. He don't act like nobody else. One of these nights they'll come get him, you mark my words."

"If she wants t' get rid o' her brats b'fore they're registered, well, that's between her and the proctors, I don't want no part of it, but when she throws 'em down *my* unit's waste chute, well!"

"Last I heard, he'd been transferred to, uh, I don't know ex-actly but might be disposal detail in, uh, the south somewhere."

"Nah, they won't investigate. She wasn't filling her quota. Why should they care if somebody cuts her throat? Saves them trouble, in fact."

"Shhh! Look out!"

The stillness spread in rings around Lockridge's uniform. He didn't have to push through the crowd like everyone else; folk pressed themselves against the walls, away from him, looked down at the pavement and pretended they were nowhere near.

Their ancestors had been Americans.

He was glad to reach an upward shaft where he could use his gravity belt. Above were levels of wide hallways, painfully clean. The doors were shut and few were abroad, for the tech-nician class need not scrabble around the clock for a livelihood.

Those people he glimpsed wore uniforms of good material and walked with a puritan purposefulness. They saluted him.

Then a file of gray-clad men passed by, with one soldier for guard. Their heads were shaven and their faces dead. He knew them for convicted unreliables. Genetic control did not yet extend to the whole personality, nor was indoctrination always successful. That these men might be trusted among the machines down below, their brains had been seared by an energy field. More efficient would have been to automate everything, rather than use such labor; but object lessons were needed. Still more important was to keep the population busy. Behind a poker face, Lockridge struggled not to retch.

He reminded himself, somewhat wildly, that no state could long endure which had not at least the passive support of a large majority. But that was the final abomination. Nearly everyone here, on every level of society, took the Rangers' government for granted, could not imagine living in any other way, often enjoyed their existence. The masters fed them, sheltered them, clothed them, educated them, doctored them, thought for them. A gifted, ambitious man could rise high, as technician, scientist, soldier, impresario of ever more elaborate and sadistic entertainments. To get anywhere, one must kick others in the teeth; and that was fun, that gave release. One did not, of course, aspire to the ultimate masterships. Those were assigned by machines, taken to be wiser than any mortal, and if a man was fortunate enough to serve close to such a person, he did so in the spirit of a watchdog.

Like Darvast, Lockridge thought. *I've got to remember who I'm s'posed to be.* He hurried on.

The sun was just rising, through carcinogenic clouds, when he left the roofs behind and flitted toward Brann's stronghold. Patrolmen swarmed about the walls, flies against a mountain. Guns crouched on every flange, and warcraft circled the burning globe at the spire. This high, the air was clean and cold, the city's growl subdued to a whisper, the westward view a sierra of towers.

Lockridge landed as ordered and identified himself again.

There followed three hours of hurry-up-and-wait, partly because he must go through the chain of command, partly because the master was not yet ready to see anyone. An officer,
of sufficiently elevated rank to be daring, explained with a
leer, "He was busy till late last night with his new playmate.
You know."

"No, I've been away," Lockridge said. "Some girl, eh?"

"What?" The Ranger looked shocked. "A female—for pleasure? Where have you been?" His lids drew together.

"In the past, and spent several years," Lockridge said hastily. "You forget your own world, back then."

"Ye-e-es . . . I understand that's quite a problem. Agents
who are gone too long, ego time, can develop some nasty devi-
ant notions."

Being still under close watch, Lockridge said, "You needn't
tell me. I've met such cases. Also among the enemy, luckily."

"It balances out," the officer nodded, and relaxed. "Well,
what's so urgent about your own report that you can't wait for
an appointment?"

"For his ears only," Lockridge said in sheer automatism.
Most of him was too astonished at the casual acceptance of his
lie. How could a Warden be subverted? Surely nothing in the
past was better than what he had seen in today's Europe.

The anti-worry chemical in him suppressed puzzlement. He
settled back in the austere little room and composed his ideas.
First, speak to Brann; then break loose. There was a time gate,
open on this year, in the foundations of the tower. He'd go
back to a period before the rise of the Rangers. They might
chase him the whole way, kill him, and somehow fail to return
until after their lord had departed. On the other hand, he
might elude them, flit to Europe, find one of the several corridors he had been told about, and get home free. Perhaps, at
this very moment, he was greeting Auri in Storm's palace. That
was a thought to cherish here.

A voice from the air said: "Guardsmaster Darvast. The Director will see you."

Lockridge went through a wall, which dilated for him, to an

antechamber armored in steel and force. The soldiers there made him strip, and searched clothes and person respectfully but most thoroughly. When he dressed again, he was allowed to keep his diaglossas—not, though, his gravity belt or weapons.

A double door beyond opened on a wide, high-ceilinged chamber, draped and carpeted in gray, airily furnished. A viewer showed the immense spectacle of Niyorek. On one wall, a Byzantine ikon glittered gilt and bejeweled. After the crampedness everywhere else, Lockridge had an odd brief sense of homecoming.

Brann sat next to a service machine. The lean black-clad body was at ease, and the face might have belonged to a statue. He said quietly, "You must have realized that no such person as you is close enough to me to be known by name. However, the fact that you could get by identification is so significant that I decided to interview you as requested. Only my Mutes are overseeing us. I assume you have no ridiculous assassination scheme in mind. Speak."

Lockridge looked upon him, and the drug must be wearing off, because the fact struck shatteringly: My God, I met and fought this man six thousand years ago, and yet this is the first time he's ever seen me!

The American gulped for air. His knees wobbled and his palms grew wet. Brann waited.

"No," Lockridge got out. "I mean . . . I'm not a Ranger. But I'm on your side. I have something to tell you that, well, that I believe you'd want kept secret."

Brann studied him, sharp features unmoving. "Take off your helmet," he said. Lockridge did. "Archaic type," Brann murmured. "I thought so. Most would never notice, but I have encountered too many races in too many times. Who are you?"

"Malcolm . . . Lockridge . . . U.S.A., mid-twentieth century."

"So." Brann paused. All at once a smile transfigured him. "Be seated," he said, as host to guest. He touched a light on the machine. A panel opened, a bottle and two goblets appeared. "You must like wine."

"I could use some," Lockridge husked. Remembrance came to him, how he had drunk with Brann before, and made him toss off his glass in two swallows.

Brann poured afresh. "Take your time," he said leniently.

"No, I have to—Listen. The Koriach of the Westmark. You know her?"

Brann's calm was not broken, but the mask slid back over him. "Yes. In age after age."

"She's mounting an operation against you."

"I know. That is, she disappeared some time ago, undoubtedly on a major mission." Brann leaned forward. His look grew so intent that Lockridge's eyes must seek escape in the stern serenity of the Byzantine saint. The deep voice cracked forth: "You have information?"

"I . . . I do . . . master. She's gone into my century—my country—to drive a corridor here."

"What? Impossible! We would know!"

"They're working under cover. Native labor, native materials, starting from scratch. But when they're finished, the Wardens will come through, with everything they've got."

Brann's fist rang on the machine. He bounded to his feet. "Both sides have tried that before," he protested. "Neither has succeeded. The deed isn't possible!"

Lockridge made himself regard the figure towering over him and say: "This time the operation looks likely to work. It's masterly well hidden, I tell you."

"If anyone could, then she—" Brann's voice sank. "Oh, no." His mouth twisted. "The final thrust. Firebolts loosed on my people."

He began to pace. Lockridge sat back and watched him. And it came to the American that Brann was not evil. In Avildaro he had spoken—he would speak—well of his Yuthoaz because they were not needlessly cruel. His anguish now was real. Evil had created him, and he served it, but behind those gray eyes lay a tiger's innocence. When he demanded facts, Lockridge spoke with near pity:

"You're going to stop her. I can tell you just where the corridor is. When its gate here opens, you will strike down it. She'll only have a few helpers. You won't get her then, she'll escape, but you'll have another chance later."

More or less truthfully, he related his own experiences until he came to his arrival at Avildaro with Storm. "She claimed to be their Goddess," he went on, "and presided over a mighty vicious festival." As expected, the Ranger was not aware that the Tenil Orugaray, far outside his own field of cultural manipulation, did not practice ceremonial cannibalism like their neighbors. Also, perhaps, he assumed Lockridge disapproved of orgies, which was untrue but useful.

"That was what began to change my mind about her. Then you came, at the head of an Indo-European war band, and captured the village and us." Brann's fingers opened and closed. "I escaped. At the time, I thought that was luck, but now I reckon you kept me loosely guarded on purpose. I made my way to Flanders and found an Iberian trading ship that took me on as a deckhand. Eventually I got to Crete and contacted the Wardens there. They sent me to this year. Mainly I wanted to get home. This isn't my war. But they didn't let me."

"They wouldn't," Brann said, self-controlled again. "The primary reason is superstitious. They think her sacred, you know, an actual immortal incarnation of the Goddess, like her colleagues. You, the last to meet her, are now too holy yourself to be profaned by becoming an ordinary citizen of an era they despise."

Lockridge was jarred at how smoothly the story the Wardens had concocted was going over. Could Brann's idea be *true?*

"They treated me pretty well otherwise," he said. "I got, uh, very friendly with a high-ranking lady."

Brann shrugged.

"She told me a lot about their intelligence operations, showed me the gear and everything. Showed me too damned much of their civilization, in fact. It's not fit for a human being. In spite of the propaganda I was fed about the Rangers, I began to think you were more my kind of people. At least, you might send me home; and mercy—" Lockridge had to use English there— "but I'm homesick! Got obligations as well, back yonder. So finally I wheedled her into letting me go along on a survey mission last night, even dress in one of your uniforms. Since I knew about the fake Darvast identity—" He spread his hands. "Here I am."

Brann had stopped prowling. He stood utterly still for a minute, before he asked, "What is the precise geographical location of that corridor?"

Lockridge told him. "After my story," he said, "I wonder why the Wardens didn't go back a few months and warn her."

"They can't," Brann replied absently. "What has been, must be. In practical terms: a Koriach, even more than a Director like myself, has absolute authority. She does not divulge her plans to anyone she does not choose. For fear of spies, this one probably told no person except the few technicians she took along. Time enough to do that when the corridor was ready. Now, with so little advance notice and so much to occupy them elsewhen, there is no time to organize a substantial force of Wardens capable of operating efficiently in the past. Such as could be sent have doubtless been baffled by the uncertainty factor; they emerged too early or too late. That is, if any were sent at all. She has rivals who would not be sorry to lose her."

He considered Lockridge for a while that grew. Finally, slowly, he said: "Assuming your account true, I am grateful. You shall indeed be returned and well rewarded. But first we must establish your bona fides with a psychic probe."

Fear rose in Lockridge. He was getting very near the moment beyond which his future was unknown. Brann stiffened. Sweat, pallor, a pulse in the throat—what was the stranger so nervous about?

"No," Lockridge said feebly. "Please. I've seen what happens."

He had to give a reason for his flight which would not make Brann too wary to watch for Storm's gate and lead his troop through it. But the terror in his guts was real. He had indeed seen that darkened part of the Long House.

"Have no fear," Brann said with a touch of impatience. "The process will not go deep unless something suspicious emerges."

"How do I know you're telling the truth?" Lockridge rose and backed away.

"You must take my word. And, perhaps, my apology." Brann gestured.

The door opened. Two guards came in. "Take this man to Division Eight and have the section chief call me," Brann said.

Lockridge stumbled from the room. Remote as the heaven they watched from, the saint's eyes followed him out.

The men in black led him down an empty hallway. Sound was muffled, footfalls came dull, and never a word was spoken. Lockridge drew a breath. Okay, boy, he thought, you know you're goin' to make it as far as the time corridor. His dizziness left him.

The shaft he wanted came into sight, its opening an oblong in the blank wall, its depths whistling with forced air. The soldiers led Lockridge past.

Their energy guns were drawn, but not aimed at him. Prisoners never gave much trouble. He stopped short. The blade of his hand hewed into the Adam's apple on his right. A helmet jerked back, a body went to all fours. Lockridge spun to the left. He threw a shoulder block, his full weight behind. The guard toppled backward. Lockridge got a grip on him and hurled them both into the shaft.

Downward they tumbled. An alarm shrieked. That many-eyed machine which was the building had seen the unusual. In a voice nearly human, it cried what it knew.

Featureless, walls converging on a bottomward infinity, the tube fled by. Lockridge clung to the Ranger, arm around the throat, fist pounding while they fell. The guard went loose, his mouth slackened in the bloody face and the gun left his fingers. Lockridge fumbled at his belt controls. Where the furious hell—?

Door after door whizzed upward. Twice, energy bolts sizzled from them. And now the bottom leaped at him. He found the plaque he wanted and pushed. Unbalanced force nearly tore him from his grip on the Ranger. But they were slowed, they were saved from that bone-spattering impact, they were down.

The base of the shaft fronted on another hallway. An entry stood opposite, to show a room whose sterile white made the rainbow shimmer of a time gate all the more lovely. Two guards gaped across leveled weapons. A squad was dashing down the passage.

"Secure this man!" Lockridge gasped. "And let me by!"

He was in uniform, with potent insignia. The castle had not seen details. Arms snapped in salute. He sprang into the anteroom.

Around him, the air woke with Brann's voice, huge as God's. "Attention, attention! The Director speaks. A man dressed as a guardsmaster of the household has just entered the temporal transit on Sublevel Nine. He must be captured alive at any cost."

Through the gate! The twisting shock of phase change made Lockridge fall. He rolled over, his bare head struck the floor, pain burst through him and for an instant he lay stunned.

The fear of the mind machine brought him awake. He hauled himself erect and onto the gravity sled which waited.

Half a dozen men poured through the curtain. Lockridge flattened. Pale stun beams splashed on the bulwarks around him. He lifted a palm and covered the acceleration control light. The sled got into motion.

Away from the Rangers, yes. But they were on his pastward side. He was headed into the future.

The wind rasped in his lungs. His heartbeat shook him as a dog shakes a rat. With his last reserves, he mastered panic enough to risk a look aft. The black shapes were already dwindling. They milled about, uncertain, and he remembered Storm Darroway, seated by a fire in a wolf-haunted forest: "*We ventured ahead of our era. There were guardians who turned us back, with weapons we did not understand. We no longer try. It was too terrible.*"

I served you, Koriach, he sobbed. Goddess, help me!

As from far away, echoing down the vibrant whiteness of the bore, he heard Brann's command. The guards assumed formation. Their gravity units raised them and they gave chase.

The corridor reached on beyond sight. Lockridge saw no gate ahead, only emptiness.

The sled halted. He flailed the control panel. The machine sank inert. The flyers swooped near.

Lockridge jumped off and ran. A beam struck the floor behind, touched his heels and left them numb. Someone shouted victory.

And then the Night came, and the Fear.

He never knew what happened. Vision went from him, hearing, every sense and awareness; he was a disembodied point whirled for eternity through infinitely dimensioned space. Somehow he knew of a presence, which was alive and not alive. Thence radiated horror: the final horror, the negation of everything which was and had been and would be, cold past cold, darkness past darkness, hollowness past hollowness, nothing save a vortex which sucked him into itself, and contracted, and was not.

He was not.

16

Again he was.

First he was music, the most gentle and beautiful melody that ever had been, which with a drowsy delight he knew for *Sheep May Safely Graze*. Then he was also a scent of roses, a yielding firmness under his back, a body at peace with itself. He opened his eyes to sunlight.

"Good mornin', Malcolm Lockridge," said a man. "You are with friends," said a woman. They spoke Kentucky English.

He sat up. They had laid him on a couch in a maple-paneled room. There was little decoration, except for a screen where colors played through soft strange shapes, but the proportions were so right that nothing else was needed. Beyond an un-closed doorway he saw a garden. Flowers grew along graveled walks and willows shaded a lilypond from the heat of high summer. On the far side of a turf-green lane stood another house, small, bedecked with honeysuckle, simply and sweetly curved.

The man and woman stepped close. They were both tall, somewhat past their youth but still with backs erect and mus-cles hard. Their hair was bobbed below the ears and held by intricately ornamented bands. Otherwise they wore nothing except a pocketed band on the left wrist. Lockridge saw that he was equally nude. He felt for his own bracelet-purse. The woman smiled. "Yes, your diaglossas are there," she said. "I don't believe you'll want anything else."

"Who are you?" Lockridge asked in wonder.

They grew grave. "You won't be with us long, I'm sorry to say," the man replied. "Call us John and Mary."

"And this is . . . when?"

"A thousand years afterward."

With a mother's compassion, the woman said, "You've been through nightmare, we know. But we hadn't any other way to turn back those devils, short o' killin' them. We healed you, soma and psyche, while you slept."

"You'll send me home?"

Pain crossed her tranquility. "Yes."

"Right away, in fact," said John. "We have to."

Lockridge got off the bed. "I didn't mean my own home. Europe, in the time of the Wardens."

"I know. Come."

They walked out. Lockridge fumbled for understanding. "I can see why you don't let anyone in from the past. So what am I to you?"

"Destiny," said John. "The ghastliest word a man can speak."

"What? You—I—my work's not finished?"

"Not yet," said Mary, and caught his hand.

"I must not tell you more," said John. "For your own sake. The time war was the nadir of human degradation, and not least because it denied free will."

Lockridge strained to hold onto the calm they had somehow instilled into him. "But time is fixed. Isn't it?"

"From a divine view, perhaps," John said. "Men, though, are not gods. Look into yourself. You know you make free choices. Don't you? In the time war they rationalized every horrible thing they did by claimin' it was bound to happen anyway. Yet they were themselves, directly, responsible for more tyranny, more death, more hate, more sufferin' than I can stand to count up. We today know better than to look into our own future, and we only go in secret, as observers, to the poor damned past."

"Except for me," Lockridge said with a flick of anger.

"I'm sorry. That's a wrong we've got to do, to prevent a

greater wrong." John gave him a steady look. "I console myself by thinkin' you're man enough to take it."

"Well—" Wryness touched Lockridge's lips. "Okay. I certainly am glad you interfered there in the corridor."

"We won't do so again," said Mary.

They came out onto the lane. This seemed a fair-sized town, homes stretching off among high trees. A machine tended one lawn. Folk were about, handsome people with unhurried gait. Some were nude, others evidently felt a light tunic was more comfortable in the warmth. A couple of adults passing near bowed with unservile respect to John.

"You must be an important man," Lockridge remarked.

"A continental councilor." Love and pride lay in Mary's tone.

Several children whooped by. They shouted something which made John grin and wave.

"Uh . . . me bein' here . . . you've kept that quiet?" Lockridge asked.

"Yes," Mary answered. "The fact of your comin' is known. We prepared ourselves. But the—call them the time wardens —never released details. For your own sake. Someone might've told you too much." In haste: "Not necessarily awful. But a sense o' destiny makes a slave."

I've somethin' crucial ahead o' me, Lockridge thought. They don't want me to know how I'm goin' to die.

He wrenched free of that by seizing on a word. "Time wardens! Then my side did win." With a look around, a breath of woodland odor, a sense of cool turf underfoot: "Sure. I should'a guessed. This is a good place."

"I think," said John, "you'd do well to remember what one of our philosophers wrote. *All evil is a good become cancerous.*"

Puzzled, Lockridge followed him in silence. They came after a while to an area walled off by a hedge. John touched a leaf and the branches parted. Behind lay a torpedo-shaped vehicle which the three of them entered. The forward cabin was a transparent bubble, with no controls visible. Aft, through a doorway, Lockridge saw—machines? shapes? Whatever they were, they had no clearly understandable form, but seemed to follow impossible curves to infinite expansions and regressions.

John sat down. Silently, the carrier lifted. Earth fell away until Lockridge overlooked the eastern seaboard entire beneath a darkened sky. Mostly the land was green—how long had men needed to repair the work of the Rangers?—but southward a complex of buildings spread across miles. They were tasteful, the air was clean around them, and he identified parks. "I thought the Wardens didn't build cities," Lockridge said.

"They didn't," John replied shortly. "We do."

"Man also needs the nearness of his fellows," Mary explained.

Lockridge's disturbance was interrupted by the sight of a silvery ovoid lifting over the horizon. He estimated distances and thought, Good Lord, that thing must be half a mile long! "What is it?"

"The Pleiades liner," John said.

"But, but they couldn't reach the stars . . . in Storm's era."

"No. They were too busy killin' each other."

The vehicle picked up speed. America vanished in the ocean's unchangeable loneliness. Lockridge started to ask more questions. Mary shook her head. Tears blurred her eyes.

The time was short until Europe hove into view. In some fashion, as it moved down, the carrier did not batter its way through the air. Lockridge would have welcomed noise, to get his mind off his pastward future. He strained ahead. They were still so high that the coast unrolled like a map.

"Hey! You're aimin' for Denmark!"

"We must," John said. "You can go overland to your destination."

He stopped and hovered in sight of the Limfjord. The country was mainly woods and pasture. Lockridge saw a herd of graceful spotted beasts, were they from another planet? But near the head of the bay stood a town. It wasn't like the one he had just left, and that gladdened him a little. He had never liked the idea of the world blanketed with dead uniformity. Red walls and copper spires reminded him of the Copenhagen he had known.

Okay, he told himself, whatever I've still got to do, I reckon it'll be in a good cause.

"I wish we could show you more, Malcolm," said Mary gently. "But here we leave you."

"Huh? Where's your corridor?"

"We've found a different means," John said. "This machine'll carry us."

Fire crawled among the shapes aft. Blackness sealed the cabin. Lockridge took heart. He needn't really be doomed. This couple might only feel sorry for him because he had some fighting left to do. At the least, he'd soon see Auri again. Not to mention Yuria and her cousins; what a party that would be! And afterward Storm. . . .

The transition ended. John's countenance had tautened. "Get out quick," he said. "We can't risk bein' spotted." The machine fell to a shockless landing. He gripped his passenger's hand. "Fare you well," he said roughly.

"Oh, fare you well," cried Mary to Lockridge, and kissed him.

The door slid back. He jumped out. The carrier rose and vanished.

17

That summery land he had glimpsed was a thousand years unborn. He stood in a wilderness as thick as any the Tenil Orugaray had known. These trees were mostly beeches, though, tall and white, their branches bare against a darkening sky. Fallen leaves rustled dryly in a chill wind. A raven flapped overhead.

He winced. What kind of friends had those people been, to dump him here naked and alone?

They had to, he thought.

Still, damnation, no purpose was served by his starving. So somebody must live nearby. He peered through the dusk and found a trail. Narrow and obviously seldom used, it wound off among brush and tree trunks toward the bay. He selected the diaglossa for this milieu by experiment and struck off with a briskness that was largely to warm himself.

A glow broke through the woods, opposite the last embers of sunset. Hunter's moon, he decided. Auri must have been awaiting him for a good three months. Poor lonely kid. Well, they had to study her anyhow, and he'd be there as soon as he could find transportation—

He stopped. The cold sank teeth into him. Far off he had heard the baying of hounds.

Well, was that anything to scare a man? Why the devil was he so jittery? He got moving again.

Dusk thickened into night. Twigs crackled and stabbed as

he blundered half blind from side to side of the path. The
wind grew louder. Ever more close, the dogs gave tongue.
And was that a horn he heard? Must be, with such a clang;
but the notes were an ugly snarl.

Probably bound along this same trail, he thought. Let's wait.
. . . No. He broke into a trot. For some reason he didn't want
to encounter that pack.

A part of him, above the growing unease, tried to understand why. If the Wardens reserved wild areas, that fitted
their philosophy. If they hunted for sport, what of it? Yet this
region was so blasted desolate. Auri's home woods had teemed.
Here he had seen nothing but trees and bushes and one
carrion bird, heard nothing but wind and the unnaturally rapid
approach of dogs.

The moon swung higher. Shafts of light pierced between
trunks turned ghostly gray, to speckle the ground with shadow.
Deeper in, the gloom was absolute. More and more he felt as
if he were in flight down an endless tunnel. He began to
breathe hard. Howling echoed, the horn blew again, he sensed
hoofbeats drum through the cold earth.

Ahead of him, the forest opened. Hoarfrost glinted on
heather and the Limfjord lay black and silver-streaked under
flickering stars. Lockridge heard himself sob with relief.

But suddenly the hounds yelped and yammered, the horn
rang shrill, and the gallop became thunder. Knowledge
stabbed: They've got my scent! Uncontrollable, the fear rose
up and took him. He ran, with horror at his back.

Closer the pack clamored. A woman screamed like a wildcat. He broke into a dazzle of moonlight. A mile away, next
the shore, he saw a black mass and a few tiny yellow glimmers.
Houses— He tripped, into whins that raked him bloody.

The fall shocked out a little panic. He'd never make that
shelter, if shelter it was. The dogs would be on him in minutes.
Storm, he wept, darlin', I've got to get home to you. The memory of her breasts against him gave him the courage to double
back.

To the forest edge . . . up a tall tree . . . stand on a branch, hug the bole, become another shadow, and wait!

Down the trail and out onto the heath came the hunt.

Those were not dogs, that score of wolfish monsters, roaring forth under the moon. Those were not half a dozen horses, they were much too huge and narwhal horns sprouted from their heads. The lunar light was so icily brilliant that he could see dark, clotting wetness on one point. They were human who rode, two women and four men in Warden uniform. Long fair hair blew wild with their speed. And that shape was also human, slung naked with a rent belly across one saddlebow.

A man winded his trumpet almost beneath Lockridge. Such dread came upon the American that he was near losing his hold, he knew only that he must run, run, run— Subsonics! flashed through his last sane part, and he clutched the tree till the bark bruised him.

"Ho-yo, ho-yo!" The leading woman shook her spear aloft. Her face was unbearably akin to Storm's.

Forth they galloped, until the hounds lost the scent and cast about with angry snufflings. The riders reined in. Through wind and beasts, Lockridge heard them shout to each other. One girl pointed eagerly at the woods. She knew what the quarry had done. But the rest were too drunk with motion to go beating the bush. After a while they all lined out eastward across the waste.

Could be a trick, Lockridge thought. They figure me for comin' down, as I've got to, and they'll be back to catch me then.

The horn sounded anew, but already so far off that most of its mind-destroying effect was lost. Lockridge slid from the tree. They might not expect him to make for yonder hamlet immediately. He wouldn't have that much coolness left him, if he were some ignorant *slogg*.

Where did he get that word? Not from his diaglossa, which held so carefully little truth about this half of the world. Wait. Yes. Storm had used it.

He filled his lungs, pressed elbows to ribs, and started running.

Moonlight flooded the earth, the heather was frost-gray and the waters gleamed, surely they would see him but he could only run. Bushes snagged and scratched, the wind blew straight against him, but he could only run. Naught else was left in all the world, unless to wait for fang and horn and lance. Did terror, or something put in his veins by John and Mary, lash him to the pace he made? This part of his flight was no dream eternity; he reached the shore in one sprint.

The settlement was a mere huddle of huts. Though their walls were concrete and their roofs some glistening synthetic, they were more cramped and poor than those of the Neolithic. Through ill-fitting shutters and doors trickled those gleams he had seen.

He beat on the first one. "Let me in!" he cried. "Help!"

No answer came, no stir, the house closed in on itself and denied that he was real. He stumbled across bare dirt to the next and hammered his fists raw. "Help! In Her name, help me!"

Someone whimpered. A man's voice called shaken, "Go away."

Remote on the heath, the noise of the hunt was checked. It lifted again and began to sweep closer.

"Go away, you filth!" bawled the man within.

Lockridge cast himself at the door. The panel was too strong. He rebounded in a wave of hurt.

Into the hamlet he lurched, shouting his appeal. At the middle was a sort of square. A tau cross rose twenty feet high near a primitive well. Upon it was tied a man. He was dead, and the ravens had begun to eat him.

Lockridge went past. Now again he could hear the hoofs.

At the far end of settlement lay some fields that might have borne potatoes. Plain in the relentless moonlight he saw the tracks of riders. A cabin even meaner than the rest stood hard by. Its door creaked wide. An old woman stepped forth and called, "Here, you. Quickly."

Lockridge fell across the threshold. The woman closed and locked the door. Above his gasps, he heard her drunken grumble: "They're not like to come into town. No sport, killing a boxed-in man. And I say a Wildrunner is a man. Let her get wrathy as she likes, if she finds out. I know my rights, I do. They took my Ola, but that makes me his mother holy for a year. None less than the Koriach can judge me, and my lady Istar won't dare trouble Her over so fiddling a matter."

Lockridge's strength crept back. He stirred. The woman said hastily, "Now remember, if you make any fuss, you, I need but open the door and holler. I've strong men for neighbors, who'd be glad to get their hooks on a Wildrunner. I don't know if they'll tear you to pieces themselves or send you out for Istar to chase, but your wretched life is in my hands and don't you ever forget that."

"I . . . won't . . . be any bother." Lockridge sat up, hugged his knees, and looked at her. "If I can give you any thanks—any return—"

She was not so old at that, he realized with an unexpected shock. The stooped gait, in her drab gown, the gnarled hands, weather-beaten skin, half toothless mouth, had fooled him. Her hair, braided to her waist, was still dark, her features not much wrinkled, her eyes drink-hazed but unfaded.

The one-roomed cabin behind her was scantily furnished. A couple of bedsteads, a table and a few chairs, a chest and cabinet . . . wait, that kitchen corner held apparatus that looked electronic, and there was a communicator screen on the wall . . . opposite a little shrine with a silver Labrys—

She started. "You're no Wildrunner!"

"I suppose not. Whatever that is." Lockridge cupped an ear. The pack had veered off again. He drew a ragged breath and knew this was not his night to die.

"But, but you come naked from the woods, fleeing them, yet still you're barbered, and talk better'n I do—"

"Let's say I'm an outlander, though no enemy." Lockridge spoke with care. "I was bound this way when the hunters chanced on me. It's important that I get in touch with, uh, the Koriach's own headquarters. You ought to be well paid for saving my life." He rose. "Uh, could you lend me some clothing?"

She looked him up and down, not as a woman at a man but with an immemorial wariness that slowly yielded to resolution. "Very well! Might be you lie, might even be you're a devil sent to trap poor *sloggs,* but I've scant to lose. Ola's tunic should fit you." She rummaged in the chest and handed him a shabby one-piece garment. As he took it, she stroked a hand across the fabric. "His spirit must still be there, a little," she said low. "Might be it remembers me. If so, I'm guarded."

Lockridge slipped the tunic over his head. "Was Ola your son?" he asked as softly.

"Yes. The last. Sickness got the rest in their cribs. And this year, when he was no more than seventeen, the lot chose him."

With a gruesome intuition, Lockridge blurted, "Is he the one on the cross?"

Anger flared back. "Hold your jaw! That was a traitor! He cursed my lady Istar's lover Pribo, who did no more than rip a fishnet of his!"

"I'm sorry," he stammered. "I told you I was a stranger."

Her mood changed with intoxicated swiftness. "Ola, now," she said, "he got to be the Year Man." She knuckled her eyes. "Goddess forgive me. I know his life is in the land. If only I could forget how he screamed when they burned him."

Lockridge found a chair, slumped, and looked into nothingness.

"You're so pale," the woman said. "Would you care for drink?"

"Christ, yes!" He meant no blasphemy: not of that god.

She poured from a jug into a glass. The wine was rougher than what he had drunk at the palace, but he felt the same peace stealing along his nerves and thought, Sure, they need somethin' to make them endure.

"Tell me," he said, "is this Istar your priestess?"

"Why, indeed. She's the one you should call. Not before tomorrow afternoon, I think. She'll be out late, hunting, and'll sleep late, and no matter how important you are, she's no good person to get out of bed." The *slogg* drank from her own glass and tittered. "Into bed, now, well, I hear that's another matter. The lads aren't supposed to talk about the springtime rites, but they will, they will."

"Uh, these Wildrunners. Who are they?"

"What? You must be from afar! They're the naked ones, the woods dwellers, the wretches that skulk in to steal a chicken or waylay any man unwise enough to go out yonder by himself. I really don't know why I let you in, when I believed you was a Wildrunner. Unless maybe I'd been sitting here alone remembering Ola and . . . and of course they must be hunted, not just to keep them down but because their life goes into the land . . . yet even so, I sometimes wonder if the Goddess won't ever make us a better way."

Oh, yes, Lockridge thought sickly, a better way can be made.

Though not in this age. I see it quite plain. I see that bewildered old workman I knew, two thousand years ago, laid off because he couldn't handle a cybernetic machine. What do you *do* with your extra people?

If you're a Ranger, you dragoon them into a permanent army. If you're a Warden, you keep them ignorant serfs, with some out-and-out savages as a check, and a religion that— No, there's the worst of the matter. The Wardens themselves believe.

Do you, Storm?

I've got to find out.

Vaguely, he heard the woman say, "Well, sinful though I am, Ola makes me holy till the next Year Man be chosen. He must have guided me to let you in. What else could have?" With quick eagerness: "Stranger, I helped you. In return, might I see the Koriach? My grandmother did once. She came flying across this very land, Her hair black as that storm She ofttimes calls Herself, oh, in sixty years they've not forgotten! If I might see Her, I would die so happy."

"What?" Exhaustion and the drug were upon him, but he jolted to wakefulness. "The same? That long ago?"

"Who else? The Goddess doesn't die."

A trick of some kind, maybe using the time gates. But Brann had spoken of combatting her throughout all history—and so few were fitted to go through the corridors. Their leaders, at least, must have to spend a total of years or decades in every milieu— *How many?*

The glass fell from Lockridge's hand. He got up. "I can't stay here," he exploded. "I'm going to call for someone to come get me."

"No, wait, that set only goes to Istar's keep, you don't think the likes of me has a direct line to the Goddess, do you? Sit down, you fool."

Lockridge brushed the woman aside. She sank onto a bed and poured herself another tumblerful. He covered the single call light. The screen came to life with a young man bored, sleepy, and resentful.

"Who are you?" the Warden demanded. "My lady is a-hunting."

"Your lady can hunt herself into Chaos if she wants," Lockridge snapped. "You connect me with the Westmark Koriach's palace."

The beardless chin dropped. "Are you possessed?"

"Listen, pretty boy, if you don't jump I'll nail your hide to the nearest barn, with half of you still inside it. Get me the Warden Hu, the Lady Yuria, any of the court that's available. Tell them Malcolm Lockridge is back. In the Koriach's name!"

"You know them? Forgive me! One, one, one minute, I beg you." The screen blanked.

Lockridge reached for the jug but pulled his hand back. No, he wanted his wits tonight. He stood for a time and raged. Outside, wind gusted under the eaves. The woman watched him, and drank unceasingly.

Hu's face appeared. "You! We took you for lost!" He showed more astonishment than gladness.

"It's a long story," Lockridge cut him off. "Can you trace this call to where I am? All right, come fetch me." He broke the connection.

The crone was too drunk now to show much of the fear that had come over her. She did shrink from him and mumble, "Lor', par'n me, I di'n' know—"

"I still owe you my life," Lockridge said. "But the Koriach is gone away for a while. I'm sorry." He couldn't remain in this hut where a boy's bed stood so neatly made. He lifted the mother's hand to his lips and went outside.

The wind streaked around him, with a rattle of dead leaves. The moon was high and seemed shrunken. Immensely far off, he heard the hunters. None of it mattered.

I've got to be careful, he thought once. If nothin' else, I've got to get Auri home again.

He didn't know how long he waited. Half an hour, maybe. Two green-clad men swooped from the dark and saluted him. "Let's go," he said.

And over the land they went. Mostly he saw it as one immense night. Here and there lay villages, ringed around the brilliant upwardness of a palace-temple but separated from it and each other by miles of nothing. Often he spied the ankh that was a factory. Sure, he thought, the Wardens live by machines just as much as the Rangers. They only dress the fact up a little more.

I wasn't meant to see any o' this. The idea was, I'd go straight to a corridor, if I lived, and get wafted straight to her sanctuary.

It rose before him, even now so splendid that he knew pain to think this must perish. His guides set him down on a terrace where jasmine perfumed an air kept warm and a fountain sang. Hu stood waiting, in a robe that cascaded like a firefall.

"Malcolm!" He seized Lockridge's shoulders. His enthusiasm did not go deep. "What ever happened? How did you escape, and go that far north, and, and, why, this calls for the biggest festival since She chose Her last avatar in the Westmark."

"Look," the American said, "I'm nearly too tired to stand.

My mission succeeded and you can have the details later. Right now, how's Auri?"

"Who? . . . Ah, the Neolithic girl. Asleep, I imagine."

"Take me to her."

"Well." Hu frowned and rubbed his chin. "Why are you so anxious about her?"

"Has she been hurt?" Lockridge shouted.

Hu stepped back. "No. Certainly not. However, you must realize she was distraught on your account. And she's evidently misunderstood some things she observed. That's to be expected. Only to be expected. The very reason we had to study someone from her culture so closely. Believe me, we treated her as kindly as possible."

"I believe you. Take me to her."

"Can't she wait? I thought we would give you a stimulant now, and after your basic account is recorded, a celebration—" Hu gave in. "As you wish."

He lifted an arm. A serving youth appeared. Hu gave instructions. "I shall see you tomorrow, Malcolm," he said, and walked off. His robe flamed about him.

Lockridge hardly noticed by what ways he was taken. In the end, a door opened. He trod through, to find a small room with another door opposite and a bed on which Auri lay. The shift she wore was quite pretty, and she had not grown thin (the local biomeds knew how to keep a specimen in good shape), but she moaned in her sleep.

With a hand that wavered, he inserted his diaglossa for her time and stroked a soft cheek. Her eyes blinked. "Lynx," she mumbled; and then, coming bolt awake: "*Lynx!*"

He sat down and held her close while she laughed and wept and shuddered in his arms. The words torrented from her, "Oh, Lynx, Lynx, I thought you must be dead, take me away, take me home, anything, this is where the wicked dead must go, no, I was not beaten, but they keep people like animals, they *breed* them, and everybody hates everybody else, always they whisper, why do they want to own the others, every one of them does, she can't be the Goddess, she mustn't be—"

"She isn't," he said. "I came here through her land, I saw her people, and I know. Yes, Auri, we will go home."

The inner door opened. He turned his head and saw the Lady Yuria. Blonde tresses did not quite hide the thing in her ear, nor did her nightcloak mask how stiffly she stood.

"I almost wish you had never admitted that, Malcolm," she said.

18

1827 B.C.

Lockridge crossed the auroral curtain. "When are we?"

Hu checked the calendar clock. "Later than I desired," he said. "The end of August."

So Avildaro has lived a fourth of a year since we broke Brann and the Yuthoaz, Lockridge thought. Auri, about as long. Me, a few days, though each one passed like a century. What's Storm done here, this whole summer?

"The uncertainty factor is what makes transtemporal liaison so difficult," Hu complained. He half turned back to the gate. "We might try again." The four soldiers who accompanied them showed alarm. One man actually started to protest. Hu changed his mind. "No. That sort of thing can entangle you in the grisliest paradoxes, if you're unlucky. I did get some couriers back and forth during the past several weeks. At last report, everything was still going smoothly, and that was little more than a local month ago."

He started up the ramp. His men fell in around Lockridge and Auri. The girl clutched the American's hand and breathed, "Are we truly home?"

"You are," he said.

In an abstract way, he wondered why no garrison of Wardens was maintained at a gate which had become as important as this one. Well, he decided, she's got a variety of reasons, includin' the fact that she needs to keep as many loyal men as possible in her own era. But mainly, I reckon she doesn't want to chance givin' the show away, in case some Ranger scout reconnoiters this far.

They emerged. The sun stood noon high over a forest rich and vivid at season's climax. A herd of roe deer, cropping the meadow, bolted and flushed a thousand partridge. Auri stood for a moment with glory in her face, raised her arms to the sky and shook back an unbound mane. Before they left, she had changed to the brief garb of her people. Lockridge noticed how startlingly her body had matured while he was gone.

He wished he'd had the nerve to ask for kilt, cloak, and necklace, instead of the green uniform given him.

"And we are free again, Lynx." Abruptly the girl must leap and shout for joy.

You are. Maybe. I hope, he thought. Me? I don't know.

They had not mistreated him, during those two days he was held in the palace before being taken here. He could stroll about as he liked, with a single guard. They asked him, quite courteously, to make his report under a drug which inhibited lying; and he had done so, spilled the whole beanpot, because the alternative could be a mind machine. Afterward Yuria had held lengthy discussions with him, not the least ill-tempered. Her position was that, imprimis, his background did not equip him to understand a totally different civilization; secundus, what he had seen was not a fair sample; tertius, tragedy must be integral to any human life which was to realize its full nobility; quartus, granted, abuses did occur, but they were correctible, and under a wiser government they would be.

He'd said nothing to that, nor accepted the favors she offered. She was too alien to him. They all were.

Hu spoke an order. The party rose and aimed for the Limfjord.

This day I'll see Storm again, Lockridge thought. His heart slammed. He couldn't tell how much was fear and how much —well—herself.

Nevertheless, she would judge him. No one else dared. Not

only was he a chosen of hers, but he had that enigmatic word from her future.

The woods fell behind. Brilliance danced on the bay, where Avildaro stood under its holy grove. Some fisher boats were out, and women at their work between the cabins. But camped to the north and spilling eastward—

Auri screamed. Lockridge ripped out an oath.

"The Yuthoaz! Lynx, what has happened?"

"By God, Warden, start explainin'," Lockridge choked.

"Be easy," Hu called over his shoulder. "This was planned. Everything is going well."

Lockridge slitted his eyes and counted. The Battle Ax people were no horde. He saw a dozen or so chariots, parked outside the tepees of their chieftainly owners. The men, gathering excited to stare at the flyer band, numbered little over a hundred. Others might be out hunting or whatever, but surely not many.

They had brought their women, though. No Orugaray female wore coarse wool sweaters and skirts. Small children scrambled among them. Older ones tended herds of cattle, sheep, horse, a wealth of livestock grazing miles over the range. Turf sheds were being erected.

The enemy had returned to stay.

Storm, Storm, why?

Hu brought them down at the Long House. View of the encampment was cut off by the huts clustered around. The open area before the doorway was deserted; no villager stirred in what had once been the jostling, haggling, laughing center of the community. Voices from afar hardly touched this sunlit silence.

The house itself was changed. Garlands used to hang over the lintel, oakleaf in summer and holly in winter. Now an emblem shone in gold and silver, the Labrys across the Sun Disc. Two warriors stood proud guard, leather armored, plumed and painted, spear, dagger, bow, and tomahawk to hand. They gave the newcomers a Warden salute.

"Is She within?" asked Hu.

"Yes, my master," said the older of the Yuthoaz, a stocky forkbearded redhead. The wolf was painted on his shield. Jarred, Lockridge knew Withucar again. His broken arm had knitted. "She makes Her magic behind the blackness."

"Keep this man here for Her summons." Hu went inside. The skin curtain flapped to behind him.

Auri covered her face and sobbed. Lockridge stroked the bright locks. "You need not stay," he murmured. "Go seek your kinfolk."

"If they live."

"They must. There was no second fight. The Storm brought back the strangers for some purpose of her own. Go on, now, home."

Auri started to leave. A soldier grabbed for her. Lockridge slapped down the man's hand. "You have no orders to detain her," he barked. The soldier stepped back with fright on his countenance. Auri vanished among the huts.

Withucar had watched the interchange with more amusement than his awed companion. His face cracked in a grin. "But you are him who got away from us!" he bawled. "Well, well!"

He leaned his spear and came over to pummel Lockridge's back. "That was a warrior deed," he said with quite genuine warmth. "Ha, how you tumbled us about, and for the sake of one little girl! What fortune had you since? We've become your friends, you know, and I've seen the gods so close these past weeks that I grow jaded and think you used no wizardry, only tricks I'd be most glad to learn. Welcome, you!"

Lockridge collected his wits. Here was a chance to get an honest account. "I went afar, on Her business," he said slowly, "And know not what's happened in these lands. No little surprised am I to find your clan returned." He planted a barb: "And to find yourself playing sentry like any common youth."

Withucar signed himself and answered with quick gravity, "Who but the highest born is fit to serve Her?"

"Uh . . . yes. Still, when did the charioteers do so?"

"Since this midsummer, or a while after. See you, we were a

frightened people, after him we thought the very Firelord was beaten and ourselves scattered by outlanders whose weapons were real metal. We counted ourselves lucky to get home, I can tell you, and made big sacrifices to the gods of this land. But an emissary came from Her and spoke to our council. He said She was not too angry with us, we being simple folk whom the giant had tricked. Indeed, She would fain use us as warriors, for Her own must go back whence they came."

Of course, Lockridge remembered. The English had to be sent home: too ill adapted to be efficient help in this age, not to mention being too noticeably foreign. Storm had dropped a remark about some idea she'd gotten, for arming this headquarters of her newest theater of operations. . . .

"Well," Withucar continued, "we were unsure. Adventurous youngsters might join Her guard for some years. But family men? So far from our own kind and gods? Then the emissary explained She wanted a warrior people to come and stay. The fishermen are brave, but untrained in order of battle and modern weapons. She wanted us, not only our hale men but our entire tribe.

"We would get land, and be honored. So would our gods be. Sun and Moon, Fire and Water, Air and Earth—why should they not wed, and be worshipped alike? So in the end, those phratries you have seen remembered how they were getting too large for their pastures, bethought themselves what could come of alliance with One so powerful, and trekked hither.

"Thus far, we've fared right well. We've skirmished just enough with the Sea People further along this shore to keep us sharp and fetch in some plunder and slaves. Next year there will belike be a real thrust, to make those places pay Her due respect which haven't already done so. Meanwhile, we are settling down in a good land; and She, Sister to the Sun, walks among us."

Storm, these Northern races were never before cursed with empire.

Harshly, Lockridge asked, "How do you get along with the Avildaro natives?"

Withucar spat. "Not so well. They dare not fight, when She has said they must not touch us. But some have stolen off overseas, and the rest are a surly lot. Why, you know what their women are like; yet if a lad of ours wants a bit of fun, his only hope is to catch one in the greenwood and force her. For we're not supposed to harm them either, you know." He brightened. "However, give us time. If they'll not often trade with us, we can manage by ourselves. In the end, we'll make them ours, even as our ancestors made those they overran into their own image." He leaned close, nudged Lockridge in the ribs, and confided, "Indeed, She intends that outcome. She promised me Herself, not long ago, there'd be weddings between the high houses of both people. And that way, you see, the inheritance goes from their mothers to our sons."

And the end of it, Lockridge thought, is Junker Erik.

No, wait. That was Ranger work.

But hadn't the Wardens laid the foundation?

He fell so silent that Withucar was hurt and returned to his post. The sun moved toward afternoon.

For all his brooding, Lockridge was idiotically glad when Hu appeared and said, "She will see you now." He almost sprang past the curtain. No one followed him.

The Long House was still fireless, coldly lit by the globes. The blackness still cut off the rear end. Where Lockridge stood, the floor had been covered with some hard material and the walls draped in gray. Furnishings and machines of the future stood among the wooden pillars like a jeer.

Storm came toward him.

The gauntness of her captivity had departed. Blue-black hair, golden skin, sea-green eyes, glowed as with a light of their own, and her gait flung her robe back against breast, hip, and leg until he must think anew of the Winged Victory. That robe was white today, deeply cut, trimmed with the blue of Crete's kingdom. The lunar crescent shimmered above her brows.

"Malcolm," she said, in his own language. "This is my true reward: that you came back." She caught his face between her hands and looked at him through a beating stillness. "Thank you," she said in the Orugaray.

He knew when a woman awaited a kiss. Dizzily, he stood his ground and tried to keep every doubt and resentment. "Hu must've given you my report," he said. "I've nothin' to add."

"Nothing you need add, my dear." She gestured to a seat. "Come. We've everything to talk about."

He joined her. Their knees touched. A bottle and two filled goblets stood before them. She gave him one and raised her own. "Will you drink to us?"

"Brann gave me wine too," he rasped.

Her smile faded. She regarded him long before she set her glass down again. "I know what you are thinking," she said.

"That the Wardens are no better than the Rangers, and to hell with 'em both? Yeah, I reckon so."

"But it isn't true," she said earnestly, never releasing his eyes. "Once you mentioned the Nazis of your time as a case of absolute evil. I agree. They were a Ranger creation. But think —be honest—suppose you were a man from the Neolithic now, transported to 1940. How much difference between countries could you have seen?"

"Your cousin Yuria used some such line of argument."

"Ah, yes. Her." Briefly, the full mouth hardened. "Someday I must do something about Yuria."

She eased, laid her hand on his thigh, and said soft and fast, "You met two, exactly two people in my future, who for their own purposes had rescued you. For an hour or so, you were in their world. They took you back to a place of their own choosing, and left you after making some calculatedly ambiguous remarks. Come, Malcolm, you have had scientific training. What sort of basis is that on which to draw conclusions? Any conclusions!

"You saw what you were meant to see. You heard what you were intended to hear. They want something to come about to which you are a key. But what is a key, except a tool? You saw merely a world that has changed. How do you know the roots of that change are not a Warden victory? I think they must be.

"For, Malcolm, a great deal of the wrong you met in my land is due to the war. Without an enemy, we would need less discipline, we would be free to experiment and reform. Yes, I know what Istar is like. But you are not so naive as to think the most absolute ruler can simply issue a decree and have her will come to pass. Are you? I must use what fate has given. It so happens that Istar supports me. Her successor—and I cannot upset the law of succession with dangerously shaking the whole realm—the one who would come after her is of another faction."

"Yuria's?" he asked from his daze.

Storm grinned. "Dear Yuria. How she would like to be Koriach! And what a poor one she would make!" She grew sober. "I don't undervalue myself, Malcolm. You have seen what I can do. By trapping Brann, with your help, I have dealt the Rangers what could be the start of a mortal blow. So few are able to mount these temporal operations, and so much depends on them. While Brann was free, most of my energy had to go simply to fending him off. Now, I know who's gotten his command, and frankly, I can think circles around Garwen.

"But our very triumph has loosed a whole new set of problems. While you were gone, faithful Hu had his spies out, and his messengers went back and forth. My rivals—oh, yes, there are more and darker palace intrigues at home than you have guessed—those who plot against me, under the hood of friendship we must wear while the war continues—they've seized on the strategic issue. Did not Yuria hint at rewards if you would be her agent in my camp?" Lockridge must nod. "Well, for purposes of rallying support, that faction maintains we must continue to concentrate our efforts in the Mediterranean and Orient. Ignore the North, they say; it has no importance; though the Indo-European conquest will surely happen in the South and East, let us keep it from becoming of real value to the enemy. Whereas I say, abandon those regions; keep only a token force there, while the Rangers tie up their best men; unknown to them, let us create in the North a thousand-year stronghold!"

He drew his attention from high-boned features and curving body to say, with less force than intended, "Is that why you've betrayed people here who trusted you?"

"Ah, yes. I've called in the Yuthoaz, and the megalith builders don't like it." Storm sighed. "Malcolm, I had you read books and spend time in the Danish National Museum. You should know the archeological facts. The new culture is coming in and will mold the future, and nothing you or I can do will remove those relics which prove it from their glass cases. Yet we can control the details, of which the relics say nothing. Would you rather the newcomers take Denmark as they are going to take India, with butchery and enslavement?"

"But in God's name, what're they to you?"

"I couldn't keep the Englishmen," she said. "They have been sent home, except for a handful who will guard that gate until it closes in several weeks. As a matter of fact, I've even sent those agents you met back to their sixteenth century. Once the basic work here was done, they were of little help. And because of my rivals' pressure, I cannot order real experts from Crete—not until I can show solid promise here."

She gestured widely. "What then will I show?" she said. "A new and long-enduring nation. A powerful folk who, under whatever mythological compromise, follow the Goddess. A source of supplies, wealth, men if we need them. A section of space-time so well defended that there we can build Warden strength against the final conflict. Given the beginnings of this —well, the other Koriachs will incline toward me. My position at home will be secured. More important, my plan will be accepted and our full force brought to bear here. And so the Ranger obscenity will come nearer its destruction—after which we can right some wrongs in our own place."

Her head sank. "But I am so alone," she whispered.

He couldn't help himself, he must take the hand that lay empty on her lap. And his other arm went about her shoulder.

She leaned close. "War is an ugly business," she said. "One

has to do heartbreaking things. I promised you, after this mission you could go home. But I need every soul who will stand by me."

"I will," he said.

After all . . . did he not have a mission unfulfilled?

"You're no ordinary man, Malcolm," she said. "The kingdom we build will need a king."

He kissed her.

She replied to him.

Presently she said in his ear, "Come on, you man. Over yonder."

The sun declined. Fisher boats returned from a west where the waters sheened yellow, smoke rose out of huts, the Wise Woman and her acolytes went forth to offer their evening oblations in the grove. Thunders beat across the meadows, where the Battle Ax men drummed their god to rest.

Storm stirred. "You'd better go now," she sighed. "I'm sorry, but I do need sleep. And this being divine takes most of my time. But you'll come again. Won't you? Please."

"Whenever you want," he answered, deep in his throat.

He walked into twilight. Peace dwelt within him. Beyond the Long House he found the Tenil Orugaray at their lives. Children still romped outdoors, men gossiped, through open entrances he saw women weaving, sewing, cooking, grinding meal, shaping pots. His passage left a wake of silence.

At the cabin which had been Echegon's, he entered. Here he could stay.

The family sat around their fire. They scrambled up and signed themselves, in a manner that not long ago had been foreign to them. Only to Auri was he still human. She came to him and said unsteadily, "How long you were with the Goddess."

"I had to be," he told her.

"You'll speak to Her for us, won't you?" she begged. "She may not know how wicked they are."

"Who?"

"Those She brought in. Oh, Lynx, what I've heard! How they

graze their beasts in our crops, and seize unwilling women, and scorn us in our own country. They raided our cousins, did you know? There are people from Ulara and Faono, my own dear kinfolk, in their camp this night—slaves. Tell Her, Lynx!"

"I will, if I can," he said impatiently. He wanted to be alone with this day for a while. "But what must be, must be. Now, may I have something to eat, and then a quiet corner? I've much to think about."

19

Like every other war Lockridge knew of, this one demanded that the bulk of effort go into the unspectacular organizing of things. Being shorthanded was equally familiar. With agents scattered the length and breadth of history, the time contenders were appallingly so. Storm Darroway was still worse off: practically alone.

She admitted that political jealousy was not the sole reason she had no support from her coavatars. Her scheme was radical, involved scrapping a considerable investment in the old, doomed civilizations elsewhere. Some of the Warden queens had been sincere when they informed her the payoff she swore could be gotten must be demonstrated before they would help. For the fact was, the time war seemed to bypass Bronze Age Northern Europe. Neither Wardens nor Rangers were known to be conducting significant operations in that thousand-year, thousand-mile stretch of space-time.

"But hey, doesn't that prove you're wrong?" Lockridge fretted.

"No," Storm said. "It could just as well mean success. Remember, because of the corridor guardians, we in our age are ignorant of our own future. We can't foretell what we are going to do next. Even such cause-and-effect circles as we used to trap Brann are rare, thanks to the uncertainty factor in the gates."

"Sure, sure. But look, sweetheart, you most certainly can

check a past era, like this one, and find out whether any of
your own people are around."

"If their work runs smoothly, what will we see? Nothing except the natives leading their everyday lives. When Warden
agents are hidden from the Rangers, they are to a large extent
also hidden from other Wardens."

"Uh . . . I reckon so. The security problem. You can't let
your own cohorts know more than they have to, or the enemy's
goin' to find out."

"Furthermore," Storm said haughtily, "this is my theater. I
will employ my own people, in what manner I see fit. The
power I get will not be used just against the Rangers. No, I've
some accounts to settle at home too."

"Sometimes you scare the dickens out of me," he said.

She smiled and rumpled his hair. "And other times?" she
purred.

"You make up for it, in spades!"

But they had not long together. There was too much to be
done.

Storm must remain in Avildaro, goddess, judge, maker of
decisions and maker of laws, until the nation she was building
had taken the shape she wanted. Hu must be her thread of
contact with home and with Crete. Ordinary soldiers were useful only as couriers or guards; in this case, the men Hu had
brought were not even required in that capacity, and she sent
them back. Trained agents could not well be spared from other
milieus. Most desperately she needed an able man to work
with the tribes.

Lockridge went forth. Withucar and some warriors accompanied him. He had gotten quite fond of the red Yutho, they'd
guested each other and drunk mead together and bragged till
far into the night. Okay, so he's not civilized, Lockridge
thought. I reckon I'm not either. I like this life.

The ultimate object was to cement the people of the Labrys
and the people of the Ax into one. That was certainly going to
happen: Jutland would come into history as a nation, and even
beyond Lockridge's century remain identifiably itself. Like-

wise for many another region. The question was, would the Indo-European incursion which the Rangers had launched to destroy the old culture do so here, or would so much of the megalith builder survive, however disguised, that the Wardens could secretly but securely draw upon the Bronze Age North? Reports from the next millennium indicated the latter might well be the case, that the Rangers' move was to recoil upon them in this part of the world.

But the founding of those kingdoms must be slow, both for lack of agents and because the event must look natural. (Must in fact *be* natural; a jerry-built empire like Alexander's or Tamerlane's was too short-lived to be of much value.) The first step was to bring the villagers around the Limfjord into a union more close and demanding than they had known before. For that, Storm had the awe of her own presence, and her Yuthoaz allies wherever force was necessary. At the same time, she had to league herself with the inland tribes, both aboriginal and newcomer. She sent Lockridge on the first such mission.

He would have preferred to go on horseback. But these shaggy, long-headed ponies had never been ridden, and it would take too long to break one. He walked. When they neared a settlement, he and Withucar got onto their chariots, set their teeth against the jouncing, and arrived in what this era took for dignity.

On the whole, though—even after what followed—Lockridge admitted he'd seldom had more fun. His pet recreation had always been to backpack into some wilderness area; now he could do it with Withucar's liege men to carry the load. When they reached people, they were hospitably received, and he was fascinated to observe details that weren't recorded in his diaglossa. (Which, gradually, he was ceasing to need, as repeated usage imprinted speech and customs on his natural memory.) In Battle Ax camps, rough ceremony was followed by feasting. The ancient agricultural villages were a little wary at first: not scared, however, for they hadn't had many clashes with the immigrants, the land being wide and thinly settled. They would begin with elaborate rituals. But they were apt to end with a celebration that would have raised twentieth-century eyebrows.

The message Lockridge bore was simple. The veritable Goddess had established Herself in Avildaro. She was not, as some had said, the enemy of Sun and Fire; rather, She was Mother, Wife, and Daughter to the male gods. The Powers desired Their children to be united as They Themselves were. To that end, the first of a series of councils would be held at Avildaro this midwinter, to discuss ways and means. All headmen were invited. Lockridge didn't add, "Or else." That would have been both antagonizing and unnecessary.

Some of what he saw and heard repelled him. But we'll fix that, he promised himself. Mostly, he enjoyed the people. He couldn't even call them less sophisticated than his own. Albeit tenuously, they had broad contacts: in the case of the Battle Ax tribes, as far as southern Russia. Their politics were almost as complicated as the twentieth century's, on a smaller scale, and untainted by ideology; their mores were a good deal subtler; if ignorant of physics, historiography, or that pseudo-science called economics, they were wise in the ways of earth, sky, and humankind.

His route took him by a holy hill which would become Viborg, over country more fertile than what he had seen in the future; north to the surf and wide strands of the Skaw; southward again along the Limfjord. A small beginning. Yet he needed almost a month. The heaths were blossoming in purple and gold, sunrise saw hoarfrost and the leaves had begun to turn color, before he reached Avildaro again.

That was on a day when the wind came brawling off the western sea, light and cloud shadow raced each other across the world, waves marched on the bay and on the puddles from last night's rain. The forest tossed and shouted; stubblefields lay yellow and the meadow grass had become hay. A flight of storks went under the sun, Egypt bound. The air was chill, with smells of salt, smoke, and horses.

Lockridge's party had been seen from afar. He rode through the Yutho encampment among lusty cheers, onto the no man's land between it and the village. No Tenil Orugaray were out to welcome him.

Except Auri. She came on jubilant feet, calling to him over and over. He made his driver stop, swept her up and hugged her. "Yes, little one, I am fine, we had no trouble, of course I am glad to see you but I do have to tell the Goddess my story first—" He would have liked to give her a lift, but the chariot scarcely had room. She danced beside the wheels the whole way.

At the Long House, trouble touched her. "I will abide in my home, Lynx," she said, and hastened off.

Withucar stared after her and scratched his beard. "A good bit of flesh, yon," he said. "How is she with a man?"

"She's a maiden," Lockridge answered curtly.

"Eh?" Dismounting, the Yutho gaped. "Can't be. Not among the Sea People."

Lockridge explained what had happened.

"We-e-ell," the chief murmured. "Well, well. But surely you're not afraid of her?"

"No. I'm too busy." Lockridge snapped his mouth shut.

"Ah, yes." Withucar signed himself, though he also grinned. "You are favored of the Goddess." That was no longer cause for undue reverence, after he and the American had tramped the hills, hallooed after deer, cursed rain and unstartable camp-fires, and faced possible death together. "This Auri," he said. "I've liked her looks erenow, but took without thought that she was yours. She does nuzzle up to you every chance."

"We're friends," Lockridge said with rising irritation. "Were she a man, we would be oath-brothers. Any hurt done her is done me, and I'll take revenge."

"Oh, yes, yes. Still, you'd not wish her left single forever, would you?"

Lockridge could only shake his head.

"And she is the inheritor of the old headman here; and you say the curse is off her—hm."

Well, Lockridge thought with an odd sinking, that may turn out the best answer to her problem.

He couldn't keep her long in mind, though. Storm waited.

In the presence of Hu and Withucar, she greeted him formally, and seemed only half to listen to his report. He was soon dismissed. However, she had given him a smile and said an English word: "Tonight."

After that, and the easy comradeship of his past weeks, he didn't want to spend the day among the Tenil Orugaray. They had changed from the merry folk he knew before, into a bewildered and sullen occupied country. A gap had opened between him and them; he was Her agent, and She had chosen to reveal some of Her more terrible aspects. He could have visited the Yuthoaz . . . but no, he would see their slaves. Auri? Well, that had become a rather difficult relationship. He hiked off alone. The sacred pool on the forest edge probably wasn't too cold for him to wash off his journey's grime.

He should have been happy. But something had gone sour. He chewed it over as the miles went past. Surely the peaceful unification of the two races was a good goal. And the Battle Ax men weren't bad by nature; just sort of overbearing. Like untrained boys. That was it. They needed the fear of the Lord thrown into them. Specifically, they needed a respect for the humanity of the aborigines. At present, they were merely adding the Moon Goddess to their pantheon, with nothing except Her command to keep them from making booty of the Sea People. And no entire culture had ever respected another which gave no good account of itself in battle.

Progress, Lockridge thought sadly. Will man be any different, four thousand years from now? We white Americans may have robbed the Indian, but because he fought back, we're proud of any Indian blood we may have. The Negro we plain despised, till my very own decades, when at last he stood up and slugged it out for his rights.

Maybe John and Mary's people don't have to have their noses rubbed in blood before they can honor a stranger. I like to think so. But how do we get from here to there?

Maybe that's my job. To lay one single brick for their house.

Only how? The Yuthoaz know perfectly well they would've

beaten the Tenil Orugaray if the gods hadn't taken a hand. They're here now, by Storm's invitation, because they make better warriors. It's fine to call a council and set up a king. But how do we escape a kingdom made up of master and serf?

Does Storm even want to?

No! Stop that!

He had been so lost in his brown study that he was almost to the pool before he saw what was going on. And they—seven young men and a girl from the village—were so intent that they hadn't seen him coming.

She was stretched on the boulder from which tools were cast as offerings. While his companions stood by with mistletoe in their hands, the seventh man raised a flint knife above her breast.

"What the hell!" Lockridge bellowed.

He dashed toward them. They scattered back. When they saw who he was, fear turned them less than human, they groveled on the earth while the girl came piecemeal from her trance.

Lockridge controlled his stomach and said in his deepest voice: "By Her name, I demand confession of your misdeeds."

He got it, in stammerings and pleadings. Some of the details were left out, but he could fill those in for himself.

"Goddess" was no good translation of the word for what She was in this culture. The Japanese *kami* came nearer: any supernatural being, from this rock, or the tree whose pardon one asked before felling it, to the vast vague Powers that dominated the elements. Dominated, not controlled. There was no formal theology, no separation of the magical and the divine; all things had some mystical strength. He, Lockridge, had a frightful amount. Withucar could be his friend, but that was because Withucar did not expect the magic to be unleashed against himself. Auri, less fortunate, had no one at all who felt easy in her presence.

These of the kindly Tenil Orugaray saw their country invaded by Her will. They could have escaped to Flanders or England, as some had already done, but the instinct of homeland was too deep in them. Instead, they would try to raise powers against Her. They had heard tales of human sacrifice among the inland people, and knew those inlanders were still free—

"Go home," Lockridge said. "I call no ill down on you. I will not tell Her about this. Better times are coming. That I swear."

They crawled off. When they had gotten some distance, they ran. Lockridge sprang into the pool and washed himself savagely.

He did not return till after sunset. The weather had thickened, a rack of clouds blew from the sea, bringing cold and an early dusk. None were abroad in the village, and skins across the doorways shut him out.

Whatever his feelings, a man must eat, and Lockridge was bumming off the house which had been Echegon's. He walked into a stillness. Smoke stung his eyes, shadows filled the corners and crowded close around the wan flicker in the firepit. Auri's kin sat as if waiting for him: her mother the widow, who tonight reminded him of that woman who sheltered him from Istar's hounds; her few remaining small half brothers; her aunt and uncle, plain fisher folk who watched him out of an absolute withdrawal; their own children, some asleep, some so far grown that they were still awake to cower from him. "Where is Auri?" Lockridge asked.

Her mother pointed to a dais. Wheaten hair spilled across the deerskin blanket. "She wore herself out weeping. Must I rouse her?"

"No." Lockridge looked from face to shut and careful face. "What is the matter?"

"Surely you know," her mother said, without even accusing him.

"I don't. Tell me!" The fire jumped momentarily high, so its light played over Auri's form. She slept with thumb inside fist, like a troubled child. "I want to help," he groped.

"Oh. Yes, you were ever her friend. But what's best for her?" the mother appealed. "We cannot be sure. We are only earthdwellers."

"Nor am I more," Lockridge said, and wished they would believe him.

"Well, then. This afternoon came that Yutho chief called Withucar and asked that she be his . . . what is their word?"

"Wife," Lockridge said. He remembered that Withucar had three.

"Yes. His alone. A kind of slave who must do his every bidding. Yet, well, you are wiser than us, and you know this man. He said we would all come under his protection. Is that true? This house has sore need of a guardian."

Lockridge nodded. Protection has a price, he thought, but didn't say so.

"Auri refused him," the mother said wearily. "He answered that the Goddess had told him he could have her. Then she grew wild, and cried out for you. We calmed her a little and sought the Long House. The Goddess saw us, after a wait, and commanded Auri to join with Withucar. But they do such things differently among the Yuthoaz. It may not be until certain rites have taken place. So we brought her home. She raved of killing herself, or taking a boat alone—that would be the same thing—but at last she slept. What do you think?"

"I will speak to the Goddess," Lockridge said unevenly.

"Thank you. I do not know myself what is best. She would be unfree with him, but are we not unfree already? And The Storm has commanded. Yet Auri could never gladly spend her life in such narrow streams. Perhaps you can tell her it's best."

"Or get her released," Lockridge said. "I will go at once."

"Do you not first wish food?"

"No, I am not hungry." He dropped the curtain behind him.

The village was very dark. He must fumble his way to the Long House. The Yutho sentries let him through without argument.

Inside, the globes still glowed. Storm sat alone at the control board of a psychocomputer. In this heated place she wore a very brief tunic, but he looked upon her without desire. She turned about, laughed, and stretched. "So soon, Malcolm?

Well, I'm tired of extrapolating trends. The data are mostly guesswork anyhow."

"Look," he began, "we've got to talk."

Her mirth went away and she sat quite still.

"We're goin' about this project wrong," he said. "I figured the original people here would get reconciled to the new arrangements. But instead, while I was away, things went from bad to worse."

"You certainly can switch moods in a hurry," she said, chill of tone. "Be more specific. You mean that friction between the tribes has increased. What did you expect? What am I supposed to do, disown my good Yutho allies?"

"No, just take them down a peg or two."

"Malcolm, my dear," Storm said more gently, "we haven't come to build a utopia. That's an impossible task anyway. What we are concerned with is the creation of strength. And that means favoring those who have the potential of being strong. Before you get too self-righteous, ask if the dwellers on Eniwetok will really want to be moved, to make room for your country's nuclear tests. We can try to minimize the pain we inflict, but someone who refuses to inflict any has no business in this world."

Lockridge drew back his shoulders and said, "Okay, you can outargue me whenever—"

Storm rose. Her look was shameless and enchanting. "Especially in one way," she said.

"No, wait, damn it!" Lockridge protested. "Maybe we do have to be bastards, we humans. But not without any qualification. A man's got to stand by his friends, at least. Auri's a friend of mine."

Storm halted. A while she stood motionless, then ran fingers down a night-black lock and said softly, "Yes, her. I thought you'd raise the question. Go on."

"Well, uh, well, she doesn't want to be in Withucar's harem."

"Is he a bad man?"

"No. But—"

"Do you want her to remain single: knowing how unnatural that makes her here?"

"No, no, no—"

"Is anyone else available to her?"

"Well—"

"Unless, perhaps, yourself," Storm growled.

"Oh, good God!" Lockridge said. "You know I—you and me—"

"Don't set yourself too high, my man. But as for this wench. If the races are to become one, there have to be unions. Marriage is too strong an institution for the Battle Ax people to give up; therefore the Sea People will have to accept it. Auri is the heiress of this community's leadership, Withucar is as influential as any in his tribe. Both in practice and as an example, nothing better could happen than their marriage. Of course she threw a fit. Are you so ignorant you think she will never console herself? Nor love her children by him? Nor forget *you?*"

"Well, though—I mean, she deserves a free choice."

"Who is there for her to choose, except you who don't want her? Nor would it help the purpose if you did. You came in complaining of unhappiness among the villagers. The English are going to be still unhappier after the Norman Conquest. But a few centuries later, there are no Normans. Everyone is an Englishman. For us, here and now, that same process begins with Auri and Withucar. Don't talk to me about free choice . . . unless you think every war should only be fought by volunteers."

Lockridge stood helpless. Storm came to him and put her arms about his neck. "I believe Auri, in her childish way, calls you Lynx," she murmured. "I would like to do that."

"Aw—look—"

She rubbed her head on his breast. "Let me be childish now and then, with you."

A Yutho voice called from beyond the curtain: "Goddess, the lord Hu asks to come in."

"Damn!" Storm whispered. "I'll get rid of him as fast as I can." Aloud: "Let him enter."

Spare and lithe in his green uniform, Hu trod in to bow. "I beg your forgiveness, brilliance," he said. "But I was out on an aerial sweep."

Storm tautened. "Well?"

"Most likely this means nothing. Still, I saw a considerable fleet beating across the North Sea. The lead ship is Iberian, the rest are skin boats. I never heard of such a combination. They're plainly bound from England to Denmark."

"At this season?" Awareness of Lockridge drained from Storm. She let him go and stood alone in the frigid light.

"Yes, that's another paradox, brilliance," Hu said. "I couldn't detect advanced equipment. If they have any, it must be negligible. But they will be here in a day or two."

"Some Ranger operation? Or a mere local adventure? These are times when the natives themselves look to new things." Storm frowned. "Best I go glance at them myself."

She fetched her gravity belt and fastened it about her waist, an energy pistol at the hip. "You may as well stay and rest, Malcolm. I won't be gone long," she said, and left beside Hu.

For some time Lockridge prowled the hall. The night was noisy with wind, but he heard a thrusting inner silence. And the gods so clumsily and tenderly hacked out of the pillars— did they look at him? Lord, Lord, he thought, what does a guy do when he can't help somebody who cares for him?

What is truth?

A woman six thousand years hence told him her son had been burnt alive. But she knew the cause was good. Didn't she?

Lockridge checked himself. He had almost gone through the veil of lightlessness. Brann had suffered and died behind it. His guts knotted. Why did they continue to maintain the thing?

Why hadn't he asked?

I reckon I never wanted to, he understood, and stepped through.

This end of the house had not been refurnished. The floor

was dirt, the seats covered with skins gone dusty. One globe illuminated the section; shadows lay in every corner. The black barricade cut off sound, too. The wind was gone. Lockridge stood in total quiet.

That which was on the table, wired into the machine, stirred and whimpered.

"No!" Lockridge screamed, and fled.

Long afterward, he got the courage to stop sobbing and return. He could do no else. Brann, who had fought as best he could for his own people, was not dead.

Little was left, except skin drawn dry across the big arching bones. Tubes fed into him and kept the organism together. Electrodes pierced the skull, jolted the brain and recorded what was brought forth. For some reason of stimulus, the eyelids had been cut away and the balls of the eyes must stare into the light overhead.

"I didn't know," Lockridge wept.

Tongue and lips struggled in the wreck of a face. Lockridge wasn't wearing his diaglossa for Brann's age, but he could guess that a fragment of self pleaded, "Kill me."

While just beyond the curtain—her and me—

Lockridge reached for the machine.

"Stop! What are you doing?"

He turned, very slowly, and saw Storm and Hu. The man's energy gun was out, aimed at his belly. The woman said urgently: "I wanted to spare you this. It does take time, to extract the last traces of memory. There isn't much cerebrum by now, he's really no more than a worm, so you needn't feel pity. Remember, he had begun to do the same thing to me."

"Does that excuse you?" Lockridge shouted.

"Will Pearl Harbor excuse Hiroshima?" she gibed.

For the first time in his existence, Lockridge said an obscenity to a woman. "Never mind your fancy reasons," he gasped. "I know how you kept yourself in my country . . . by murderin' my countrymen. I know John and Mary gave me an honest look at the way you run your own territory. How old are you? I got enough hints about that too. You can't have done every crime you have done, except in hundreds o' years, your own time. That's why they've got the knife in you, back at the palace—why everybody wants to be the Koriach—she's made immortal. While Ola's mother is old at forty."

"Stop that!" Storm cried.

Lockridge spat. "I've got no business wonderin' how many lovers you've had, or how I'm just a thing you used," he said. "But you aren't goin' to use Auri, understand? Nor her people. Nor anyone. To hell with you: the hell you came from!"

Hu leveled the gun and said, "That will suffice."

20

Rain started before dawn. Lockridge awoke to the sound of it, muffled on the peat roof of the cabin where he lay, loud on the muddy ground. Through a lattice across the doorway, he looked over pastures where Yutho cattle huddled as drenched as their herdsmen. Sere leaves dropped one by one off an oak, under the steady beat of water. He couldn't see the rest of the village from this outlier hut, nor the bay. That added to an isolation he had believed was already infinite.

He didn't want to put his Warden uniform back on, but once out from the skins, he found the air too chill and damp. I'll ask for an Orugaray rig, or even a Yutho one, he thought. She'll give me that much, I hope, before she—

Does what?

He shook himself, angrily. Having managed a few hours' sleep, after he was put here, he should now be able to hold his courage.

Hard to do, though, when everything had broken in his grasp during a single night. To learn what Storm and her cause really were—well, he'd had clues enough, had simply ducked his duty to think about them, until the sight of Brann snapped the leash she had put on him. And to know what she would make of these people, whom he had become so fond of—that was too deep a wound.

Poor Auri, he thought in his hollowness. Poor Withucar.

The remembrance of the girl was curiously healing. He

might yet be able to do something for her, if no one else. Maybe she could stow away on that fleet bound hither. It was evidently a joint Iberian-British venture, to judge from some remarks that passed between Storm and Hu while they oversaw the preparation of a jail for Lockridge. The size as well as composition was unique; but then, some rather large events appeared to be going on in England these days, of which the founding of Stonehenge might be one consequence. Storm was too preoccupied to care much. It satisfied her that everyone aboard, seen through infrared magnifiers, was of archaic racial type, no agents from the future. Of course, in this weather the fleet would doubtless heave to, and not arrive for an extra day or so. He might not be around then. But he could, perhaps, find ways to suggest the idea of escape to Auri.

Purpose restored him a little. He went to the entrance and stuck his face out between the lashed poles, into the rain. Four Yuthoaz stood guard, wrapped in leather cloaks. They edged from him, lifted their weapons and made signs against evil.

"Greeting, you fellows," Lockridge said. Storm had let him keep his diaglossas. "I want to ask a favor."

The squad leader nerved himself to reply, sullenly, "What can we do for one who's fallen under Her wrath, save watch him as we were told?"

"You can send a message for me. I only want to see a friend."

"None are allowed here. She ordered that Herself. We've already had to chase away one girl."

Lockridge clenched his teeth. Naturally Auri would have heard the news. Many a frightened eye had seen him marched off last night, by torchlight, under Yutho spears. *You she-devil, Storm,* he thought. *In the jail you hauled me out of, they let me have visitors.*

"Well," he said, "then I want to see the Goddess."

"Hoy-ah!" The warrior laughed. "You'd have us tell Her to come at *your* bidding?"

"You can tell her with respect that I beg audience, can't you? When you're relieved, if not before."

"Why should we? She knows what She wants to do."

Lockridge donned a sneer and said, "Look, you swine, I may be in trouble but I've not lost every power. You'll do as I say or I'll rot the flesh off your bones. Then you'll have to pray for the Goddess' help anyway."

They cringed. Lockridge saw foreshadowed the kind of realm that Storm would build. "Go!" he said. "And get me some breakfast on the way."

"I, I dare not. None of us dare leave before we are allowed. But wait." The leader drew a horn from beneath his cloak and winded it, a dull sad noise through the rain. Presently a gang of youths arrived, axes in hand, to learn what the trouble was. The leader sent them on Lockridge's errands.

It was a puny triumph, but nonetheless drove some more hopelessness off him. He attacked the coarse bread and roast pork with unexpected appetite. *Storm can break me,* he thought, *but she'll need a mind machine for the job.*

He was not even surprised when she came, a couple of hours later. What did astonish him was the way his heart still turned over at sight of her. In full robe she walked over the land, big and supple and altogether beautiful. The Wise Woman's staff was in her hand, a dozen Yuthoaz at her back. Lockridge saw Withucar among them. From her belt of power sprang an unseen shield off which the rain cascaded, so that she stood in a silvery torrent, water nymph and sea queen.

She halted before the cabin and regarded him with eyes more sorrowful than anything else. "Well, Malcolm," she said in English. "I find I must come when you ask."

"I'm afraid I'll never come to your whistle again, darlin'," he told her. "Too bad. I was right proud to belong to you."

"No more?"

He shook his head. "I wish I could, but I can't."

"I know. You are that kind of man. If you weren't, this would hurt me less."

"What're you goin' to do? Shoot me?"

"I am trying to find a different way. You don't know how hard I am trying."

"Look," he said with a hope wild, sweet, and doomed, "you can drop this project. Quit the time war. Can't you?"

"No." Her pride was somber. "I am the Koriach."

He had no answer. The rain hammered down around them.

"Hu wanted to kill you out of hand," Storm said. "You are the instrument of destiny, and if you have become our enemy, dare we let you live? But I replied that your death might be the very event that is necessary to cause—what?" Her resolution flickered low and she stood isolated in the blurring waterfall. "We don't know. I thought, how gladly I thought, when you came back to me, that you were the sword of my victory. Now I don't know what you are. Anything I do could bring ruin. Or bring success, who can tell? I know only that you are fate, and that I want so much to save you. Will you let me?"

Lockridge looked into the haunted green eyes and said with huge pity, "They were right in the far future. Destiny makes us slaves. You're too good for that, Storm. Or no, not good—not evil either, maybe, not anything human—but it's wrong for this to happen to you."

Did he see tears through the rain? He wasn't sure. Her voice, at least, was steady: "If I decide you must die, it shall be quickly and cleanly, by my own hand; and you will be laid in the dolmen of the gate with warrior's honors. But I beg that that need not be."

He fought against a witchcraft older and stronger than any powers her distorted world had given her, and said: "While I wait, can I say good-bye, or somethin', to a few friends?"

Then anger leaped forth. She stamped the staff into mud and cried, "Auri? No! You'll see Auri wedded tomorrow, in yonder camp. I'll talk to you again afterward and learn if you're really such a contemptible idiot as you act!"

She turned, in a whirl of cloak and gown, and left him.

Her escort followed. Withucar dropped behind. A sentry tried to stop him. Withucar shoved the man aside, came to the door, and held out his hand.

"You're still my brother, Malcolm," he said gruffly. "I'll speak for you to Her."

Lockridge took the clasp. "Thanks," he mumbled. His eyes stung. "One thing you can do for me. Be kind to Auri, will you? Let her stay a free woman."

"As far as I'm able. We'll name a son for you, and sacrifice at your grave, if things come to that. But I hope not. Luck ride with you, friend." The Yutho departed.

Lockridge sat down on the dais and stared into the rain. His thoughts were long, and nobody else's business.

Toward noon the downpour ended. But no sun broke through. Instead, mists began to rise, until the world beyond the door was one dripping gray formlessness. Now and then he heard a voice call, a horse neigh, a cow low, but the sound came muffled and remote, as if life had drawn away from him. So cold and damp was the air that eventually he got back under his blanket. Weariness claimed him; he slept.

His dreams were strange. When he rose out of them, inch by inch, he didn't know for a while that he was doing so. Real and unreal twisted together, he was wrecked in a storm-dark ocean, Auri blew past, crying his mother's name, a horn summoned hounds, he went down into green depths and heard the clangor of iron being forged, fought his way back to where the lightnings burned, thunder smote him and—and the hut was filled with blackness, twilight seeped through the fog, men shouted and weapons clattered—

No dream!

He stumbled from his bed to the door, shook the bars and yelled into the slow wet roil, "What's happenin'? Where is everybody? Let me out, God damn you! Storm!"

Drums thuttered in the gray. A Yutho voice roared, hoofs hammered past, wheels banged and axles squealed. Elsewhere, wildly, men rallied each other. From afar, a woman shrieked, under a mounting rattle of stone. And metal, bronze had been unscabbarded, he heard the sinister whistle of an arrow flight.

Figures moved, vague in the smoky dusk, his guards. "Some attack from the shore," the leader told him harshly.

"Why do we wait, Hrano?" shrilled another. "Our place is in the fight!"

"Stay where you are! Our place is here, till She tells us otherwise." Feet pattered by. "Hoy, you, who's fallen on us? How goes the battle?"

"Men from the water," the unseen one panted. "They're bound straight for our camps. Follow your standards! I go to my chief."

A sentry mouthed a curse and took off. The leader bawled after him in vain. Louder grew the clamor, as the strangers met hastily formed Yutho squadrons.

Pirates, Lockridge thought. Must be that fleet the Wardens saw. Could only be. They didn't lie to after all. Instead, they rowed day and night, and this fog gave 'em cover for a landin' up the beach a way. Yes, sure. Some sea rover from the Mediterranean's gotten himself together a bunch o' tribesmen. England's too tough, from what I hear, but across the North Sea is loot to be had.

No. What can they do, as soon as Storm and Hu start shootin' them down?

And, well, that was probably best. Avildaro had suffered enough without being sacked, without Auri's being taken for a slave. Lockridge strained at his bars and waited for the eruption of panic when that gang found they'd tangled with the Goddess.

A shape sprang from the fog, a tall blond man with furious eyes. The Yutho leader waved him away. "By the Maruts, you Orugaray chicken," he ordered, "get back where you belong!"

The big man rammed home his harpoon. The leader clutched a pierced stomach, uttered a strangled moan, and folded to his knees.

Another guard snarled. His tomahawk swung high. A second villager came behind him, cast a fishline around his neck, and tightened it with two great sailor hands. The third sentry went also down, head beaten in by tree-felling axes.

"We've got them, girl," the tall man called. He went to the door. Sufficient light lingered for Lockridge to see the water drops that jewelled his beard, and recognize a son of Echegon. He knew a few others by name of the half score who waited uneasily beyond, and the rest by sight. Two of them had been accomplices in yesterday's attempt at human sacrifice. They stood now like men.

Echegon's son drew a flint knife and sawed at the thongs binding the lattice together. "We'll have you out soon," he said, "if none chance by to see us."

"What—" Lockridge was too stunned to do more than listen.

"We're bound off, I think. Auri fared around the whole day, pleading with everyone she thought she could trust to help you. We didn't dare at first, we sat in her house and muttered our fears. And then these strangers came, like a sign from the gods, and she reminded us of what powers she got in the underworld. So let the fight last only a little while more, and we'll be on our way. This is no good place to live any longer." The man peered anxiously at Lockridge. "We do this because Auri swore you have the might to shield us from the Goddess' wrath. And she ought to know. But is she right?"

Before Lockridge could reply, Auri was there, to hail him in a shivering whisper. She herself trembled under the wet cloak of her hair; but she carried a light spear and he saw that she was in truth a woman. "Lynx, you can lead us away safe. I know you can. Say you will be our head."

The nearing battle was no more loud or violent than Lockridge's pulse. "I don't deserve this," he said. "I don't deserve you." But he had spoken unthinkingly in English. She straightened herself and said like a queen:

"He casts a spell for us. He will take us where he knows is best."

The thongs parted. Lockridge squeezed between two poles. Fog curled around him. He tried to guess where in the twilight the combat was going on. It seemed to be spread over a wide front, moving inland. So the bayshore ought to be deserted for now.

"This way," he said.

They moved close to his protection. A number of women

were with them, children clustered near or held as babes in arms. Anyone who'll take such a risk to be free, he thought, has a call on everything I've got to offer.

No. One item more. "I've a duty at the Long House," he said.

"Lynx!" Auri gripped his arm in anguish. "You can't!"

"Go on down to the boats," he said. "Make sure you have water skins and gear for hunting and fishing aboard. By the time you are ready to go, I will have joined you. If not, leave without me."

"*Her* place?" The son of Echegon shuddered. "What must you do there?"

"Something that—well, we'll have no good luck unless I do."

"I will come too," Auri said.

"No." He stooped and kissed her, a brief touch across lips that tasted of salt. Even then he caught a scent of her hair and warmth. "Everywhere else, if you wish, but not here. Go make me a place in the boat."

He ran off before she could say more.

Huts gloomed around him, where folk lay in twilit terror. A pig grunted by, black and swift. He remembered that She kept swine in Her aspect of the death goddess. The battle sounded close—savage yells, footfalls, clashings, arrow buzz and thud of ax striking home—but Lockridge went enclosed in his own silence.

The Long House stood unguarded, as he had hoped. Though if Storm or Hu were still within. . . . He had no choice except to cross that threshold.

The hall was empty.

He ran among machines and gods. At the curtain of lightlessness, he almost stopped. No, he told himself, you mustn't. He passed through.

The agony of Brann seared upward at him. He put the diaglossa of a terrible tomorrow into his ear, stooped, and said, "I am going to let you die if you want."

"Oh, I beg," the mummy voice gasped. Lockridge recoiled. Storm had said no reasoning mind was left.

Storm lied about that, too, he thought, and went to work.

Unarmed, he couldn't cut the Ranger's throat. But he yanked out wires and tubes. The blackened body writhed, with little mewling appeals. Not much blood trickled from the piercings.

"Lie there," Lockridge said. He stroked Brann's forehead. "You won't have long to wait. Good-bye."

He fled, the breath rough in his throat.

As he crossed the veil, racket rolled over him. Some part of the fight was swaying back into town. And there went the sizzle of an energy gun. Light flimmered lurid past the doorway curtain. So much for the pirates, Lockridge thought. If I don't get out of here right away, I never will.

He ran into the square.

Hu the Warden appeared at its edge. "Koriach!" he was shouting, lost and frantic. "Koriach, where are you? We must stand together—my dearest—" The gun which made fountainplay further off among the huts was not the one in his hand.

His head wove back and forth, in search of his goddess. Lockridge knew he himself couldn't get clear away, nor even back inside the Long House, before he was seen. He sprang.

Hu saw him and yelped. The pistol slewed about. Lockridge hit the green-clad body. They went over onto the earth and struggled for control of the weapon. Hu's grip on the butt was not to be broken. Lockridge pulled from his clawing and squirmed around to the Warden's back. He anchored himself with a scissor lock, cast an arm around his enemy's neck, and heaved.

A dry snap came, so loud he heard it through the tumult. Hu ceased to move. Lockridge scrambled up and saw death. "I'm sorry." He bent to close the staring eyes, before he took the gun and was off.

For an instant he was tempted to look for Storm, now that he was armed like her. But no; too chancy; one of her Yuthoaz might well brain him while he was stalemated by her energy shield. And then what would become of Auri? He owed the world to her and that handful of her kinfolk down on the strand.

Besides, he wasn't sure he could bring himself to fire on Storm.

The water's edge gleamed forth. He made out a big skinboat rocking shadowlike on the ripples, filled with shadow shapes. Auri waited ashore. She sped to him with laughter and tears. He gave her, and himself, a moment's embrace, then waded out and climbed in.

"Where now do we go?" asked the son of Echegon.

Lockridge looked back. He could still see the houses as bulks in the fog, a dim outline of the grove, a hint of men and horses where they fought. Good-bye, Avildaro, he called. God keep you.

"Iril Varay," he said: England.

Paddles bit deep. A coxswain chanted the stroke as an invocation to Her of the Sea; for Auri, who had been reborn, told how The Storm was no goddess but a witch. A baby wailed, a woman sobbed quietly, a man lifted his spear in farewell.

They slipped around the western ness and Avildaro was gone from them. A mile or so further, through the gathering night, they descried the raider fleet. The coracles had been drawn ashore, the galley stood off at anchor. A few watchmen's torches glowed starry, so that Lockridge saw the proud curve of figurehead and sternpost, the rake of yards into the sky.

It was a wonder that these Vikings of the Bronze Age were not yet in decimated flight. Storm and Hu would have separated, of course, to rally confused and scattered Yuthoaz around their flame guns. But then, for some reason, Hu had run off alone. Even so, Storm by herself could—well, that was behind him.

Or was it, really? Fate-ridden, she would not rest until she found and destroyed him. If somehow he got back to his own century . . . no, her furies could track him down more surely then than in the wide and lonely Neolithic world. That was the more so if he burdened himself with this boatload of aliens whom he could not abandon.

He began to doubt his choice of England. Other megalith builders were fleeing there from Denmark, he knew. He could join them, and live out his days in fear. It was no life to offer Auri.

"Lynx," the girl whispered beside him, "I should not be so happy, should I? But I am."

She wasn't Storm Darroway. And what of that? He drew her close. She was fate too, he thought. Maybe John and Mary had wanted no more than to give her gallant and gentle heredity to the human race. He wasn't much, but her sons and daughters could be.

It came to him what he must do. He sat moveless so long that Auri grew frightened. "Are you well, my dear one?"

"Yes," he said, and kissed her.

Throughout the night the fugitives went on, slow in the murk but every paddle stroke a victory. At dawn they entered the fowl marshes and hid themselves to rest. Later the men hunted, fished, and filled waterskins. Fog blew away on a northeast breeze, the stars next evening stood brilliant to see by. Lockridge had mast raised and sail unfurled. By morning they were at sea.

That was a passage cold, cramped, and dangerous. None but the Tenil Orugaray could have ridden out a storm they met, in this overloaded frail craft. In spite of all misery, Lockridge was glad. When the Koriach didn't find him, she might conclude he had drowned and quit looking.

He wondered if she would be sorry. Or had her feelings for him been another lie?

After days, East Anglia rose low and autumnally vivid before them. Salt-crusted, wind-bitten, hungry and worn, they beached the coracle and devoured the sweet water of a spring they found.

They had expected to look for a seaboard community that would take them in. But Lockridge said no. "I have a better place," he promised. "We must go through the underworld to reach it, but there we will be safe from the witch. Would you rather skulk like animals or walk in freedom?"

"We follow you, Lynx," the son of Echegon answered.

They made their way across the land. Progress was not fast, with small children along and the need to hunt for food. Lockridge began fretting that they might reach his goal too late. Auri had a different impatience. "We are ashore now, my dearest. And yonder grows soft moss."

He gave her a weary grin. "Not until we have arrived, little one." Seriously: "You are too important to me."

She glowed at him.

And in the end, they waded through icy meres to an island which the tribes roundabout shunned. Natives had told Lockridge, one night when the travelers stayed in a village of theirs, that it was haunted. He got exact directions.

Under bare trees stood a carelessly erected lean-to. One man waited, sword in hand. He was burly and kettle-bellied, with hair and beard falling grizzled about pocked, battered features.

Gladness jumped in Lockridge. "Jesper, you old devil!" he shouted. They beat each other on the back. When Lockridge had his sixteenth-century diaglossa in place, he asked what this meant.

The Dane shrugged. "I was fetched hither with the rest of the fighting men. The witchmaster asked for a volunteer to guard the gate this final while. I said I would. Why not do my lovely Lady a service? So here I've sat, with a bit of duck hunting and such to keep me amused. In case of trouble, I was to do something to an engine down below, that'd tell Her. Naught's happened, though, and taking you for ordinary savages, I didn't send any summons. I thought instead, more fun would be to scare you off. But good to see you again, Malcolm!"

"Isn't your guardianship nearly over?"

"Yes, in a few more days. Priest Marcus told me to watch the clock and be sure to leave when the time came, or else the gate would disappear and I'd be stranded. I'll go up to the other gate he showed me, and thence be wafted home."

Lockridge looked on Fledelius with compassion. "To Denmark?"

"Where else?"

"I am here on secret business for our Lady. So secret that you must not breathe a word to anyone."

"Never fear. You can trust me, as I you."

Lockridge winced. "Jesper," he said, "come with us. When we get where we're bound, I can tell you—well, you deserve more than life as an outlaw under a tyrant. Come along!"

Wistfulness flickered in the little eyes. The heavy head shook. "No. I thank you, my friend, but I'm sworn to my Lady and my king. Until the bailiffs catch me, I'll be at the Inn of the Golden Lion each All Hallows Eve, waiting."

"But after what happened there, no, you can't."

Fledelius chuckled. "I'll find ways. Junker Erik won't stick this old boar as easily as he thinks."

And Lockridge's people stood freezing.

"Well . . . we must use the corridor. I can't tell you more, and remember, this is secret from everyone. Good-bye, Jesper."

"Good-bye, Malcolm, and you, my girl. Drink a bumper to me now and then, will you?"

Lockridge led his followers below the earth.

He had prepared a story to fool anyone who might have been on guard here. At worst, he would have used his energy gun. But it was luck finding Jesper. Or destiny? No, Satan take destiny. If Storm happened to think the fugitives had come this way, and sought out the Dane herself to inquire, he would talk; but that was extremely improbable, and otherwise he would keep his mouth shut. Lockridge would never have gotten the idea himself, except for Auri's nearness.

He entered the gate of fire. The Tenil Orugaray gathered their whole courage and followed him.

"We need not linger," he said. "Let us be reborn. Hold hands and come back to the world with me."

He took them out along the opposite side of the same gate. That corresponded to the moment when it first appeared in the world, as it would vanish a quarter century afterward.

The anteroom, like the island, lay empty. He used the control tube Fledelius had given him to open the entrance above the ramp, and close it again. They emerged into summer. The fen lay green with leaves and reeds, bright with water, clamorous with wildfowl, twenty-five years before he and Storm were to reach Neolithic Denmark.

"Oh, but beautiful!" Auri breathed.

Lockridge addressed his band. "You are the Sea People," he said. "We will go on to the sea and live. Folk like you can soon grow strong in this land." He paused. "As for me . . . I will be your headman, if you wish. But I shall have to travel about a great deal, and perhaps call on your help from time to time. The tribes here are large and widely ranging, but they are divided. With the new time before us, coming in from the South, they will be the better for as broad a oneness as we can shape. This is my task."

Inwardly, he looked at his tomorrows, and for a while he was daunted. He was losing so much. His mother would weep when he never came back, and that was worst of all; but himself, he surrendered his country and his people, his whole civilization—the Parthenon and the Golden Gate Bridge, music, books, cuisine, medicine, the scientific vision, every good thing that four thousand years were to bring forth—to become, at most, a chieftain in the Stone Age. He would always be alone here.

But that, he thought, would mark him out for awe and power. Knowing what he did, he could work mightily, not as conqueror but as uniter, teacher, healer, and lawgiver. He might, perhaps, lay a foundation that would stand strong against the evil Storm was to bring.

This was his fate. He could only take it.

He looked at his few people, the seeds of what would come. "Will you help me?" he asked.

"Yes," Auri said, with her voice and her being.

21

And the years flew past, until again there was a day when rain grew into fog and the warriors from the west came in its cloak, up the Limfjord to Avildaro.

He whom they called Lynx stood in the galley's bow: a man older than most, gray of hair and beard, but still hardly less hale than the four big sons beside him. All were armed and armored in shining bronze. They peered at the shoreline, sliding vague in the fading vaporous light, until the father said, "Here is our landing."

The eagerness of his sixteen years beat through the tone of Hawk, Auri's child, as he relayed the order. Oars ceased to splash and creak. The stone anchor went overboard. Men stirred down the length of the ship, their battle gear clanked, they sprang from the benches into cold shoulder-deep water. The skinboats of their flint-weaponed allies grounded and were drawn ashore.

"Keep them still," said Lynx. "We must not be heard."

The captain nodded. "Belay that noise, you," he commanded his sailors. Iberians like him, dark hook-nosed round-heads, smaller and more slender than the fair tribesfolk of Britain, they needed every restraint that could be laid on them. Even he, a civilized man who had often been in Egypt and Crete, had had some trouble understanding that this was to be no piratical raid.

"I have gathered enough tin and fur to pay for your voyage

ten times over," the chief named Lynx had told him. "All is
yours if you will help. But we fare against a witch who wields
lightnings. Though I can do likewise, will your men be too
frightened? Moreover, we go not to plunder, but to set my
kindred free. Will you and yours be content with my wages?"

The captain swore so, by Her Whom he worshipped as did
these powerful barbarians. And he was honest when he did.
There was that about the blue eyes confronting him which bespoke a majesty like nothing less than the Minos of the South.

Nonetheless— Well, Lockridge thought, we'll just have to
play her as she lies. Which is a liberation. Tonight I break free
of destiny.

Not that the time in England was ever bad. On the contrary.
I've had a better, happier, more useful life than any I dared
dream of.

He made his way aft. Auri stood by the cabin under the
poop. Their other children, three girls and a boy too young to
fight, waited with her. They'd been lucky in that respect also:
a certain dolmen sheltered only one tiny form. Indeed the
gods loved her.

Tall, full of figure, the hair that fell past her Cretan gown
little less bright than in girlhood, she looked at her man with
no more than a glimmer of tears. A quarter century in which
she must be his right hand had brought forth greatness. "Farewell, my dearest," she said.

"Not for long. As soon as we've won, you can come home."

"You gave me my home, beyond the sea. If you should fall—"

"Then return, for their sakes." He caressed the children, one
by one. "Rule Westhaven as we did before. The folk will re-
joice." He forced a smile. "But I shall not be harmed."

"It will be strange," she said slowly, "to see our young selves
go by. I wish you could be with me then."

"Will the sight hurt you?"

"No. I will give them our love, that pair, and be glad for
what they have ahead of them."

She alone had come to understand what had happened with
time. To the rest of the Tenil Orugaray, that was a disquieting

magic which they gave as little thought as possible. True, it had brought them to a good country, and they were grateful; but let Lynx bear the burden of sorcery, he was the king.

Lockridge and Auri kissed each other and he left her.

Wading to land, he found himself surrounded by his men. A few were Avildaro born, infants when they fled. The rest came from half of Britain.

That had been his work. He had not gone back to East Anglia, lest rumors of him cross the water and wait for Storm Darroway. Instead, he led his company into that beautiful land which would later be named Cornwall. There they plowed and sowed, hunted and fished, loved and sacrificed, in the old carefree manner; but piece by piece, he taught them how much they could gain from the tin mines and from trade, he recruited new members from the restless tribes around, he brought in new ways of life and work, until Westhaven was known from Skara Brae to Memphis as a rich and mighty realm. And meanwhile he made alliance—with the axmakers of Langdale Pike, the settlers along the Thames, even the dour downland farmers, whom he persuaded that manslaughter was not pleasing to the gods. Now today they spoke of erecting a great temple on Salisbury Plain, as the sign and seal of their confederation. And so he could leave them; and a hundred hunters he could pick, from the many who asked to come, for his battle in the east.

"Form ranks," he ordered. "Forward."

Northerner and Southerner alike, they fell into the formation he had drilled and moved toward Avildaro.

Walking through the dank grayness, where only footfalls and the wail of curlews broke silence, he felt his throat gone tight and his heart wild. Storm, Storm, he thought, I'm comin' home to you.

Twenty-five years had not blurred her in his mind. Grown lean and wolf-gray, with the troubles and joys of a generation between him and her, he still remembered black tresses, green eyes, amber skin, a mouth that had once dwelt on his. Step by reluctant step, he had come to know his weird. The North

must be saved from her. The human race must be. Without
Brann, she could drive her Wardens to victory. And neither
Warden nor Ranger must prevail. They had to wear each other
down, until what was good in both stood forth above the wreck
of what was evil and the world of John and Mary could take
shape.

Yet he was not really Lynx, the wise and invincible. He was
only Malcolm Lockridge, who had loved Storm Darroway.
The fight was hard to hold fast to Auri, and to the fact that he
was going against the Koriach.

Hawk slipped back from his scouting. "I saw few about in
the village, Father," he said. "None looked like Yuthoaz, as
near as I can tell from what you've related of them. The chariot
people's watchfires are dim in this mist, and most lie bundled
up from the cold."

"Good." Lockridge was glad of action. "We'll divide the
bands now, each to its own part of the meadows." Their com-
manders came to him and he gave close instructions. One
after the next, the groups vanished into the dusk, until he was
left with a score. He numbered their bullhide shields and
sharp edges of flint, raised his arm and told them: "Ours is the
hardest task. We go to meet the witch herself. I swear again
that my magic is as strong as hers. But let any leave who fear
to witness our strife."

"Long have you led us, and ever we found you right," rumbled a hillman. "I stand by my oath." A fierce whisper of agree-
ment ran around the circle.

"Then follow."

They found a path toward the sacred grove. When combat
got going, Storm and her attendants at the Long House should
come this way.

Shouts lifted through cloudiness.

Lockridge stopped by the dripping trees. Noise grew and
grew on his right: horns and horses neighed, men whooped
and screeched, bows twanged, wheels groaned, axes began to
thunder.

"Will she never come?" muttered his son Arrow.

Lockridge felt strained near breaking. He had no guarantee of success. One energy gun could scatter a host, and the thing that weighed in his hand was matched against two.

Feet thudded from Avildaro. A dozen Yuthoaz burst into view, out of the fog. Their weapons were aloft and their faces furious. At their head ran Hu.

I'm not goin' to kill you this time, Lockridge thought with a shiver.

The Warden jarred to a halt. His pistol lifted.

The same weapon flared in Lockridge's grasp, upon itself. Red, green, yellow, deathly blue, fire sleeted. The Yuthoaz flung themselves on the Britons, who scattered back in supernatural dread.

"Koriach!" Hu shouted above the crashing energies. "They are Rangers!"

He did not know Lockridge in the man who confronted him. And within this hour, he would lie dead before the Long House. Lockridge stood frozen with the terror of it. Hu stepped closer. A Yutho howled and swung his tomahawk. The hillman who had spoken of oaths fell before him.

That broke Lockridge's paralysis. "Westhaven men!" he yelled. "Strike for your kindred!"

Arrow bounded forth. His bronze sword flashed in the fires, drove home and came back bloody. Hawk took a blow on his helmet, which belled like his own laughter as he struck. Their brothers, Herdsman and Sun Beloved, rallied to them; and so did the rest. They outnumbered the Battle Ax men. Short and unmerciful was that fight.

Lockridge drew blade on Hu. The Warden saw his troop go down, lifted off the ground, and was lost in the mists. Above the war in the fields, he could be heard shrieking for Storm.

So she took another route. She's out yonder, Lockridge thought. "This way!"

He came onto the meadows. A chariot careened by, aimed for a line of his men. Trained by him, they stood fast until the wheels were almost upon them, then parted, and smote the chieftain from the sides. Masterless, the horses ran into twilight and were lost. The Britons charged those Yuthoaz who followed on foot. To Lockridge it was all a shadow play. He hunted for Storm.

Over the stricken field he went with his band. From time to time he saw a piece of the battle. A Yutho dashed out the brains of a Westhaven warrior, and was cut to pieces by an Iberian. Two men rolled in the mud like dogs, seeking each other's throats. A boy named Thuno sprawled in blood, eyes turned empty to the hidden sky. Lockridge hurried past. His scabbard slapped his leg. Helmet and corselet grew heavy upon him.

After some part of eternity, he heard cries. A group of his people loped by, lips set against panic. He hailed their leader. "We met her, at the edge of town," the tribesman gasped. "Her flames slew three before we could get away."

They had not bolted, though. They were following his instructions to retreat and seek another opponent. Lockridge sped the way they had come.

First he heard her voice: "You and you and you. Find the clan's chiefs. Have them come to me. I shall abide here, and when we have conferred and brought some order into our ranks, we shall destroy these sea bandits." Her voice was husky and lovely.

He advanced into the clouds. They seemed to part, and she was there.

Several Yuthoaz were at her side. Horses stamped before the one chariot, where Withucar stood with halberd ready. But Storm was alone, ahead of them. She had thrown no more than a tunic across her huntress body, and the moon crescent on her brows. The hair gleamed wet in what light remained, the countenance was vivid with life. He fired on her.

She was too quick. Her shield went up. Rage upon rage, the energies spent each other in flame.

"Ranger," she called across the roaring fearsome beauty of rainbows, "come and be slain." Because he wore his diaglossas, for the first time in many years, Lockridge understood. He moved nearer.

Her Valkyrie face broke in horror. "Malcolm!" she screamed.

His sons egged on their men. Sword, spear, and tomahawk flew free.

From the edge of an eye, Lockridge saw Withucar swing his long ax down upon Hawk. The boy dodged, sprang up onto the chariot, and stabbed. Withucar's half-grown driver cast himself between the blade and his lord. As he crumpled, the chief drew a stone knife. Hawk could not pull his weapon out in time. He threw arms around the redbeard. They tumbled off and fought by the wheels.

Elsewhere, the Westhaven men closed. They met brave, skilled foes who stood fast, shield to shield, blow for blow. Battle shocked the darkening air.

"Oh, Malcolm," Storm sobbed, "what has time done to you?"

He could only be remorseless, advance on her with gun in one hand and the other one free that should have held a sword. At any moment she could flit off like Hu. But her men were being driven back by greater numbers. She retreated with them. Lockridge could not get to her, in the ruck that boiled around. When a space opened briefly between them, he and she made defense, and flames crowned her. Otherwise the grunting, panting, bestial struggle held them apart.

In among the huts they moved. The Long House appeared, black above roofs.

Abruptly, Arrow and Sun Beloved crashed through the Yutho line. Their feet spurned the men they had killed. Whirling about, they cut from behind. Their folk poured through the gap. The fight broke into knots, back and forth between those humble walls.

Lockridge saw Storm before him. He leaped. So bright grew the radiance that they were both momentarily blinded. His hand chopped in a many-colored darkness. She cried in pain. He felt her gun spin loose. Before she could take off, he had dropped his own weapon and seized her.

They went to earth. She fought with hands, nails, knees, teeth, till blood runneled down his skin. But he pinned her beneath his weight and metal. The dazzle cleared from his eyes. He looked into hers. She lifted her head and kissed him.

"No," he choked.

"Malcolm," she said, her breath quick upon him, "I can make you young again, immortal, with me."

He voiced an oath. "I'm Auri's man."

"Are you?" She lay suddenly calm in his grasp. "Then draw your sword."

"You know I can't do that." He got up, removed her belt, helped her to her feet and kept her arms pinned behind her back. She smiled and leaned close.

The fight had ended around them. When they saw their Goddess taken, such of the Yuthoaz as still could threw down their axes and fled. Wounded men ululated on the earth.

"We have the witch," Lockridge said. It sounded in his ears like a stranger talking. "Now only her warriors remain."

His sons approached, glaives ready. He felt ashamed of being no happier than he was to see Hawk with them. He let Storm go. Bruised, smeared, and captive, she looked imperially at them all and said, "Is this the destiny you want?" But she spoke in English.

Lockridge couldn't meet that gaze, he dropped his own and sighed, "It's the one I've got."

"Do you imagine for a minute you can escape revenge?"

"Yes. When they don't hear from you, of course your spies will come to learn what happened. They won't find you. They'll hear about a raid where you evidently perished: not Ranger work, as far as they can tell from the confused native accounts, just an attack by an ambitious chalcolithic chief who'd heard Jutland was in trouble and saw his chance and was so lucky that stray arrows got you and Hu before you could drive him off. More than ever, your successors will think this is a bad period to meddle with. They've got plenty to do elsewhere and elsewhen; they'll leave us alone."

Storm stood quiet a while. "You read shrewdly, Malcolm," she said at last. "What a hero you could be for us."

"I'm not interested," he said without force.

She straightened her garment until it clung. "But what will you do with me?" she murmured.

"I don't know," he said in his trouble. "As long as you're alive, you're a mortal danger. But I . . . I can't hurt you. I'm so thankful you came through this business that—" He blinked hard. "Maybe we can hide you someplace," he said roughly. "In honor."

She smiled. "Will you come see me?"

"I shouldn't."

"You will. We can talk then." She brushed aside the sword of Herdsman, Auri's son, came to Lockridge and kissed him again. "Farewell, Lynx."

"Take her off!" he rapped. "Bind her. Be careful, though. She must not be harmed."

"Where shall she be kept, Father?" Arrow asked him.

Lockridge prowled a little beyond, into the square before the Long House. Hu's body looked shrunken at his feet.

"In there," he decided. "Her own place. Post a guard outside. Lay out the dead and do what you can for the wounded."

He watched her until she had been led through the doorway.

War pealed in his ears like the pulse within him. On an instant, he could no longer be still. He ran through the village and shouted.

"Avildaro men! Sea People! We have come to set you free! The witch is fallen. They fight for you out in the meadows. Will you lie there and strike no blow for yourselves? Come out, whoever is a man!"

And they came: household by household, hunters, fishers, riders of the sea, they gathered beweaponed around the newcome deliverer. He called his sons to join. They went fifty strong through the holy grove and fell upon the Battle Ax ranks.

And broke them.

When the last chariot lay splintered and the last Yutho was chased out onto the heaths, Lockridge ordered all captives brought before him. Mostly those were women and children, who stumbled through the desolation of their hopes. But Withucar lived. Hands lashed behind his back, he knew Lockridge and defied him.

A dying fire had been fueled until it lit the wet dark as wildly as the Tenil Orugaray were dancing. Lockridge saw the misery that faced him and spoke with much gentleness:

"You will not be hurt further. Tomorrow you may go. This is our place, not yours. But a man from us will depart with you, to talk of peace. The land is broad; we know of ranges unpeopled for your use. At midwinter, the tribal chiefs will hold council here, when we will seek ways to meet our common needs. Withucar, I hope you will be among them."

The Yutho dropped to his knees. "Lord," he said, "I know not what strangeness has touched you this night. But for your ruth, we are still sworn comrades, you and I. If you will have me."

Lockridge raised him. "Take off his bonds. He is our friend."

Looking across his people, he, Lynx, knew his work not ended. Westhaven was strongly founded. In the next twenty or thirty years—however much time was granted him—he must build the same kind of league in Denmark.

If only Storm—

A man dashed to him and fell on his face. "We did not know! We did not know! We heard the noise too late!"

Night closed on Lockridge like a fist. He cried for torchbearers and ran the whole way to the Long House.

By the unmerciful light of the globes, she lay. Her beauty was gone; one is not strangled to death without blackening skin, tongue swollen between teeth, eyes half bulged from the skull. Yet something lingered, in sheening hair and carven face, in body that had fought to the last and in bound hands which once touched him.

Brann's corpse was across her.

I forgot him, Lockridge thought. I couldn't stand to remember. So he came through the veil, with death on his heels, and saw her, his torturer, helpless.

Storm, oh, my Storm!

The Sea People grew hushed when their lord wept.

He had them bring wood. He himself laid her to rest, with her lieutenant and her great enemy at her feet, and put the torch to the Long House. High and loud sprang the flames, to make another day out of darkness. We will build a sanctuary here, he thought, to the worship of Her Who one day will be called Mary.

But for him there was only one place to go. He returned alone to the ship.

Auri's arms enfolded him. Toward sunrise he found peace.

God, or fate, or whatever you wanted to name it, be thanked for work.

The Bronze Age, the new age was coming. What he had seen in his own unborn yesterdays gave him to believe it would be a time rich, peaceful, and happy: perhaps more happy than aught men would know until that distant future he had glimpsed. For the relics that afterward remained did not show burning, slaughter, or enslavement. Rather, the golden Sun Chariot of Trundholm and the lur horns, whose curves recalled Her serpents, spoke for the Northern races become one. Then widely would they fare; the streets of Knossos would know Danish feet and men depart from England for Araby. Some might even touch America, where the Indians were to tell of a wise kindly god and of a goddess named Flower Feather. But most would return. For where else was life so good as in the first land the world ever saw which was both strong and free?

In the end it would go down, before the cruel age of iron. Yet a thousand fortunate years were no small achievement; and the spirit they brought to birth would endure. Through every century to come, the forgotten truth that men had once known generations of gladness must abide and subtly work. Those who built the ultimate tomorrow might well come back to the realm that Lynx founded, and learn.

"Auri," Lockridge whispered, "be with me. Help me."

"Always," she said.